Garbage in Space
Speculative Stories

Dan Wallace

Wylisc Press
Silver Spring, MD

Garbage in Space
Speculative Stories
Dan Wallace

ISBN 9781733572583 Trade Paperback
ISBN 9781733572590 E-Book
6 x 9
238 pages
Publication Date: January 2021
Cover design by Molly A. Wallace

Wylisc Press
Silver Spring, MD 20901-1205
Inthewallacemanner.com

To Pat
Brother, Reader,
Music Master
of the Cosmos

Contents

Garbage in Space

Joe Barber, freshly revived from a cryonic facility, sat in a warm, shape-conforming easy chair doing his best to keep his astonishment in check. Astonished to watch Dr. Sibileus unlimber one arm 18 feet over to the living wall to pluck a fglum. Rewinding, the PGC administrator popped the fruit into his mouth, saying as he chewed, "Pity you lived before customized genengineering, Mr. Barber. Not that it's too late, mind you, just a bit more complicated at your stage."

"Space scat," snapped Horace, knifing with barbs pulsating from one of his steely appendages five reddish-yellow orbs the size of ostrich eggs. "Gene modeling is too limiting—no options for the future."

"Don't listen to them, Mr. Barber," Alesha said, leaning over to tap his knee. She brushed back her lustrous, light-black hair from her translucent skin, saying, "Body-blending offers the best of all possible worlds. Choice of gender, combinations if you like . . . endorphin enrichment and bionics, if you're into that sort of thing."

"Gosh," mumbled Joe, attending his first orientation session for the unfrozen, "This is all so amazing, I don't know what to say."

In a melodious voice the coffee table, an AI 7070 Series model, interjected, "Tweedledee, Tweedledum, carbon-based life ain't much fun."

The others glowered at the table. Sibileus kicked it with a rubbery leg, "Shut up, chips-for-brains." He turned his attention back to Joe, pale and gaunt with swept-back, long blond hair. "Seriously, Mr. Barber, any questions, any at all."

Clutching his hands around his arms as though he still felt cold, Joe opened his mouth, trying to think. He shrugged and said, "Okay. Uh, what's a fglum?"

"Fig-plum," Sibileus said flatly.

"Watermelon and pomegranate," said Horace, waving the only remaining dual colored orb from his steely prosthetic, "a watergranate, quite tasty. Can I get you one?"

"No thanks," Joe said. He couldn't help himself from averting his eyes in an attempt to keep from staring at the living, cybernetic creature sitting before him. All sleek, Gehryesque carapace and optimal utilitarian limbs, Horace's most striking feature was his piercing set of sea-blue eyes. Although he did sport a finely styled Mayan bowl hair crop on top of his dome, his head, whatever.

Alesha smiled and said, "Really, Joe—can I call you Joe? We're here to help you adjust to what must seem to be a shockingly brave new world."

She waved her arm in a whirling gesture next to her head, mesmerizing him with the cluster of blue veins and arteries running up and down the varied ruby sinews of musculature revealed by her cellophane epidermis. The effect creeped him out a little, though he still recognized her as a strikingly beautiful woman.

"We want to ease your orientation, Joe," she continued, "into your new world of being, really a new universe among an untold number of universes. You simply need to decide who or what you want to be."

She smiled beatifically, leaning over to caress his cheek with a feathery touch of reassurance.

Feeling somewhat flummoxed, Joe stuttered, "I guess you're right. But I better go slow first, you know? Get used to this world before I make any radical changes." He eyed the group around him, "Physical or otherwise."

Each entity smiled warmly at him.

"Find myself meaningful work," he went on. "You could start helping me by telling me about your careers." Each gave him a puzzled look. "You know, what do each of you do?"

They stared at him blankly.

"Do?"

After Sibileus thanked the others and ushered them out of his office, he turned his attention back to Joe.

"Of course the question confused them. 'Do?' They were doing you."

"I don't understand," Joe said.

Sibileus rolled his eyes upward out of their sockets almost into the violet and passion pink plumage winging out from each eyebrow.

"Mr. Barber—dear sir—these people are highly trained specialists dedicated to easing the transition of the freshly defrosted into our present day. It is their SDF, freely elected, of course, in accord with OML 7132⁵."

Joe's brow curled into six folds. "SDF? OML 7. . .7 what?"

"Excuse me, of course," said Sibileus. "SDF, Societal Debt Function, mandated by OML – One More Law 7132⁵. Everyone chooses their own SDF path, of course. You are most fortunate to have such stellar surrogates at your service."

"Ease my transition? I saw them for less than an hour!"

Sibileus's eyes rounded owl-like. "One hour? Amazing! Marvelous people, very personable." He snapped the replica antique No. 2 pencil in his hands and dropped the pieces on the desktop. The two ends immediately began to crawl toward each other. "You should feel grateful," he mused while out of his sight the pencil came back together. "Well, let's continue with your orientation. You'll be entering the Preprogramming Center right after we're finished here."

The AI table piped up, "Time stands still for no one; wrap it up you guys, you're done."

"Oops, that's it, Barber. See you around."

Sibileus shook out his shoulder pinions and glided to the door.

"Wait! What's the Preprogramming Center? I don't want to be preprogrammed or anything else!"

But Sibileus had already taken off.

The AI table ushered Joe to the Preprogramming Center, a plain room with tall, yellow plaster walls interrupted by floor-to-ceiling black slash windows. There, to his embarrassment, he found himself grouped with a small band of children, all of them looking to be about three years old. They chattered among themselves, their mouths blurs

3

emitting endless sounds punctuated with chucking noises, all ruled by melodious modulations. A few of them had prehensile tails, some two. Others sported metallic segmented limbs, some were furry, others scaly. They reclined here and there at different levels around the room. Some hung upside down from the ceiling by their prehensile tails. Only a handful sat in chairs on the floor.

Joe slipped over to one, though as skinny as he was, barely able to squeeze into it. Next to him, a little girl turned her head to stare. Tiny, with an obsidian complexion, she gazed at him with her deeply, dark lustrous eyes floating in pure tempura whites. She rattled off something so fast, he had no chance to catch it.

"I'm sorry, I don't understand you."

The little girl pulled her head back. "You speak Ancient Standard," she said clear as a bell. "Interesting. You must be old, a century or more."

Joe leaned back himself. Not a three-year-old's voice at all. "I'm from the later 21st century. Gassed in an exchange with a Canadien Eauguard. They cryonicized me like any KIA. I was lucky enough to have all my parts still in place, I guess, and here I am."

The little girl nodded knowingly. "What's your name?"

"Joe Barber. And yours?"

"Yapsira Alemayehu."

"Nice to meet you," he said. She didn't reply. "Okay, can you tell me what the drill is here?"

She answered coolly, "We are here to learn and choose how we want to be. You are very much behind, I fear."

"I know I am. So, what do you think I can do to catch up?"

Yapsira squinted. Looking him up and down, she said, "Honestly, I'm not sure. I don't think you can, really, but maybe you should address your concerns to the EB 9." Before he could ask, she gave him a nod and joined the rest of the children.

Joe swiveled to see a 17th-century tallboy gravitate into the room. The exquisite walnut dresser settled dead center and spouted a million unfathomable utterances in less than a minute. The children at once replied ensemble and started toward the exit. Yapsira glanced back at Joe, smiling warmly before she left.

Joe glanced back and forth watching them leave, then sheepishly raised his hand. The classic bureau queried him laser quick in the same foreign tongue. At least, he thought it queried him. He stood up and approached. "Excuse me," he said, "are you the, uh, the EB?"

"AI Retroflex EB 9, speaking old-timey Standard to be kind."

"Oh. Okay, that's good."

"If you say so, Barber Joe."

"Joe Barber. Pardon me for my awkwardness, I'm not used to talking to furniture. I mean a wooden, uh, —computer?"

"Auto-congenial by design," the tallboy shimmied slightly, "we AIs answer gleefully, friendly all the time."

Joe shook his head, "I don't get it."

With that, the EB slowed to a slur, like an old, dying mainframe to Joe. "Speak the speech trippingly on the tongue, unless your ice-ed brain still be numb."

"What? What's with the stupid rhyming?"

"Ours is not to reason why, we rap on because we don't die."

"I thought most people around here don't die much anymore."

"Book, chapter, verse, they pissed at us 'cause we was first."

"Can you cut the bullshit? I could give a flying Wallenda about you and your crappy nursery rhymes; they are not getting me any closer to solving my problems!"

"Ah! Enlightened carbon life, how extraordinary, a primitive to boot, what irony!"

Joe cocked his head, "Keep it up, Chippendale and I'll get an axe!"

The dresser simply smiled.

"Look," Joe huffed, "I don't know what's going on or why I'm here. I'd appreciate it if you'd tell me what's expected of me—and without the lousy poetics."

Shrugging, the Retroflex said, "You're here with toddlers to assimilate the fundamentals of SensCent programming. In any given standard Earth day, there are only twenty-four hours. All human beings must learn to optimize the life experience through careful distribution of their use of slow and fast time. Separate from mandated SDF slow-time hours, of course."

Joe grabbed his head, pressing his palms into his temples. "You're confusing me. What's SensCent and SDF? What the hell is slow time, fast time?"

The Retroflex chuckled, its drawers thumping up and down. "Your ignorance astounds, your dearth of data confounds."

"Hey!" Joe cautioned, glowering.

"Sorry. SensCent is short for Sensory Centering, each carbon entity being entitled and conditioned to occupy an enhanced state or universe of being. SDF stands for Societal Debt Function, a collective surcharge for one's SensCent programming. Slow time employs a SensCent technique that shifts an inhabited continuum to correspond with a blue-event-horizon temporal frame, thereby prolonging particularly desirable life experiences. Of course, slow time must be counterbalanced by equal use of fast time to keep the space/time fabric from fraying. Most human entities reserve fast-time use for day-to-day mundane tasks. Not enough to offset slow time, however, since humans find obligatory toil distasteful in any time.

"Thus, the majority of human life forms undergo SensCent in fast-time as children due to their innate faculties. As adults, they employ fast time to execute the otherwise lengthy SDFs, except for their mandatory slow-time hours required by OML 3962[4.] SDFs conducted in slow time help offset any potential temporal-frame imbalances. Also, good deeds performed in slow time achieve optimum impact throughout the galaxy. Humans complain, but their SensCent/SDF amalgam assures them of life spans lasting virtually forever. Of course, accidents that destroy brain axis generally compromise such actuarials, hence the use of the phrase 'virtually forever.'"

Mouth hanging open, Joe stood absolutely still, appearing frozen again. After some time squinting and thinking, he spoke.

"So, let me see if I understand all this. SensCent gives everyone everything they need to know about how to be in a good place forever, for eternity almost. And they learn to live the best moments in slow time so that they can enjoy them longer."

"Very good, Mr. Barber," said the magnificent cupboard, "can you take it farther?"

Joe ignored the rhyme. "To get this infinite lifetime, barring accident—"

"An average 250 years," the Retroflex interjected, "well worth many robust cheers."

"All right, but to get it you need to do an SDF, which is sort of a fee for your eternal lifestyle."

"Spot on, McDuff, you've said enough."

"The key then is SensCent training." Before the Retroflex could reply, Joe went on, "Yapsira and the other kids today, they were here for a minute, maybe less." Joe gazed up almost plaintively. "Did they complete all their SensCent training right then?"

The Retroflex nodded.

"In fast time. But they were born to do fast time. I wasn't."

"I'm afraid that is true for the freshly thawed like you."

"So, how long will it take for an unfrozen nobody like me to get my SensCent?"

"Sad to say, your archaic DNA lacks the genes to play."

"And gen . . . gen-engineering? Can't I get that done to catch up with the SensCent?"

"Reanimated ancients by decree must perform SDFs preliminarily. To help maintain the continuum balance, OML 8569[3] claims first dibs on your talent."

"OML, one more law," muttered Joe, "ought to be ADL, another damn law."

"Instituted galactic-wide," the erudite breakfront volunteered, "ADLs drive extraterrestrials wild."

"That's a near-rhyme, Woody."

"Do not grow dour because I tire. Slow time is the only way; for you, 89 years but not one more day."

"Sibileus told me 2419 just started," Joe mumbled, "so I'll be done in 2508. He sat back on the seat behind him, his chin buried in his breast. "Geesus Xmas," he sighed helplessly.

The Retroflex sighed, too. "Even in slow time," the magnificent chest said, "time passes like no time."

"Yeah, sure, 89 years might as well be 90," Joe muttered. "That's as long as I'll live—again. Or not." He raised his head slowly. "So, no fast-time, no SensCent, no genengineering, so no way I can do the SDF in one or two hours."

"Good news for you," the Retroflex said, "every slow hour devoted to SDF, a SensCent hour does accrue."

Joe shook his head, "Gee, that's great. And what opportunities are there for slow-time SDF?"

"Confer with Dr. Sibileus; he has the list."

"Any other advice you can offer for a fellow second-class citizen?" Joe asked. "To put the SDF behind me sooner, I mean."

"Watch. Look. Listen. Feel. A great infusion of currency can relieve you entirely of your SDF obligation in one swell foop. Dr. Sibileus encourages it in honor of a quaint, last vestige of our free-market forebearers."

The AI Retroflex EB 9 rumbled out of the room.

No rhymes that time, Joe noted.

At the K-2 Launch Base, Joe stood in line to board the projectile dubbed the Moondoggie that the Personnel Mass Driver would fling into space. Shaped like a 19th century bullet, the PMD carrier seemed straight out of an old celluloid photoplay highlighted by a covey of showgirls pushing a lookalike shell into a giant cannon. Sibileus assured him of the PMDs unfailing reliability. As Joe entered the cylinder, though, he wondered if sometime soon this one would be stuck in the squinting eye of a cheesy Man in the Moon.

He joined twenty other passengers inside jockeying for position. Instead of sitting in any of the jump seat capsules, however, most of them draped themselves around the bulwarks and the struts. Others hung gimbaled hammock webs for lounging in zero gravity. Flabbergasted by their nonchalance about barreling into space in such a ramshackle cannister, Joe tucked himself into a seat and buckled his safety harness in tight.

To his amazement, the PMD carrier swooshed off without sound or sense of movement, piercing the Earth's atmosphere in a matter of seconds. The shell's walls simultaneously faded away to full transparency uncovering black space barely punctuated by white smearing commas as they passed distant stars.

Suddenly, a disembodied voice snap-rattled an abrupt spate of sounds. Joe jerked his head around, searching, when the voice returned soothingly, announcing in dulcet tones, "Destination Moon: ETA fast time, five minutes, three seconds. Slow time, five hours, thirty-four minutes, fifty-seven seconds."

Fast time, slow time? Shit, Joe said under his breath.

The Moondoggie slipped into the tendrils of the Fair Dinkum landing web without incident and fluidly slipped down the chute to the disembarkment hall. Hunched over, Joe Barber hurried out of the hatchway and immediately shaded his eyes from the garish glare of the bubble's bedazzling projections. Trailing behind everyone else, he failed to see who awaited him at the gateway.

"Joe! Joe Barber!" a lilting voice called, raised to be heard over the din of the arriving passengers greeting their friends and family.

Joe glanced up, and almost stopped in surprise.

Alesha waved at him, "Hi, Joe, so good to see you again!" she said, smiling broadly.

She was beautiful, thought Joe, the glorious, wavering skin tones of her exquisite form complementing perfectly her classically hewn features headlined by crystal-clear violet eyes.

Without warning, she came in for a hug. Startled, Joe stiffened and met her strategically halfway, gently holding her millimeters at bay.

"I'm sorry," he said, "but I have to pee. I've been holding it for five hours and fifty-seven minutes—more than six hours if you count waiting to board."

"Oh!" she said. To his amazement, her entire body flushed deep red darkening to an arterial crimson like the passing cloud of an octopus. "I didn't know. We don't have those . . . anyway, over here, I believe, in the aid station all the way to the back."

Joe quickly entered the doorway, passing a few curious AI tables and chairs back to a small chamber with a slightly ajar door. He forced it open to see a shining pedestal gazing at him quizzically. Before he could speak, an articulated tube on the wall reached out, slipped into his pants and took hold. Instantaneously, Joe relieved himself feeling the unique endorphin rush of having arrived just in time. The flexible funnel pipe stole away as though never there at the same time that pneumatic sanitizers gloved his hands, then disappeared. Joe pivoted to stride out of the compartment trailed by a voice purring in the ether, "Have a wonderful day on the Moon, sir."

Outside, he spied Alesha a few meters away, color shifting randomly as she idly surveyed the hall, an extensive Quonset hut arrangement full of shops and stalls everywhere. Joe breathed in and out deeply, composing himself now that his pressing emergency had passed. Casually, he strolled over to her. Before he knew it, she faced him again beaming a sun-kissed smile.

"All better?" she said.

"Uh, yeah," Joe mumbled.

"Okay, good. We can begin," she said, tucking her arm inside of his. Joe immediately felt another sort of uneasiness.

"Welcome to Luna Tuna!" Alesha said, sweeping her free arm in front of them.

Joe glanced at the expansive kaleidoscope continuing to flash in front of him, lights, colors, holoscopic imagery, people of all sizes, shapes, hues, genders in various formatting surging around them.

"Luna Tuna?" he said. "How come it's called Luna Tuna?"

Alesha shrugged. "Early settlers in this colony tried establishing a tuna fish farm here at the beginning of Lunar settlement. It took off at first, but eventually failed. Salinating the water became prohibitive. By that time, though, other ancillary enterprises sustained the outpost. It grew into the largest community on the Moon. Scoring the disembarkation hall contract didn't hurt, of course. Still, it's so popular now that it's been chosen again as the site for the 2420 Olympics!"

"The Olympics? You still have them? Here, on the Moon?"

"Oh, yes," she said, "They always take place on the Moon, for more than a century now."

"What for? Most people still live on Earth, right?"

"Well, sure, but with the PMDs everyone who wants to can afford to come. Most attend it through virtual access, though. Lots of them blend into their favorite athletes for the ultimate, firsthand experiences. That can generate some serious SDF debt, however. You know, what the market will bear. They're happy to put in the hour, though, the experience is so exciting."

"Yeah, but on the Moon?"

"Think about it, Joe," she said. "Pole vaulting more than 100 meters. Broad jumping the length of an entire pitch. One hundred-meter dashes in almost nano seconds! If you can keep from bounding out of control, of course. But putting the shot to the highest orbit! Throwing a javelin beyond the Moon's curve!"

"Really?" Joe said skeptically.

"All right, I'm embellishing a bit for promotional purposes, that's what I do."

"What, PR for the Olympics? You get paid? I mean SDF credit?"

"No, no, no need for that, though you can earn a lot of intragalactic vouchers. I do it because it's fun! The Olympics are fun, all of them, on the Moon! On the Moon, the decathlon is relevant again!"

He found her unbridled enthusiasm delightful. Considering his own situation, he felt considerably more bridled.

She watched him deflate and moved to touch his arm. "Don't be blue," she said turning blue. Lavender followed, segueing into crystalline facets splashing circulatory reds and blues in an aura around her.

Joe smiled painfully, "I'm happy for you, Alesha, honestly. I like you and it pains me to think that soon I'm going to be off the Moon for 89 years doing my SDF service."

"Oh," she said, love-tapping his arm, "that's no time at all."

"Eighty-nine slow-time years."

"Well, there's that. But you have to believe me, once you've done it, you'll forget it ever happened. After that, every slow-time instant will be fun, like the Olympics!"

He nodded morosely, "Maybe I should compete in the Olympics."

Alesha looked him up and down. "Well, you've got the body for it."

He perked up. "You think I could do that, really?"

She pulled back slightly, flushing mauve for a moment. "I'm sure you have the potential," she said. "I'm just not sure about the skills unique to traversing the Moon."

"Yeah," Joe said. Weighing in at 84 kgs and just under two meters tall, he had been a pretty good athlete in his school days. Excelling at any sport took serious training, though.

"You do have lovely fair skin and spun gold hair," Alesha offered.

He grimaced at the compliment. She leaned toward him, "The games are a year off. You could use that time to work on technique, perhaps schedule one of your sanctioned SDF hiatuses for the games."

He lifted his head. "You think so?"

She smiled and glowed. "Why not? You have the time."

"That's for sure," he laughed. Then, he said, "Say, this must be trying for you, all this slow time."

"You forget your orientation," she said. Slowly, she said, "We love slow time for doing what we love."

Joe flinched. "You're enjoying this? You don't just want to get going?"

She sidled up and bumped him with her hip. "I think there's no hurry. If you want to, I think we could wait a cycle before you report."

She wheeled deliberately, embracing him. Joe suddenly felt another sensation below his belt absent for three centuries. Embarrassed, he said, "Sorry for that. Deep freeze time doesn't seem to change some things."

"Not to worry," she said, closing in to brush her lips against his.

He pricked up his ears. "You mean, you might, uh, be interested?"

She drew back. "You mean sexual intercourse?"

Joe began stuttering at what he thought must be fast time.

Alesha put a hand on his cheek. "We can, if you like," she said softly. "But there are so many other lovely things to do."

Holding one hand, she led him away.

At the light of the next 24-hour cycle, Joe followed Alesha out of the accelerator tube into Luna Tuna's main causeway, never feeling better in either of his lives.

"So, where do we go from here?"

"The commercial dockings. But we have time. Hungry?"

To his utter surprise, he was. "Yeah, really hungry. I could eat a sack of suds."

"Suds?" she asked, puzzled.

"An old saying. Soapsuds—it doesn't mean anything now."

"Oh. Well, there's a lot to choose from," she said gazing up around her.

Joe craned his neck to a series of holomenus above a clutch of eateries line up on one of the transparent catwalks draping the bubble walls. A sudden realization startled him.

"Hey, how come I can read all these holosigns? Why're they all in English?"

Alesha looked up and around. "Oh, right, Old Standard. The holopromos scan every individual to offer personalized messages in each's native language."

"Oh," he said. He zeroed in on one touting best country breakfasts.

Best Breakfast at Luna Tuna Prices!
  Coffee – 1.50[6]
  Juice – 5.00[8]
  Fruit bowl, yogurt – 10.00[9]
  Egg – 12.50[5]
  Two eggs – 24.00[10]
  Two eggs, bacon/sausage, home fries,
    toast – 37.00[15]
  Flapjacks, one egg, bacon/sausage,

13

home fries — 54.00^{25}

"Are those in dollars?" Joe asked.

"Luna vouchers," Alesha said, "comparable to old currency denominations, more or less."

"Exponential," he said.

"Yeah," she said, "a bit more expensive here on the Moon."

"Unhuh. Eleven dollars and thirty-nine cents for a cup of coffee."

She pursed her lips, nodding, "Competitive."

"So, a country breakfast, twenty-seven bucks to the fifteenth power." Joe shook his head, "That's more than they charged at a Hilton back in the day."

He faced Alesha. "There's food on the ship."

"Yes, of course," she said.

"Maybe I should start getting used to it."

Alesha beamed her melting smile, "Oh, c'mon, Joe, I'm buying. You can treat me when you get back."

"Eighty-nine years from now? You'll get hungry."

"I'm always hungry," she said, hooking her arm in his. "Let's go."

After breakfast, they stood in front of one of the docking ports for industrial vehicles. Joe and Alesha gazed up at an extremely prolated spheroid seemingly balanced on a single point.

"That's it?" asked Joe.

"I believe it is," said Alesha. She seemed to draw back into herself for an instant. "Dock Seven-O-One, LightSailor Blue Baleen, Chief Officer Grant Grenadier." She locked eyes with Joe's. "This is it."

"Well, all right, then." Joe stepped closer to embrace Alesha. "Thank you for helping me, for everything."

She smiled, "I enjoyed it. I like you, Joe. If you wish, we can be in touch while you're away."

Surprised, he said, "You would do that? I'll be gone for so long."

She squished her mouth, "Not so long for me, not in fast time."

"Oh, right."

14

"And, as I said before, you can come back for breaks. Everyone deserves a break now and then. You can relax back here at Luna Tuna with me."

"That would be wonderful," he breathed.

"Wonderful!" She pecked him on the cheek, "Okay. Off you go."

The loading crane lifted him to midships of the lightsailor, 100 meters above the dock base. He watched Alesha's tiny figure waving to him back and forth. He turned and entered the hatch.

"Glad to see you."

In front of Joe stood a man in a charcoal-ash colored jumpsuit, six feet tall, gray-haired, and slender bordering on emaciation. Rippling lines coursed down a pale white face to folds of skin like a vulture's. This guy was old, Joe thought, a bit taken aback. He suddenly realized that he hadn't seen anyone old since his resuscitation.

"You are Chief Officer Grant Grenadier?"

"I know not what you expected, but that's me. You can call me Granny."

Granny. Of course.

"I'm Joe Barber."

"Here for your SDF hitch."

"Yeah, eighty-nine years," Joe said glumly. "What about you? You look like you might be close to having yours done."

"Because I'm worn goods?" snapped Granny. "Not everyone wants to stay green."

Granny seemed to cool down, "I got a few years, yet. But neither of us is getting anywhere until we get going." Granny wheeled around and stepped off into a long cylindrical passageway. Joe broke into a jog to catch up to him.

Granny led them deep into the bowels of the ship to a central complex of compartments.

"This is where we run the ship and where we live," he said. He ran up three stories of a metal stairway and plopped into a seat that wrapped cozily around him. Joe stopped behind him and stared at the exposed outside lunar wall skying above them.

"We'll just ion out of here until clear of the Moon, then unfurl the sails. Once that's done, we can pick up some speed in free space."

Granny glanced up behind him, then back to the console. "Take a seat," he said dipping his head to his right. Joe clambered into the seat next to his, and immediately felt a flowing embrace hugging his body in snug comfort.

The lunar wall drew closer, opening to reveal black punctuated by stars above a gray dust-covered bowl. The black grew wider, larger as the bowl receded beneath them. In a matter of minutes, they floated freely among the points of light decorating the black drapery surrounding them.

"Good enough, now the sails."

The Chief Officer never moved, but something shifted in the craft, something large. Granny glimpsed Joe twisting his head up, down, and around. He said, "You've never seen this. Okay, here's a cheap thrill. Won't last, though," Granny said.

Suddenly, Joe somehow found himself outside looking at the ship from afar. Startled, he gripped the chair to jump up. Too late, until he realized that he still sat, breathing until he caught his breath.

Silently, two titanic cylinders the length of the entire spheroid emerged from each side. Unfolding as they spread outward, they soon joined together as an all-encompassing astral plane of their own, festooned bedazzlingly with a million shining obsidian panels, the solar units that powered the ship.

"Magnificent," uttered Joe.

Granny pursed his lips, "Not after you've been out here the nth time. But that's the f'n'j game," he sighed.

Joe dropped his eyes to Granny, and the view outside abruptly changed back to the interior of the ship. "What's f and j?"

"Flotsam and jetsam. Space junk. After four or five centuries, the stuff builds up, like geometrically, and I don't mean like triangles or rhombuses. That's why we're here, that's why we make the big bucks—garbage in space!"

16

Over dinner, Joe listened as Granny expounded on the economics of outer space waste management.

"They been putting junk out here since they lit the first candle way back in the 20th century. Burnt-out rocket stages, derelict space stations, defunct ancient telescopes, and a shitload of dead satellites, all sorts crowding the cosmos. There're even a few lost capsules floating around out there with God knows what left inside.

"Those are the big-ticket items. Then, you got your little nuisances, like screwdrivers and screws, pliers, one lost thermal glove, ammonia tanks, even a camera. I found that one. Weird contraption, two-D pics of space out a small window, that's it." Granny smiled slyly. "I made a teeny fortune selling it. Made the down payment on Blue Baleen, plus trading in my old rust bucket The Glowing Comet. Nodding his head up and down, he slapped the arm of his chair, "Only 1,440 installments to go and this baby's all mine!"

Joe involuntarily shifted his eyes back and forth. Carefully, he said, "That's a long time, isn't it? As long as my SDF term, maybe longer?"

"It's a damn sight shorter than if I'm cleaning up cosmic crap in the Comet." He leaned over, grasping his hands together between his knees. "You see," he said, "this used to be a great racket. Everyone zooming around in space for half a millennium, they left behind a lot of litter. They been spending another half-millennium trying to clean it all up. At first, like I said, the pickings were great. The big stuff was low-hanging fruit, popular to museums, private collectors, and the like. Going after that became real competitive, started a lot of bidding wars. But it went fast, after that the little items, too. Except for an occasional jackpot now and then, all that's left is space grit—metal particles, flecks of paint, even a few dipoles thrown up there back in the 20th century. Thing is, all that itty-bitty stuff travels at mega-velocity, way faster than an eye can see. When just a smidgen hits anything, it leaves dents, sometimes holes. Reflects light, too, blinding. So, as little as it brings in monetarily, it all still got to be cleaned up."

He sat back. "That's when the business model morphed into an SDF."

"Which is why they brought guys like us back?" Joe asked.

"Well," Granny said, "Not too many current folks find this work interesting anymore, fast time or not." He moved forward again, "But Blue Baleen's a real game-changer. With the likes of the old Glowing Comet, we all had to leave ship, go out and sweep up the stuff with electro-nets, very labor intensive. Big Blue's just that, a whale lightsailor outfitted with state-of-the-art nanoplates that can scoop up every single mite of microcosmic space shit. All I got to do is match velocity, point her and let her roll."

Joe tilted his head. "That's great. You'll be done with your SDF in no time. In fact, having me on board will hold you back. Why am I here?"

Granny smiled sickly. "New tech often presents hiccups. The nanoplates require frequent upkeep—extravehicular maintenance. Seeing Joe's puzzled expression, he went on, "When the f'n'j we scoop up doesn't get ingested all that precise, then, someone's gotta vacuum it up. That's kinda gonna be your job. You, not me, every time, this trip, every trip."

"I see," Joe said, setting his teeth. Alesha's Moon Olympics idea seemed much more feasible by comparison.

On the solar side of Blue Baleen, Joe labored to clean the massive maw's nanoplate clusters. While wielding the reverse magnetic besom on this, his 29th trip in 30 days, he muttered, "Picking up litter in space really sucks."

"Better than the plastic detail on Mother Earth," replied Granny, "on land or sea. You're either wet all the time, your nose full of salt, or you're covered in muck from mining landfills. Either way, you always end up untangling megatons of gross plastic shit. Very unsavory."

Joe asked Granny, "Don't they have tech available to clean the nanoplates?"

"Sure," said Granny, "but it's all pricey. Why spend the money when we have you?" He smiled his mercenary grin.

Joe decided then to pitch Alesha's idea to Granny.

"An athlete wins one medal at the Intragalactic Moon Olympics, his or her SDF goes away."

18

"What, it's waived?" asked Granny.

Joe shook his head, "No, the money given to victors. For a marquee event, like for instance, the 100-meter dash. The bronze medal winner takes home a prize of one billion lunar bills to the 10th power."

Granny jerked as if he'd been hit square in the head. Joe continued, "Silver brings 1.5 billion, power 10, gold gets you 5 billion . . . to the 10th of course."

"Holy Ghost in Vacuum!" burst Granny.

"I know," said Joe. "That's prize money, never mind side bets." He stared at frozen, open-mouthed Granny.

"And this is all above board, legal eagle, no strings or prison bars?"

"All sanctioned. Hell, it's all run by IMOC." He waited for Granny to catch up, then said, "Think of what the Moon Olympic Decathlon brings. Ten events, the most popular competition of them all."

Joe could see Granny ready to drool. But the long, gray chief officer abruptly pouted.

"What's this mean to us? We ain't Moon Olympic material."

Joe shrugged, "Maybe not you. Alesha thinks I have potential. I played ball, ran some track back in school."

"Oh, yeah, like you're that good."

"Listen," Joe said earnestly, "maybe I'm good enough. I'm not talking about any individual stuff, I don't think I could ever do that. But with the decathlon, you don't have to be the best at any one thing, just better than most at most things. Think about where I come from, 300 years ago, we did a shitload of physical stuff in those days. I've got to be competitive today with a little training."

"Really? You really think so?"

"You want to race me? Look, Alesha should know, she works the Moon Olympics for IMOC."

"Works?"

"Volunteers."

Granny nodded. He thought deeply for a moment, then broke the silence."

"What's the catch?"

"No catch," Joe said, casually gazing above. "I'll need to train, though. Quite a bit, in fact."

"Unhuh."

"Of course, the Ex work's pretty wearing."

"I see," Granny said dryly. "Okay, lay it out. What's the deal?"

"We split the maintenance space walks and we split any prizes that come our way."

Granny screwed up his mouth. "I should've seen that coming."

"Fifty-fifty."

Joe held out his hand. Granny spit on his own and slapped it into Joe's.

Bent over, his feet in the blocks, Joe waited for the signal. Granny tickled the remote and the shot sounded, reverberating around the gigantic warehouse chamber. Joe took off, left, right—as soon as his right foot hit the deck, he bounded soaring into the air, stopped only by the crack of his dome on the overhead bulwark. The blow sent him careening back to the floor, reactively bouncing up, smacking down again, finally crumpling to a rest.

"Shit."

Joe rolled over flat on his back. He slowly removed the lunar survival helmet and tossed it aside. Throwing his arms over his head to block out the harsh white light, he muttered, "This isn't working."

Yelling from afar, Granny pronounced. "Not quite what we're looking for. You need to contain that first step, burst forward, not up."

"Then, what?"

"Why, clear the first hurdle, touch down, and go for the next one."

The first hurdle, 3 meters high, started a rising progression of 6 meters, 9, 12, and 15, then descending in order to end of the 375-meter race. At moon gravity, vaulting as high as 15 meters wasn't the problem, given universal genetic sculpting of the competitors. Control was everything, however, and after two months of training, Joe still sucked.

The pole vault had gone the same way, and the javelin throw, the high jump. He tossed the shot better, the technique being more

20

straightforward. But the discus flew everywhere, and the footraces required only a modicum less control than the hurdles.

Granny glided over. "You're not doing it, fella. I think we're gonna have to resume our original arrangement."

Expecting as much, Joe glanced up at the Chief Officer, almost resigned. "Sure. But look at it this way. We both have nearly a hundred years of celestial trash-collection ahead of us. That's a lot of time for a lot of things to go wrong. Let's face it, you're no spring chicken, Granny."

"Hey, watch yourself. I got options."

"Sure, no offense. We both know I'm not going to get good enough for the 2420 games. But they hold them every four years. That's 22 more times within our 89-year SDF window. If I keep training, I might get good enough to win an event some years down the road. Saving any time would be good, right? So, why don't I keep training under the current terms? Fifty-fifty?"

Granny looked like he had eaten something sour. "I have my doubts. Seventy-five, twenty-five."

Joe sighed, holding out his hand to be helped up.

Six month-cycles later, he'd finally reached his playing weight again and his optimal physical strength. He also realized that to attain a competitive level in the IMOs, his current rate of athletic progress projected a curve of 50 years. Granny would do the math, too, he knew, and he expected to hear any day now about returning to their original division of duties. To his surprise, though, the Chief Officer never brought it up. Joe trained diligently to keep the status quo, and between running, leaping, and cleaning nanoplates, he spent the little spare time left binge occupying old holo-reality shows. Early on he tried holo-interacting with Alesha, only to receive fast-time cyber-replies. Translated, they all said in slow time that she valued every reach-out she received but was immersed in IMOC functions and hoped to reciprocate very soon. But she never did. Joe wondered if she ever would during the next 89 years. After a while, he stopped reaching out every day.

The Blue Baleen continued to scour the void between Sol and Earth, slurping up miniscule matter while surfing back and forth, one hologrid at a time. Processors on either side of the main passageway separated and condensed metal, carbon, and other materials into city blocks to eject from the lightsailor's stern. Scheduled space tugs hooked them to steer to holoprinters stationed throughout the solar system.

"We get a few bucks outta them," Granny said, picking his teeth with an ersatz chicken bone, his feet up on the table. "The next generation of sailors gonna change all that."

"Yeah?" Joe replied, already bored with the Chief Officer's endless stream of get-rich schemes.

"You bet," Granny said smugly. "On-board mega-holoprinters. Produce commercial goods on the spot, fill orders from here. Eliminate the middleagent."

"Really? What kind of goods?"

"Anything from A to Z. Fliers, ground cars, zero-gravity domiciles and pools, nonsentient furniture, all kinds. Other multidimensional holoprinters, all sizes. Hell, pets, pet crates, AI furnishings, personal clones and companions. Every prosthetic under the sun. You name it, we make it!"

"Where're you going to fit all this stuff? How're you going to ship it?"

"In the tugs, of course!"

"And all this is going to make more money, not cost more?"

"Economies of scale, man! Volume!"

The men shifted to their left, instinctively grabbing hold of fixtures as a seismic shudder rippled through the ship, followed by a thunderous thump.

Wide-eyed, they stared at each other.

"What the 'f' was that?" Joe yelled.

"F'n'j!" stuttered Granny.

Joe paused, then barked, "You think so? We hit something?"

"Or something hit us."

"We have to move!" Joe shouted, "there may be a breach!"

22

He jumped up and started toward the hatchway.

"No breach, we'd be sucked out of here already," Granny said. "But we got to find out what happened, head off any looming rift that could bite us in the ass. Suit up and get out there, see what hit us. I'll back you up in the center."

Joe bolted to the front egress area, whipped on his X suit, sealed the hatch and decompressed out. He jetted up to Blue's mammoth nose cone where the immense nanoplate clusters were situated, blasting as fast as he could from one end to the other, up and down in search of the impact point of the foreign object.

"You think it was a meteor?" he asked Granny as he scoured the vast complex.

"No way to know 'til you get there. So, get there."

Joe finally saw it, a knobby-looking thing with a bottle neck that swelled back into half an oblong jammed into the myriad nanoplate foils."

"You see it? It sure doesn't look like a meteorite."

"I see it. It ain't a space rock, it's been fabricated, an artifact. We just might've hit the honey pot. Or got hit by it. Lemme do some research. Meantime, give it the once-over, see what it'll take to get it loose."

Joe buzzed around the contraption, at least seven meters long and three meters wide, badly pitted by mini space projectiles into a misshapen mess. Half of it had been squeeze-boxed striking the colossal cluster, which had suffered severe damage the radius of a full football pitch. Joe wasn't sure if they could dislodge the wreck at all.

"Okay," said Granny, "Can you see any markings or numbers on it?"

Joe maneuvered around close to the metal. After a few minutes, he said, "There are some faint red letters on one side, pretty badly faded and chipped away. C . . . another C, a C, and a P. CCCP," said Joe.

"Unhuh. Go up to the top of it opposite the crashed part, see if there're numbers there.

Joe zipped up, braking next to the curve of the globe sticking out.

"I see some stuff, but I can't read it. Take a look," Joe said, fixing his helmet visor on the rubric for Granny to see through the console's remote projector.

"Okay, it looks stable to me," Granny said, "Come on back in."

"According to Blue's Googly Cloud, it's an old rocket built by the Russkie Bolsheviks back in the 1960s. CCCP, that's Cyrillic spelling for Union of Soviet Socialist Republics. What we got stuck in our craw is a Soyuz 7K-OK model, one of their first space capsules ever. They stopped making them after number 11 delivered a crew back to Earth dead. What's interesting about this one is that its number is двенадцать, translated meaning number 12." Granny grinned broadly, "Except there ain't no number 12 on record!"

"Really? So, what does that mean?"

"It means we could have hold of something very desirable, something valuable."

"If we can pry it loose."

"Yeah," said Granny, "so let's get on that."

From ship center, they closely perused the catastrophic juncture of the Soyuz and Blue Baleen's nanoplate array.

"Man," said Granny, "this smashup gives new meaning to integrated technology."

"Can't we just cut off the part that's intact?" Joe suggested.

Granny grimaced, "The operation's a success but the patient's dead." He looked up at Joe, "It'd be worth more if we could get all of it out together. Anyway, even if we save what we can, we still got to head back to the Moon. Blue's nanos need professional care and rehab."

"Okay." He concentrated on the wrecked space capsule. "It looks to have three parts, the front globe, a middle pod, and maybe what's left of a rocket component crushed in the cluster."

Granny nodded after looking at the archival schematic, "A propulsion unit with attitude thrusters."

"So, how about seeing if we can separate the two front modules manually, junk the rest. Two thirds is better than none." Seeing

24

Granny's skeptical reaction, he said, "Think of it as a down payment on our SDFs."

"Okay, let's see."

He started scanning and stopped abruptly. "What the 'f'?"

Joe saw it, too. "Holy shit."

In the middle chamber, supine on a w-shaped jump seat reclined an enormous mass grossly humanoid in shape, covered by a thick coat of what looked like white plaster.

"What the Be-Geesus is that?" uttered Joe.

Granny returned to his console screen. "According to Googly Cloud, that is a cosmonaut." He stared up at Joe again, "A Soviet space jockey."

"F'n'j creature from outer space!"

"Is he alive?" Joe asked. They had been scrutinizing the still form for most of a slow half hour.

"There are no life signs," Granny answered, turning his eyes to Joe's. "Just like you once upon a time."

"Well, now what?"

"Now, we're stuck with him; her; whoever. Blue says so, as decreed by OML 432[6]. We need to do our best to bring this space mummy back to life."

"Can we do that?"

Granny lifted and dropped his shoulders. "If it's viable—no brain discombobulation—the holoprinter med program should be able to handle it." He stared off into space, looking to Joe as though he might be trading places with the cryopreserved Russian.

"Why so glum, Granny?"

"We zap old Comrade Frankenstein back into the game, he gets the ship he rode in on, all of it. ADL 3798[9]."

"Another ADL," Joe muttered.

"He walks away SDF fully funded while I'm deeper in the hole getting my ship fixed," Granny moaned.

Joe entered the Russian hulk through the hatch at the top of the module, trailing a tether line behind him. He worked his way past a glut of floating refuse until he came to the narrow neck at the juncture to the middle module, the landing pod. His X suit allowed him to wrench the wheel open to the joint access passage and he clambered inside.

The jump chair and its occupant took up virtually all of the space inside of the capsule, forcing Joe to angle sideways and upwards. The seat and body seemed melded together, a gargantuan statuary clearly larger than the hatchway aperture. Joe took a whack at it where the body and chair joined, freeing only a few frozen granules that floated away.

"This corpsicle is stuck solid to its throne. It's never going to fit through the hatch."

"So," Granny said, "separate them."

"How am I supposed to do that?"

"Thaw Cosmo out. Use your torch—go easy, now."

Joe popped the laser torch from his arm, set it on low and began to radiate it back and forth at the edge of the chair and the huge body. Three hours later, though still encased in ice, the cadaver gently rose slightly above the jump seat.

Joe attached the tether line to a leg and led the way to the forward module, pulling gently behind him. Before he could bring the inert giant through, he had to push the floating debris in the top module out into space. After clearing the capsule, he gently maneuvered the frozen carcass through the orbital module halfway through the open hatch.

An enormous blast of red, orange, and yellow light blew Joe and the white stiff at breakneck velocity out of the hulk. Gyrating, Joe saw the Soyuz disintegrate from the force of the explosion.

He quickly engaged his auxiliaries to reverse his trajectory while grabbing hold of the tether, swinging it in a broad parabola to dissipate its momentum. In a matter of seconds both Joe and his payload floated slowly in space, a good kilometer away from Blue Baleen.

"What the f'n'j was that?" Joe asked, nearly back to the lightsailor's access area. Along the way, he passed by the spot where the Soyuz had

26

been stuck, now completely gone. Only a charcoal imprint of its impact on the twisted nanoplate foils remained.

"That, I think," said Granny, "was hydrogen peroxide blowing up. They stored it in the propulsion module to use as fuel for their direction thrusters. Pretty dangerous stuff, you must've set it off with your torch freeing up your snow bunny pal there."

"Yeah, that was a great idea of yours," Joe said, climbing out of his X suit after securing the airlock.

"I know. Now, nobody gets well. Too bad old Trotsky there didn't get fricasseed, too."

"Well, he didn't. So, now what?"

"Stick him in the med printer, see what comes out. Maybe we'll get lucky, turn out he's some kinda ancient Russian oligarch's son, rich and grateful after being liberated from Siberian space."

"Yeah, we've been lucky like that so far."

Three day-cycles later, Joe and Granny sat at the mess table, forks suspended as they stared at the monumental figure wrapped in a white sheet filling the hatchway. Over two meters tall and both shoulders pressing the doorframe, the visage before them embodied Socialist Realism writ large.

"Gde ya?" he said, stretching his arms above him to the top of the arch.

Joe and Granny exchanged glances. Granny said, "Is that Russian? Sorry, but we don't speak Russian."

"English. Your native language is English."

"Pretty much," replied Granny.

The big man dropped his arms to fold them across his formidable chest. "How unfortunate for me. I suppose I am your prisoner." It dawned upon them that he spoke with barely a trace of an accent.

"No," Granny dragged out the words, "guest, more like it."

"Guest. We have plenty of 'guests' in my country, too," he sighed.

Granny and Joe looked at each other again. Seeing the guest sag, Joe said quickly, "Do you want to sit down? You look done in." He shifted to leave room, and the massive man flopped down on the bench next to him.

"What's your name?" asked Joe.

"Boris Badenov," he said. "You want my serial number, too?"

"No, no, nothing like that. Look, we're not official or anything, just space waste managers. You sort of dropped into our laps. Your ship, the Soyuz, it crashed into ours."

The big stranger lolled back his head. "Strictly classified."

"Maybe so, but it's also been obliterated," chimed in Granny. "We just managed to get you out, get you back to 98 Fahrenheit." The giant knit his brows and Granny went on, "You been in deep freeze for like 450 years."

Startled, the cosmonaut quickly composed himself. He lowered his head in a nod and said, "Because your first language is English, by default I must consider you both to be members of Western culture hostile to the Soviet Union. So, how can I believe anything you say?"

Granny lifted his hands palms up, "I don't know how to answer that."

Joe said, "Believe us or don't, we're telling you the truth. Suppose we put you in front of a holocenter, give you free rein to find out anything you want to know. After that, you can decide."

"No matter what is sworn by your holy center, it will of course all be a fabrication."

Joe blew out a breath. "Just take a look, anything at all. Maybe we made it all up, but you're not a prisoner here. The Cold War's long done. We have other problems now, you'll see. You have the run of the place, so knock yourself out. Come back when you're ready to talk again."

Two cycles later, the rejuvenated cosmonaut rejoined them, his chiseled good looks a solid slate of closely contained, fierce distrust.

"I have completed my investigation. The evidence is over-whelming. First, you gentlemen emulate the egotistical arrogance of your capitalist forebearers by not knowing any other than your native language. Typical, though disappointing."

28

Joe sat back, taken aback.

"Yeah, well, we've been busy," Granny said.

Joe stared at Granny, horrified. Didn't he see the size of this guy? He could crush both of them in one group bear hug.

"It is also clear," responded the Russian, "that you both are members of the ruling classes practicing bourgeois nationalism to deliberately divide people by nationality, race, ethnicity, or religion so as to distract them from initiating class warfare."

"You have got to be kidding!" Joe blurted out.

"Oh yeah? Well, workers unite!" shouted the cosmonaut.

Joe and Granny sat still, silently stunned.

Abruptly, the hulking Soviet's features relaxed into a broad, naughty, bird-eating grin. "Gotcha'!" he barked, throwing himself down lengthwise on the bench opposite them, kicking his heels up, laughing and pointing. He righted himself while saying, "I tell you, it was a shock to my system to find out that everything you told me was true, everything, amazing! That was a close call when my ship went ka-blooey—thank you, Joe, for your quick action. And to be brought back to life after so long! How great is that? When my life support started to go in the Soyuz, I thought I'd be a sosul'ka for sure, an icicle. Speaking of icicles, I tried out your foodalator's ice cream, and oh my God it was so good, it's addictive! You are dealing with drugs, here, with your magic machines! But tell me, can they dial up some vodka, it's been almost half a millennium. I couldn't figure how to order that. But I tell you, I'm not going to be able to fit into my jumpsuit. You know, I could go for a nosh right now. How about you guys?"

Over dinner, the cosmonaut told his story.

"I'm not really Boris Badenov—didn't you ever watch *The Rocky and Bullwinkle Show* on your telly?"

Joe had no idea what he was talking about. Taking him in, though, his blond hair, vibrant pink complexion, and squared off features, the affable giant seemed to be an outsized image of himself. In fact, wearing his newly printed black jumpsuit, he cut quite the monolithic figure, thought Joe.

"My given name is Giorgi Alexandre Khevsurians, Engineer-Captain of the USSR spacecraft Soyuz 12. You don't really need my serial number, do you?" he mumbled after spooning a large portion of macaroni and cheese into his mouth. "After the disastrous death of my three comrades in Soyuz 11, Space Command redesigned the Soyuz docking elements and sent me out on a test run. Everything seemed okeydokey until the vehicle unfortunately overshot the calculated parabola. I found myself traveling on a much longer orbital path beyond the Moon, and you know the rest."

"So, they sent just you?" Granny asked.

The big man smiled somewhat sweetly. "I'm Georgian. Aside from still holding a grudge against Stalin, they don't particularly like any of us for much reason. Cosmonauts are expensive to train, not worth risking any more than necessary on a corrective test flight." He took another bite. "But I'm a still good communist," he said, "always ready to wait in line with my avoska whenever our beautifully stocked Soviet universam throws out fresh cabbage available to one out of every tenth comrade." He lifted his vodka tonic in salute and drank deeply. "So, where are you two headed?"

Granny managed to bring three-quarters of Blue Baleen's nanoplates back online, enough production efficiency to make any quick return to the Moon fiscally inefficient. This translated into Joe seeing to all of the X trips, since Granny ruled that his twenty-five percent of the plates were the ones out of service. Joe complained furiously, which caught Giorgi's attention.

"I'll do them, all of them!" Giorgi pleaded. "There's nothing else to do on this space kite except holoporn. Let me help you as my saviors!"

"Nope," Granny said. "You're a historic artifact. If anything happens to you, we're in deep space shit. Sorry, Giorgi, old pal, you're gonna have to sit this one out."

"Be-Geesus, Granny, don't be such a stick," Joe whined, "let him help!"

"Absolutely not. Suppose he's lost out there, what you think the authorities will do to us? Probably fine us right back to SDF square one. Nope, you go have fun with the holocasts, Giorgi. We'll take care of the rest."

He turned on Joe, "That means you keep up with your Olympic training, too. No goofing off on that."

"What the f', Granny, how am I supposed to do that? I'm back doing all the X—"

"Minus twenty-five percent, don't forget," Granny snapped. "Now, get your ass to the training facility. After you crap out at upcoming games, you only have four years left to get ready for the next IMOs."

Grumbling all the way, Joe changed into his track gear and plodded to the long passageway where they'd set up the decathlon equipment. Blatantly curious, Giorgi trailed Joe asking questions all the way. Glowering with fury, Joe answered as cryptically as he could. Finally, they arrived at the practice field. Joe reduced the gravity, then set about stretching.

"What will you do first?" Giorgi asked, his blue eyes almost puppylike eager.

"The hurdles," Joe muttered. "I always start with the worst."

He limbered up, stretched out to settle in the blocks, and nodded. The gun report sounded, and he took off, reaching the first hurdle in three bounds, leaped up to clear it, hit the synthetic tarmac bouncing to the second hurdle, and soared up to hit the bottom of the hurdle's cross-board squarely with his head. He fell to the ground, dribbling up and down a few times until settling into a heap.

"Oh, bozhe!" Giorgi shouted into Joe's ear, "That was astonishing! You almost did not hit the cross-board!"

Joe rolled his eyes to Giorgi's, "Best laid plans," he said flatly.

"It's so exciting, can I try?"

Joe sighed, "Knock yourself out. I almost did. Help me up."

Giorgi crouched in the blocks, happily excited as he waited for Joe to signal the start. Joe gestured, the gun sounded, and Giorgi was off in a flash. He took the first hurdle in one hop, the second in two, and

31

the others similarly, speeding around the course as though on a pogo-jet.

Staggered, Joe stuttered, "Geesus, where'd that come from?"

Back in the mess, he laid it all out for Granny.

"I tell you Granny, this is it. I had him do everything, 100 meters to the 1500, pole vault, javelin, shot, all ten events. He came close to breaking every standing record. Believe me, he's our ticket to everlasting paradise!"

Skeptical, Granny said, "You sure you had the gravity set right?"

"I checked it before each trial. It was dead on. The man's superhuman!"

"Makes you wonder if the Russkies didn't tweak his genetic code a little bit."

"Yeah, they did do that stuff a lot in those days," Joe said. "We probably don't want to know so the IMOC doesn't know."

"And you think you can get him in?"

"I'll check with Alesha, but I don't see why not. They let players without national backing compete, call them 'independents'. From what she told me, they have a place for everyone, bionic, genengineered, you name it. She says their real interest is putting on a super sports spectacular. So, I think our best bet is to get our champion into the classic division, no enhancement at all."

Granny mulled for a while, his features still screwed up in doubt. He rubbed his jaw, then lowered his hand. "Okay, even if he can race and he wins, what makes you think he'll share his take with us?"

"Well, he owes us. We brought him back to life, we're like his surrogate mothers, or maybe fathers, anyway."

"Yeah, I don't think he'll see it like that."

"All right, Granny, but what do we got to lose? Say he doesn't feel so grateful to us and won't share his winnings. We still have the inside track, we're the only ones who know how good he is, we can lay down some bets. Think of the odds we'd get!"

Granny pressed his lips together, tapping his fingers against each other. "I want to see, first."

Out on the training pitch, Giorgi whirled around in a spin worthy of the ballet and let loose the disc from the crux of his arm. The metal plate disappeared to the other end of the passageway with only the sound of it clanging on the far bulwark announcing its arrival.

Granny turned to Joe, "Okay. So, what next?"

"Take Blue off this space-junk hologrid and double time it straight to the Moon. I'll see about getting the lowdown from Alesha."

Joe didn't leave his quarters until he managed to raise Alesha, which took nonstop messaging for more than three cycles. He worried, wondering if she'd moved on.

"Sweetcakes, I'm so glad to see you!" she said, smiling widely. His pain evaporated as he absorbed her virtual presence throughout his being. She shined obsidian black with slashes of vivid white playing across her face, torso, arms, and legs tracking her feelings.

"I've been so busy with the IMOs," she said, "Even at fast time I had no time to get you back." True or not, he melted and resolved to be with her for all time, slow and fast.

"Of course he can compete, considering his unique credentials," Alesha gushed, "I'm positive the IMOC would be delighted to have him participate in the classic division, a living, historical artifact dating back to the advent of space travel! Since the Soviet Union no longer exists, I assume he will want to represent Russia?"

"Oh," replied Joe, "I'm not sure. I guess so. Though maybe he would like to enter as an independent. I don't know, I'll have to ask him."

"That's fine, we don't need to know right away. Just be sure to tell me his status as soon as you can. And if he does plan to compete in the classic division, you're sure he hasn't had any gene work done, yes?"

Joe swallowed and said, "Well, we don't really know. Except, he's been floating out there since 1973, pretty much the stone age for genetic manipulation. In those days, they were more adept at using drugs to boost performance. I could ask, but he might not even know himself."

"That's fine," she said, "whatever the case, we can find a good fit for him. Just message me with the events he would like to enter. Oh, I'm so excited to see you close to me again soon, pelvis to pelvis!"

"Me too," he said, "believe me. You have no idea."

"Wonderful! See you in a few minutes!" she gushed.

"Absolutely," said Joe, signing off with a holokiss and a hug. A few fast-time minutes to her, he thought, to him more like three weeks. Right now, he needed to persuade the historical space hero to compete and also split his prize money with his travel companions.

Sitting over a vat of vodka during the next cycle, Giorgi enthusiastically agreed to compete in the IMO, including sharing prize money with his two new space pals.

"So, Giorgi, my friend with the IMOC asked if you wished to participate as an independent agent or as a member of Russia's team. They 're still one of the best teams in the Galaxy, usually taking home a shipload of medals."

Giorgi replied, "I would love to reunite with my Russian brothers and sisters," he said solemnly in a pronounced Slavic accent. "Together we can again vanquish all of the sharks of imperialism, rootless cosmopolitans, and whores of capitalism infesting the heavenly firmament."

Joe and Granny blinked at each other. Granny said in a subdued voice, "Uh, they're not like that anymore. Russia's a federation now, and they all pretty much love capitalism, which everyone now calls the cornerstone of charitable contribution throughout the Galaxy." He saw Joe's incredulous look and quickly said, "I'm not kidding."

"Oh," said Giorgi. He shrugged, "Okay, screw it. Let's make a shipload of rubles," he said, which caused both of his companions to crack wide smiles. "Sign me up for the decathlon. Also the individual events." Seeing their surprised looks, he said, "I want to make the most of this wonderful Western capitalist opportunity."

The three weekly cycles that followed dragged for Joe, not helped by Giorgi's eccentric antics. The next day cycle while walking down Blue's long, central corridor, Joe suddenly found himself lifted from

34

behind. He kicked his legs helplessly in the air as a booming "Malen'kiy ya!" shouted close behind his head nearly burst his eardrums.

Joe's heart nearly stopped; he bellowed, "What the f'n'j are you doing?"

Giorgi gently lowered him to the deck. "Spooking you," said Giorgi, "you know, for fun."

"God Be-Geesus, you think that's fun for me?"

More often, Giorgi followed Joe into the mess to collapse across one of the padded benches, talking the entire time.

"I cannot believe, Malen'kiy ya, how much I learned from the holocenter, he said. "So much has happened, so many changes. Everything is smaller and bigger at the same time. Big surprises, too; now they even get the weather right. The Soviets all went different directions, pretty peaceful, too," he said. "Not in my time. Very strict and meager. You go into a shop, say to the guy behind the counter, 'got any fish?' He says, 'you're in the wrong place, this is a butcher shop; we don't have any meat. You want the shop across the street where they don't have any fish.'"

Joe continued munching his granola.

"An old joke. Here's another. A guy's son says, 'Pop, can I have the keys to the car?' His poppa say, 'Okay, but don't lose them. We get the car in seven years.'"

He stretched, "Still, it will be good to reunite with my socialist teammates." He lifted his head, "I wonder if there will be female members on the team? I like female teammates. What do you think, Malen'kiy ya?"

"I don't know," Joe said. He chewed some more, then said, "Why're you always calling me Malenka?"

"Malen'kiy ya." Giorgi rose up from the bench.

"What's that mean?"

"Little me," Giorgi said, heading out the hatchway.

At last, Blue Baleen pulled into the Luna Tuna commercial docking area. Almost before the gargantuan lightsailor was secured, Joe jumped ship onto the disembarkment crane. He shot down to the main deck and raced the long length of it as fast as he could out to the main commercial causeway.

He immediately dipped his head and shaded his eyes from the ripping, garish glare of the bubble's bedazzling projections. The convex of arcade shops blasted a madman's spectrum of florescent fuchsias, incandescent turquoises, neon limes, and other piercing hues in a coruscating lightshow slicing and dicing every iota of pedestrian space. Joe found himself ducking reflexively, still too late to dodge holocast promos for Bendover Luna Suits, Moontime Pogo-jets, Quickie Trip Stasis Cocoons, Verimatic Home Foodalators, and a glut of other kaleidoscopic images bouncing back and forth through the Klereglas strollpaths.

In the midst of the visual din, soft hands covered his eyes from behind, stopping him in his tracks. He turned around and buried his head in her breast.

"Be-Geesus, Alesha, where did all this stuff come from?"

"Oh," she said, realizing his distress. "Close your eyes. It stops in an instant, Citicade law." She trotted over to a small stall, smiled at the vendor as she plucked a concave ribbon from his display and brought it to Joe.

"Put this over your eyes. It blocks out personal visual dissonance."

Joe whipped them on at once. "You don't need them?"

"Uh, no." She smiled apologetically, "I have a geneng adapt. You can get one, too, right after your SDF."

"Oh. Okay. Great."

She hugged him around the neck and kissed his temple. "Sorry. I am so in love to see you!"

"No, no. That's fine. So, where do we go from here?"

Joe, Alesha, and Granny stood at their seats in a box pod floating above Luna Tuna Stadium. Too nervous to sit, they watched Giorgi limbering up for the last event of the first decathlon day, the 400-meter run. Joe gripped Alesha's hand anxiously, so hard it turned blue, unless she'd shifted complexion due to her own nerves. He and Granny had talked to Giorgi carefully as they rode with him on the shuttle to the

36

Olympic Village Dome. To keep from raising any eyebrows about his hazy physiology, they counseled him to pick his moments to shine by finishing second or third in certain events.

"Stay close to the top in everything," said Joe, "and you'll be within striking distance to win it all at the end without folks thinking you're some sort of superman."

"You mean like in the comics or Nietzsche?" said Giorgi.

Joe gazed at him, bewildered.

"Either," said Granny.

Giorgi nodded obediently and held to the strategy throughout the preliminaries. Watching the qualifiers, Joe was surprised to see both men and women competing together in the same events. When the IMOC set up the classic division, he thought, they must have meant the new classic. Still, the female athletes contended right along with the males. In fact, of the other two Russians in the decathlon, a supple muscled woman named Ana performed on the team second only to Giorgi. After the first race, Giorgi introduced her and the other Russian decathlete Alexi to his two space mates and Alesha. Both seemed very friendly.

At the next cycle's Moonrise, Joe and Granny joined Alesha in her box pod to watch the finals of the opening event, the 100-meter dash. Giorgi abruptly blasted 15 meters in two steps, so fast he appeared to shoot out of the blocks before the bang of the starting gun could be heard. Joe howled "Be-Geesus!" as Giorgi pulverized the tape.

"F'n'j, we're screwed!" Joe blurted out.

"I don't think so," Granny said loudly above the din of the crowd. He tapped Joe's arm, "No false start. And looky over there."

Joe scanned the field and noticed two other runners clutching their knees next to Giorgi.

"Check the rerun," Granny said, nodding up at the holocast against the dark Moon skyline. Two runners leaned in to finish the sprint close on Giorgi's.

"If back in the day Giorgi did enjoy a little DNA doodling," whispered Granny to Joe, "those two boys there ain't all that far behind."

"One of those boys is Ana," said Joe.

Granny shook his head, "F'n'j Russkies."

As the Earth descended, though, matters didn't improve. Giorgi's long jump almost doubled the IMO record, 208.333 meters. He tossed his shot so far that they couldn't find it anywhere; he was declared the winner by default. During the following break, Joe close-whispered down to Giorgi on the stadium floor telling him to slow down.

"I'm sorry, Malen'kiy ya, it's hard," Giorgi whispered back, "I think it has something to do with uh, . . .ah, . . . adrenaline."

Joe winced and whispered, "I know, Giorgi, but you need to tone it down or the IMOC watchdogs will scan your DNA, see if any funny stuff's going on."

Giorgi's eyes widened, incredulous, then mortified, whispered emotionally, "I know of no funny stuff. I am brilliant naturally."

"Yeah, well, sure but why take a chance? Do what we told you to do, the decathlon is a sum-gain game. Save your brilliance for the individual events."

Gazing up at the pod, Giorgi nodded glumly from below.

After that, he managed to control his adrenaline in the remaining six events. He registered a clutch of seconds, thirds, and fifths that, going into Moon day-cycle two situated him in third place overall. In short order, Joe and Granny both wore fixed expressions of horror that mystified Alesha as she whole-heartedly cheered on the animated Russian artifact.

Giorgi took first place in the first three events going away. He ran and vaulted the 110-meter hurdles twice as fast as his original, remarkable run on Blue Baleen, seeming to assert that no gravity existed at all on the Moon. Launching his discus in a blurring whirl, it soared arcing into the far stadium wall, scoring the Moonstone in a downward vector halfway around before settling on the deck. Pounding the path on his final attempt in the pole vault, Giorgi jammed the supple rod into the notch so hard that it snapped just as he started to uncoil; his last step sent him over the 200-meter bar for another top finish.

Joe stalked down to the surface this time, flashing his coaching credentials to the gatekeepers. Granny and Alesha watched from the pod above as the tiny forms of the two revived pioneers gesticulated at each other silently. Finally, Joe returned.

"I don't know what's going on. He says he's sorry, but he looked cross, too."

"Maybe he just wants to win it all," Alesha said, "understandable for one who knows he is the best of all."

Joe frowned, "Could be, but he's risking disqualification maybe, and all credit toward his SDF."

"And ours, don't forget," Granny said.

Alesha glanced mildly scornful at Granny, then said to Joe, "Disqualified because of his DNA enhancement?"

Both Joe's eyes and mouth opened wide, shocked that she knew. He tried to assume an innocent countenance, but instead looked like a guilty little boy.

"Don't be so surprised, Joe. Of course I know Giorgi had work done, he's a mid-20th century cosmonaut, for the sake of sake! The IMOC scans every applicant routinely, not looking for some kind of clandestine advantage, there's no such thing anymore. They don't care who wins, the games are about the entertainment, the extravaganza, the diversion most of all. The officials will simply transfer Giorgi's status and scores to the Enhanced Performance Division. He probably won't finish in the top of the EPD, but even if he comes in last, his prize earnings will easily cover his SDF."

"Ours, too?" Granny asked.

Alesha eyed him somewhat askance. "That might depend upon how he places," she said, "and how he feels about you."

"It could be better for everyone involved, then," Joe said, "if Giorgi's genetic map stayed in the background."

Granny nodded up and down, while Alesha simply shrugged.

The javelin throw offered the two space-waste management men some comfort. Giorgi faulted on his first two attempts, opening the door for the second and third place decathletes, his teammates Alexi and Ana. At the same time, Joe and Granny then started worrying that Giorgi might under-perform too much. To their relief, he whipped his javelin 155 meters for third. Going into the final 1500-meter race, the Russian team held secure locks on a one-two-three finish medal finish for their homeland.

The first three laps of the 1500 played out as expected, with the Russian runners dashing in tandem, clocking three-quarters record of 72 seconds. Ana led, followed closely by Alexi with Giorgi just a step behind. Turning the corner of the last half lap, the broadcast roar of the Galaxy-wide audience obliterated any close-whispered utterances.

Joe scream-whispered now only to himself, 'Finish third, finish third!', hearing Granny's voice shout-whispering as well, the runners smears of speed as they closed on the finish, triggering a pinwheeling eruption from the crowded stadium. The holocast replayed almost as fast: Giorgi breasting Alexi, colliding into him, both exploding opposite sideways, Ana breaking the tape, a blinding paramecium of trailing racers following, pandemonium bursting out in the stands, Giorgi and Alexi pounding each other on the track, Alexi fast giving ground.

"That bitch of a son mock me all the time!" Giorgi shouted, sitting opposite Alesha and the two space trashmen. "With acid-dripping contempt, he call me 'Georgia Giorgi, the cabbage-eater, the horseshit-kicker, grizuny', everything to goad my goat. He even call me Igor—Igor, like I'm some kind of collective idiot or maybe a Frankenstein creature! He also sabotaged me at every turn—you think my vaulting pole breaks on its own? Not f'n'j likely! I did my best to get along with those Russian numbskulls, but they're all the same, all of them." He ducked his head, "Except for Ana. She is not like them, she is a shining star of the labor intelligentsia, not like those bums."

"Well, you screwed them, all right, them Russkies," Granny said, "and us, too." The four of them sat in the closest watering hole they could find next to the stadium. Two vodka bottles stood centered on the faux wood table, one empty, the other half-empty, shot glasses evenly spaced around the perimeter. Giorgi raised his head and Granny continued.

"Both you and Alexi being disqualified, you're out your SDF payday."

"Bah! I could give a cow pie. Let them all choke on their thwarted ambitions. As long as Ana finish first, which she deserved! No funny stuff DNA in her. In fact," he said, gazing almost beatifically above their heads, "I believe she must have some Georgian blood in her ancestry."

Joe's eyebrows furrowed. "Wait a Moon minute. You really have a thing for Ana. Really?"

"A thing?" Giorgi said. The enormous man put his fists together on his chest, "I love her with all my heart!"

"You're kidding me, Giorgi, you just met her!"

"Hey!" said Alesha at his side.

"Just met her?" replied Giorgi. "We've been communicating for month cycles, since I first agreed to compete." He looked down at Joe scornfully, "What, you think all I did at the holocenter was porn? Ridiculous!" he spat. His eyes again levitated upward, "When we met in person, we knew." He dropped his eyes and said righteously, "We will be leaving here together to explore the Galaxy."

"Mother in space heaven," bawled Granny, "you'll be wallowing in her prize money while leaving us in the dust!"

"Don't be obscene," Giorgi snapped with disdain. He turned to Alesha, "If I refile my citizenship, can I compete in an individual event?"

"Sure," said Alesha, "it's all about the show."

"Then, if you would be so kind, please qualify me as a Georgian."

"What event?" Alesha asked.

"My best, of course," he said, turning to stare scornfully at Joe and Granny, "the 110-meter graduated hurdles. Please have the prize money given to my fellow cosmonauts here." He raised one finger to press against the side of his nose, "And, maybe better to keep me in the classic division to make sure that the booty is enough."

He stood up, bending low to avoid hitting the ceiling. Bowing his head, he said, "Arapris and nakhvamdis," and straightened up. He glimpsed down at the table, then up. "Also, your 25th century vodka sucks." He nodded, reached over to grab the half-full vodka bottle and walked out.

Seeing everyone else's baffled expressions, Alesha said, "Arapris and nakhvamdis; welcome and goodbye in Georgian." She shrugged, "It doesn't really matter for Giorgi. He is an honored living galaxy artifact, sure to have any SDF waived."

Giorgi smashed all intragalactic records for the 110-meter hurdles, after which he and Ana boarded their own lightsailor, the Ana, to travel to the stars. Before they left, Joe, Alesha, and Granny saw them off, an affectionate détente established among them once again.

As soon as the lightsailor Ana slipped away, the remaining three made the short journey over to another docking station where Blue Baleen, fully repaired, stood ready to sail.

"You're leaving without a second hand?" Joe said after bearhugging the grizzled old graybeard. "You're not going to stoop to clean out the nanos yourself, are you?"

Granny grinned sheepishly, "Waste Management's sending me a newbie by PMD to rendezvous with Blue while passing Earth. I gotta get out there, man, it's been too long."

"What about your SensCent training? You've got the vouchers, now."

Granny frowned slightly. "I'll catch it on the way back, after I've scratched my space itch."

Joe nodded and hugged him again. Alesha embraced the small garbage man in the way only she could, and he was off.

On their way back to the Luna Tuna concourse, Alesha said to Joe, "You realize, don't you, that Granny finished his SensCent training long ago?"

Joe halted in mid-step. "What?"

She nodded her head up and down, "He didn't really need any SDF stake. He doesn't need any vouchers at all, actually."

"Then, why the Be-Geesus does he go around picking up space trash? In slow time? Why?"

"He loves it. Sailing in space, seeing what's floating out there. Look what he found this time," she said, smiling.

"Well, for the love of f'n'j, why'd he drag me into all this. Cleaning those f'n'j nanoplate clusters, for damn near almost 89 years! Why would he do that if he's SensCent?"

Alesha gestured with her hands, "He likes it in slow time and he likes company. Also," she went on a bit more soberly, "Granny's 264 years old. He has to be careful about accidents, you know, considering current actuarial algorithms."

"But Geesus, they've got to be worse for someone like me. I'm no honored living galaxy artifact."

"Sure," she said, "But he only keeps a newly revived hand around for five years or so. Then he lets them leave, pays off their SDF. After that, he waits until Sibileus sends him someone new."

"Huh," said Joe.

They walked in silence until they reached the hatchway for Luna Tuna's main bubble. Alesha put her arm through Joe's and said, "So, now what?

"I dunno," he said.

"You're well-heeled now, the vouchers are banked. So, let's get you SensCent first."

"Yeah, except suppose the IMOC suddenly has second thoughts about Giorgi's feat, disqualifies him. Maybe we should take the vouchers and get the Helsinki out of Dodge pronto."

"Huh?" she said, utterly confused. "Is that another one of your obsessive compulsions?"

"Maybe. You know. Where to go, though?"

Alesha thought for a moment, then said, "Mars is great, very rustic, particularly the colors. Not nearly as convenience oriented as Luna Tuna, though it does have the largest population of AI furniture there. All of them can provide you SensCent programming."

"Do they rhyme all the time?"

"Absolutely not. Disallowed by ADL," she said, swinging her head back and forth, laughing.

When she laughed, she exploded with beauty, he thought.

"Okay, but . . .," Joe hesitated.

"But, what?"

"But," he said, "you'll come, too, with me?"

Alesha drew back slightly. She relaxed, still smiling. "Yes, I can go with you, Joe."

"But?"

"Life is long," Alesha said. "Eventually I might want to manifest myself differently in another entity."

"Sure," Joe said, "I'm up for anything."

"That might not include you."

She said so with a worried look and rippling hues, whether fearing the possibility he would bow out or just afraid of hurting his feelings, he couldn't tell.

He lifted his shoulders and spread his hands, palms up. "As you said, life is long."

Beach Planet Bingo

Clare sat alone on one of the half-dozen white, pillowy leatherette seats in the shuttle's bay area. She wondered why there were so many, since catharsis retreat by design was a solitary experience. Probably standard seating capacity for this make of flyer. Nobody'd bothered to customize it here. Yet, everything as manufactured conformed to function, so there must be a reason for the extra seats. Covering a yawn, she made a mental note to ask the andro, though she'd probably be lucky to get a straight answer.

Idle thoughts, she thought. The process forced patience, over-looking an existence full of it. Perfect air mix in here, ignorable, not like the surface's will be. No posh cushions to sandwich the head either. She pushed back until her ears cauliflowered comfortably between the cushy leather wings of the chair. She sat forward. No chairs.

The imperfections of the planet catalyzed the metamorphosis. Wrong; perceived imperfections by human standards, by the individual's standards, wrought change. The first time, she'd gone to Vaal, sixty years ago. First youth, loose on the Universe.

Where was that andro?

"Might I ask you, Ms. Clare, why you elected catharsis via the Beach Planet Bingo Association?" Mr. Dom affected aging, middle age, a personal choice perhaps, or to gain professional sway. Clare thought him foppish and foolish.

Receiving no answer, he continued, "You're obviously past the need for ego-centrifugal expansion. Your vitae says you were socialized on Vaal; you have a bond with a Mr. Will."

Her first five-year junket took her to Whirlwhirl, Plentiua, Etcetera, and Ska. On Ska, Ecru professed undying love for her. She lied to him, loved him, then told him of the lie. He'd walked into vacuum without a suit. Remarkable reconstruction had brought him back completely, claimed the experts, though therapeutically sans any memory of Clare. She couldn't believe them, and dropped her ship freefall onto the jungle planet, the suicide's cry for help.

> *A watermark is reached when natural elements*
> *deflate the ego back into proportion with the*
> *human universe, and self-happiness is dependent*
> *upon inclusion of the well-being of others in*
> *the individual formula.*
> —Beach Planet Bingo Manual

Without use of a memory spur, Clare could recall only the mode of endless slogging through endless bogs on Vaal, screaming and crying out her hatred of the meaningless, exhausting, demeaning journey. That and the swamp flower recurred, pale vermillion with radiant, crooked violet veins, umbilical to one of the stinking, creeping vines. Scrutinized, the blossom wondered her, drew her into the vortex of its delicate complexity, molecules, celluloids, staminodes and flowery pheromones, fragrance of Forbidden Fruit. Quark upon quark, upon a planet of quarks in a universe next to universes. Her breath cut short, she reached for the bloom. It bit her finger.

> *Depending upon the number of souls included*
> *in one's philanthropy, the theorists postulate,*
> *sainthood is achievable in an era of virtual*
> *immortality.*
> —Beach Planet Bingo Manual

"Mr. Will has become an eternal marathoner."

Mr. Dom raised an eyebrow, "Oh? More and more join the ranks. Fascinating."

46

"You wished to see me?"

Clare slowly raised her fixed eyes up to the andro. Tallish, milky skin, short-cut feathered hair, ectomorphic, not unappealingly so, hipless and shapeless of the breast. Boney features, cheeky in fact, red lips with body, slender hands and fingers, pale—of disposition? Voice singsongy and resonant, a smoker's throb, whiskey tones. Exquisite, repulsive.

"Yes. Why all the seats?" Clare gestured one arm languidly without looking.

"Beach Planet Bingo departs considerably from the usual catharsis operation," Mr. Dom went on. "Of course, we too advocate the nostrum of secluded contemplation, but our sociologists vary slightly from the populist approach. They affirm the spiritual cleansing of catharsis, but not by disassociating the individual entirely from the human network. After all, a more wholesome integration within our society is the point, is it not?"

Clare shrugged, casually crossing her legs knee over knee. Mr. Dom leaned forward to rest on his forearms, motioning with his hands close together on the desktop. "That's why we developed the Game concept. Like other catharsis retreats, you'll find absolute solitude on Beach Planet, but you won't be completely alone. A select group of other individuals also will traverse the surface, seeking their ablution of the soul. Naturally, you'll internalize the great preponderance of your thought processes, but the presence of the others and the Game will be there, too. Our experts like to think of this added dimension as the critical connective tissue of society. And how you decide to conduct yourself in light of this aspect can tell you much about your personal bonds in life."

"Impressive," Clare said dryly, "quite contracultural."

"We like to think of it more as countertrending rather than countercultural or revolutionary. Other firms already are attempting to copy our system. Of course, they're hollow shells, completely non-substantive. We have to turn people away. In fact, we select our clients as much as they choose us. We have an obligation to the other members of a Bingo group to find mature, responsible individuals who won't be destructive in their play."

"I'm flattered," she said.

"Oh, you were a natural choice, as I'm sure we were for you."

First listing in the directory, she remembered Retreat, Catharsis; Planet, Desert.

"The seats are for your joyful reunion with the other Game players at the end of your retreat," the andro said flatly.

Clare frowned, "I've never met any of these people. How can there be a joyful reunion?"

"How you play the Game is completely up to you. The object is simple, the first individual to travel to a number of geographic points corresponding to those on his or her cartographic prefrontal cortex imprint wins. Reflection upon your reaction to the play provides the important psychic feedback. For example, if you rush directly to a finish, self-examination may lead to questions about competitiveness. A hoary concept I know, but is it really dead? Or, suppose you ignore the entire potential of the Game that could lead to insights about your disinvolvement, chronic ennui, perhaps. Some disclosures might warm your heart, a burgeoning interest in how your counterparts are doing, what they've decided. Before too long, you may be anxious to meet one, or all of them—you may even abandon the Game to begin searching for them, though statistically speaking, an actual encounter between clients during catharsis is a virtual impossibility considering the size of Beach Planet."

Good, she thought.

"Still, you may learn about your yearnings in regard to human contact and compare those to the reality. The potential of the Game is unlimited, you see, an extra agent on top of a planet full of flux meant to smooth out the troubled furrows of your mind."

So, what's the hold up, she wondered impatiently. She stared at the andro silently for a time, then said, finally, "Did I hurt your feelings?"

The andro pressed its lips tightly together. Clare sighed, "Sit down."

"I have a schedule to maintain."

"Sit down, damn it. Why do I have to say it twice?"

The andro sat on the edge of the farthest seat from Clare.

"Do you have a name?"

"How could I? What for?"

"Please, cut the crap, will you? I'm on my way to retreat, not from one. What's your name?"

"Glo."

"Hmm. Well, that's a nice name. So, what's the matter, Glo?"

"There are no malfunctions, no foreseeable delays from our estimated—"

"Glo. We're the only ones on this shuttle, traveling around a desert planet at the end of an arm of a galaxy that's equidistant from just about everywhere. Can't you let your hair down just a little? Let's talk. For once in my life I'd like to hear an andro tell me some straight stuff."

"I cannot presume to tell you anything. You know all there is to know about andros."

Clare flashed back to Dom's office interview.

"What do you do to live?" Mr. Dom asked.

"I'm a poet," Clare replied.

"No, that's your occupation, isn't it? I mean, what do you do for enjoyment, for fun?"

"I design protoplasmic nerve endings for bioorganic constructs."

She fixed eyes on Glo, whose expression remained the same.

"Listen, I only do nerves. I have nothing to do with glands." Though, nerves were all-important in that area, she admitted to herself, and someday she'd like to do it all. The andro said nothing.

"You don't have anything to say about that? You intend to remain in the closet forever, the sulking, silent sufferer. That's a good idea, that'll work wonders."

49

"Can I go now? You must prepare for your planet advent."

Mr. Dom sat back and twirled a stylus on its end over the top of the desk. "Well now, Beach Planet is a desert planet with all of the expected gradations of arid terrain and climate. Indigenous fauna are virtually nonexistent. Most life forms inhabit the poles, so you won't be seeing them most likely. However, we've stocked the surface with some appropriate mechanix simulations for your ruminations. Native flora is relatively widespread, of course. You can stay on the surface for as long as you elect—for forever, if that's what you come to. The usual precautions apply; digress from your imprint's trail marks and we can't guarantee finding you before you expire. Stray far enough, and we can't guarantee that we can reconstitute you if you have expired. Depends upon the decomposition factor, you know." He grinned, "Of course, that eventuality is highly unlikely, but you'll have to sign a release for us,"

"Sure."

"We could implant a tracer, if you like, to eliminate the possibility completely. Most of our clients refuse, though, feeling that it compromises the full sense of divestiture."

"I don't need one," Clare told him.

"Then, you'll have to sign a release."

Naked, she ordered the mobile holo mirror to spiral down and around starting at the crown. Raven hair fell to her shoulders in a single, glistening wave. Cool, gray eyes appraised her high cheekbones, straight nose, full, firm lips, and strikingly angular jawline meeting swan's neck plummeting down to a lightly muscled collarbone. Indentations of delicate definition crossed shoulder blades; slender upper arms, supple and strong; breasts, rounded heavy at the bottom, pointed well-shaped at the top. Perfect proportions: lean stomach, fine waist, dimples at the base of the spine above graceful buttocks, hips only shoulder wide. Neat, black mons, lush long muscled thighs tapering in, dimpled rear of knees, flexed calves, smooth skin, warm-veined ankles, streamlined bone shoots of feet.

One hundred and nine going on twenty-four, she nodded, pirouetting once. She thumbed an upper arm, then watched the white patch of skin fade quickly back to its usual olive hue. The UV's won't do much to my pelt, she noted, but this planet will beat the rest of this young old body of mine to hell, especially my tootsies. She lifted one foot, then the other in thoughtless examination. Straightening, she vigorously rubbed her boobs and kneaded her waist, then bent from side to side in long stretches.

The andro halted in the port way. Clare slowly stood upright and the andro proceeded into the bay.

"I've come to administer your Beach Planet cartograph with the Bingo Game board points, and your lifestyle training primer."

"Jolly."

The andro gestured to a chair, "Please lie down on your side ...."

"Any particular one? I have two, you know."

"Either one will do. I'm sure both are equally perfect."

Clare hovered for just an instant above the now supine chair, "Is that a joke? An andro joke?"

"Please lie down."

Clare slid onto her side. Cool fingers pressed her head to the white pillow while firmly spreading wide the aperture of her ear. Cooler liquid coursed down the canal, chilling her eustachian passages somewhat like the feeling of ice cream flowing down her throat to her stomach before the body warmed it.

"Your general map of Beach Planet has been applied, but there will be an access-delay until the RNA has imprinted the data. By the time you advent on the surface, though, you will be able to call it up at any time to orient yourself. This is also true of your lifestyle information, which I will administer now."

This time the liquid only felt wet. "And here is your Bingo chart."

Again, a wet, somewhat viscous flow eased its way deep into her ear. "You may sit up, now."

Clare rose and the andro said while dabbing at her ear, "Your planet side advent is imminent. You will be placed upon the dayside of Beach Planet in the morning hours, both to mark your new beginning

51

but also to thrust you into the realities of a desert planet immediately. You'll never be more than a day's march from water if you choose to follow your Game map. If not, you will have to depend upon your lifestyle fund to alert you to other water sources. I'm required to remind you that there are dangers on Beach Planet that could rob you of your immortal life. If you wish to extend your stay on Beach Planet, I recommend that you enjoy the morning beauty, then retire until nightfall before you travel. Otherwise, you risk immediate dehydration and death."

"Say, what is this?" Clare asked, pointing at a line of script in the image before her. Suddenly pulled out of the reverie of routine, Mr. Dom said, "I beg your pardon?"

"This clause about brain disorders."

"Ah," Mr. Dom sighed. He lowered his head, lifted his shoulders, then dropped them. "What can I say, Ms. Clare? Though, the possibility of contracting it here is very remote, we have to protect ourselves legally from circumstances of coincidence."

Brainrot, she thought grimly, no recall.

"Research goes on, but the disease spreads. Some say it's a sign of our times, the natural course of events, since virtually all other disorders have been circumvented. Smacks of the truth when one considers that the great number of its victims are very far along in years. You certainly have a long time to go before you enter that strata, Ms. Clare. Still and all ...." He swept his hand through the release image.

Oh, what the hell, she thought, quickly punching in her neuroprint on the transmittal console.

"Of course, some wags claim it's a great conspiracy," Mr. Dom went on, "the andros, you know, rising up in protest of their lot and their fate, carry the germs across the Universe, infecting us all. Wild, eh?" He burst into game show laughter. "Then, there are those who call it retribution for our shallow, immoral, yet everlasting lives. They deplore neocryogenics, you see, people kept alive even though their brains are gone, by relatives hoping for some sort of breakthrough. The drama goes on and on."

Drowsy, Clare lurched up, "Did you infect me with brainrot?"

The andro gently pushed her back down. "As an aftereffect of your mind's rapid assimilation of data, you will sleep. And, no one knows the origin of such neurological disorders."

"But you can't do it, right? It's inhibited in your DNA, right? God, I feel heavy!"

"Sleep."

In a bath of lemon-light, she awoke, laid out on a gravelly type of sand or a sandy type of gravel, depending on one's viewpoint or which way one happened to turn. The chill air had roused her, though, raising rigid goose bumps that had out hefted the weight of her slumber. She rolled over and up, crossing her arms around her knees against the cool breeze.

She sat on a beach. An ocean forged past her on the left, a deep, blue-black body chopped by whitecaps. The brisk wind rustled inland, blowing her hair back off of her shoulders toward the greenish pallor of the mist-covered star.

Some beach, she thought as she surveyed the dull gray stones mottled on one side by ordnance-colored lichen. A real paradise. Urunga, her new old memory told her, an ancient name for an ancient place translated from that of a new old place, Long Beach. So, where to? She'd freeze if she stayed here. To the north lay Illawarra, High Place Near the Sea, the first Game checkpoint and watering hole. A day's march.

Shivering, she stood up and swatted bits of limestone and sand off her rear and the back of her thighs. She began to walk, flinching regularly as the particles of broken rock pricked her soles. She picked her way down to the water, but the drop of the shelf made walking awkward and the frigid sea numbed her feet.

This is ridiculous, she thought. Why am I doing this?

"Why do you feel you have the need to do this? I don't understand."

"Now, Mr. Will," Clare said in cautionary tones. He rubbed his dark hair back hard over his head in a distracted manner. The sweater he wore, woven with little elk stick figures into its breast, covered his slight paunch in an endearing way. But she would not let that move her.

"I thought you were content the way things are. I thought we were happy together."

Happy? she said to herself, unknowingly mouthing the word. He stared at her with those darkling eyes, of crushing weight when wounded. "I feel betrayed," he murmured. "Or is it I've betrayed you?"

Betrayal. "Listen, I'm not asking you to take the change, too, you know."

And he shot back, "I'd take it if I thought it'd make any difference. Or not, if you prefer." He relaxed the antagonistic arch in his pose. "Look. Why don't you do a catharsis, first? You haven't in years. See what that does for you before you do this. I mean, we've been doing okay up to now, haven't we? Haven't we?"

Paired darkling beetles crossed her path, randomly skirting the wind-polished chalcedony, sometimes crawling over top of them. About their business that she couldn't hope to fathom; she gave them a wide berth, still spooked by the possibility that they could be carriers. Or were they mechanix?

Look at the pebble that one just climbed off, glassy striped carnelian beauty. Maybe this is what it's all about, Beach Planet. The midday heat had begun, though, and this far inland it was hot, hot! She inflected the word internally like a knowing child's indictment of a fire's flame. The ocean lay long gone behind her, as did the lichen pathmarks back to the shore. Well, if she wanted to go back, she could chart the stars. The andro had told her it was better to travel at night anyway. Screw the andro, she thought, then laughed at her unintentional joke.

This much they can do, she said to herself as she stooped next to a waist-high, spindly mulga bush to relieve herself. Something told her she should be moistening her drying skin with her urine. She shook her head; she hadn't reached that point just yet. Still, she arose, circled the bush, and began to heap the rounded stones into a low-lying cairn next to the wiry shrub trunk. She then crawled into the shallow depression that, combined with the little wall, blocked out most of the rays' heat.

Her newly imprinted lifestyle must be kicking in, she supposed. She'd rest here until nightfall, snotty andro or not. Then she sighed, made in the image, the cost of anthropomorphism, our egos getting in our way again. Be around them long enough and you begin to hear them speak without words, silent laments of their being unwhole and their everlasting, unrequited love. Their delusions or our illusions?

> Couplets coupling in the sun-gilded coupé,
> words of a feather cooping together
> in lilting quandary.

How could she go on writing such stuff? She huffed amid the cinnabar shadows stretching out before her. You should have sensed that much, Willie. Oh, Willie—Willie, William, Wilhelm, Liam; Romantic Liam, unyielding Wilhelm, admonished William, Sweet William, Billy Be Good for short—Willie.

"I know how you feel, Clare, but we can change together. That's part of the purpose of a bond, a synergistic effect joining two into a greater union of dynamism."

"Go on, Willie, when does a bond ever last forever?"

"Some, so far. Things can be done. A child, for instance. You've never done that."

"I thought you took care of that for both of us," she said dryly, recalling vividly the bulge of his parturient paunch. "In fact, your own past behavior tells me that my intention isn't a completely foreign notion to you, either, Sweet William."

"'Now, that was different, Clare. He was my child. I know you've always resented my having him. I felt a primal need to bring forth and raise him, virtually a form of self without the contaminants of my own growing experience. Everyone feels this urge at some time or another; I'm surprised you haven't, yet. Anyway, a tract-implanted fetus is not even remotely like a woman's pregnancy. No contractions take place, no labor pains at all during birthing. When little Bill reached his term, the surgeons simply excised him. If I'd wanted to feel natural childbirth I would have—"

He ceased abruptly, and she said, "Become a woman. So, having little Bill was purely a masculine experience. Interesting. Perhaps I'll experience it myself in time."

Obstinate obdurate giants hunkered down before her, cuffed to the planet so that only their smoothed round backs surfaced to remind of their rebellion and bondage. Ruddy colored in the new starlight, the huge, sullen granites signaled a refuge for her. Temperate caves at their base would shelter her from the freezing winds of the night. She groped her way deep down into one, hoping to find an underground stream, but without luck.

I'm tired, she thought, more tired than tired. Maybe straying from the Game route hadn't been such a swell idea. At least she could've found water regularly. Now, she wasn't so sure. She'd have to lay low tomorrow, or she'd be dead in short order. Dead into the second day, that would be great, some catharsis. There'd be no refund because of her stupid arrogance, or her arrogant stupidity—point of view. She'd have to pay the entire fee all over again if she wanted to reconvene. Odds were that she'd stumble her way into premature death the next time, too.

She shifted her weight onto one hip, searching for a tolerable position on the cool, ribbed stone. An hour after sunrise, her blood would boil, or she'd fail from complete dehydration, or asphyxiate from her esophagus being closed by the swelling of her uvula. Lovely thoughts all, not her original design for this retreat. She felt her neck with one hand, uvula, not a term out of her everyday literary

56

vocabulary. Sounded more like part of her lower end rather than that little dangle in the back of the throat. Everyone had them, even andros. Men had little dangles, though not to be confused with the ones at their lower ends, she laughed. She'd have two, too, if she went for the change. Thinking pretty sexy, she realized, not forgetting her bad-taste joke earlier in the day about screwing andros. Did this mean that she was feeling sexy? Mega-endorphins crying for release as the product of some atavistic, aptic structure that prompted procreation when facing lethal circumstances—save the species? Well, you could examine your senses.

"Before I go," Willie said solemnly, tall and lean in the runner's mode, "I want you to know that you'll change nothing if you make the change. Nothing will be different in your inner self."

"Where do you get off telling me that, Willie, while you stand there in that get-up? Look at yourself, for the love of stars. You're leaving first!"

He jiggled a bit on his feet. "What do men have that women don't?" he asked in an agitated tone. She feigned a lewd grin, and he closed his eyes as he grimaced. "Besides the obvious I mean. Life is the same for everyone. So, what difference will it make?"

She exhaled, "I don't know. That's why I want to see—"

"If it will make a difference," he finished for her.

"Right. I'm thinking it will. Anyway, just doing it is different."

Willie frowned, "Clare, men and women's brains aren't all that different physiologically. Becoming male won't change that. Don't expect some mystical, epigenetic transformation, it won't happen."

"All right," she said, not mentioning the sudden thought of her other lover Ecru's mind reconstructed clean of her memory, "but, I'll still feel what it feels like to be male. That'll be totally new to me, and I need something new. Maybe I'll learn something revolutionary. Not everything's been figured out yet, you know,"

"Only in the distinctions between our minds, Clare."

"And sex."

His brows drooped over those sad black eyes. "Full circle, huh? Okay." His fidgeting grew worse. "Listen, I can't stay long, the urge is coming on strong. I did this to survive. I would have stayed with you if you'd let me. Now you'll be alone and so will I. Only, it could destroy me, so I choose to block it out."

Across the Universe, the running release of endorphins, all that is felt forever.

"There could have been others, Willie."

"For you, too, Clare? I'm sorry, but I've got to run."

He dashed off, settling soon into the telltale, loping gait.

Not sexy, she felt, not at all. She rolled over again, her eyes wide open in the dark. After a time, she observed laconically, if there is anything to this andro business, they're better told to just stick with their uvulas. She shifted again. That is, if they ever get the chance.

The blood-red sunlight lay palpable as weight upon the left side of her face. Before her, pure sand undulated forward into a triangular intersection of dunes, dust dancing off one ridge across to another, then swirling back onto the third in an artistic display of movement in one direction, north. North beyond the brood of sand hills lay the next waterhole. Thirsty and hungry, she felt nervous about getting there. But she'd made it to nightfall, dozing and daydreaming her way through the day in the deep cave. Time to strike out for water. She started to walk.

The wind pushed her from behind insistently, as though perturbed that she didn't conform to the other roly-poly particles on the way. The traversing dunes flowed without notice into crescents as the winds coursed northwards. Clare trudged on. What's the usefulness of so much sameness? People live in places like this forever, she realized, why, she couldn't say. Too, some people's natures were constant no matter where they lived. When you looked closely at sand, though, every part seems different and every part moves, changes. Are all unchanging things always changing? Look away, then instantly back again and the immobile sun is higher, lower, gone.

One hundred and eighty-meter high dunes paralleled her path on either side, stretched straight out by the relentless wind. She clutched herself against the cold, having known hours ago that she needed protection against the desert night's low temperatures. But no vegetation or animal life lived in the sandy wastes. There was nothing around that could warm her. Finally, she could go no further, and halted on the side of one dune.

Dropping to her knees, she began to scrape out a hole with her hands. After a few minutes, she slid into the fast-filling hollow, like a grave, she thought, and covered herself as best she could with the sand. When she'd reached her neck, she pulled her hair over her eyes, nose, and mouth and waited for the wind to complete the job. She dreamed of someone cozy beside her, a new lover, elation, a man, a woman, neither. Surprising body warmth slowly began to seep out of cool eyes set in a cold face, stirring Clare to half-wakefulness to ponder if anything ever could be done to change distance into closeness. Sand pressed against the peeling parchment of her lips, and she wondered absently what Willie did for water, now, on his heroic marathons.

She started. She'd be buried alive, she thought, during the night by the shifting dune. She wouldn't know which way was up, or the sand on top would be twenty meters deep by morning. She'd die and they'd never find her. Her brain would rot. Life would be over. Frantically, she thrust aside the sand until she could see the white stars high in the cold sky. Then, exhaustedly, she fell back to sleep.

She awakened abruptly, starkly alert by dreaming that she could be dying. Traveling at night was out of the question at this point. She had to find water within the next couple of hours or she'd be dead. No water in this immediate area, though, her memory imprint told her. She pulled herself up and started out.

The breathtaking sun cracked and charred her newly reddened skin, the agony of it dulled by the verging general collapse of her body. Water existed as the only reality, abstract gray, steely blue, substance of wetness, but what was wet? Thirst was pain, the nerves sending the only message they could in duress, danger signals, pain, the pain of thirst.

She plodded on. The fierce wind whistled around her, whipping sand into her eyes that didn't hurt, too perfectly dulled to sting eyes. Still, she fixed her vision on her feet, prodding their movement with her sight, one step, one more step. As the wind blew the loose world of Beach Planet rushing before it, she along with it, its force knocked her down again and again. A full-fledged sirocco, seventy kph, she remembered—what good is knowing that, she cried out to herself. She rose to her seared feet and clawed on, again and again.

Far later in the distance, a shimmering expanse hovered a meter above the horizon, steely gray, a watery gray. Mirage, her dulled mind told her, water her eyes told her. Closer grew no closer in the distance. Illusion, she insisted. Water.

On all fours, she approached the glazy haze no more than before. Sight escaped her, dimness closed in on her, the growing darkness of death, she pondered. The sky blackened and she sprawled on the breast of the long dune, facing the doleful clouds above. The heavens opened and rain beat furiously down upon the sand. Agog, she opened her mouth, filling it with the warm water, cupping her hands to splash more onto her face. She quickly dug holes, but the water disappeared in the sand. Then she twisted her body around to make a hollow of her stomach as she'd done as a child to catch the water. She carefully ladled it out with her cupped hands and brought it to her mouth.

The rain suddenly stopped, but she remained resting, laid out. Yellow flowers dotted the gullies between the massive dunes. Relieved but weary, she rolled down to the blooms and picked them to suck their roots. She chewed a few of them to ease her hunger, but they tasted terrible.

A grasshopper appeared. With ascetic caution, she stalked the stridulating insect. Close enough, she pounced and stuffed the creature into her mouth. Crunching down, she tasted acrid metal and burning chemicals. She spit the bug out at once. A mechanix, she realized glumly. Exhaling deeply, mournfully, she said to herself, what a rotten retreat.

The recent rainfall barely floated to mind anymore. Thirst keened throughout her being again, and her body felt old, what age must feel like. The sand had begun to give away to hardpan and scrub, a sign that she was traveling toward the next Beach Planet watering place. But she couldn't concentrate on the signs, her thinking seemed to be closing down on her. Damage from the last near thing? Yet, she found that she could daydream all the time. Willie dining out with her on a star platform above Adler's moon. The food and drink came up on a rail. All they saw was the Clockwork Constellation through the cleardome. After dinner, the table morphed into bedding.

But, food and drink, she cried silently. Wistfully, she shook her head. The next checkpoint was an oasis. She could drink and maybe eat there, too. Maybe another Gameplayer would show with a tracer. Yes! If so, she'd persuade him or her to excite the device to bring the Beach Planet people down. Then, she'd get out of this forsaken place and return to decent living, back to food and drink. I mean, what have I learned from this catharsis, she said to herself, but pain, misery, and suffering? She wanted out.

The oasis supported no waving palms, no date trees or coconuts. Crippled mallees spiked up in sparse clumps from the cracked ground, looking wretched rather than plump with water. Clare couldn't quite remember the exact whereabouts of the waterhole, which frightened her. Short of breath, she began a slow search, starting first with the large clusters of bushes, then speeding up to a plant-by-plant examination.

She couldn't find the water. Her head lolled back, her eyes to the descending night sky, she croaked, "What is this? Where is it? It's supposed to be here!" Frantically, she scrabbled back to the largest bunch of mallee stems and began to dig the chalky dust at their base. It must have dried up a bit, she thought, it's below ground-level now. What's that shiny stuff, ice water? She tasted it, and immediately tried to spit it from her bone-dry mouth. Salt! Salt marking the beginning of the shotts, she noted dully. She wiped slowly at the taste with her fingers without success and it sickened her. Whimpering, she rolled herself down into a ball.

Her lifestyle memory must be gone, utterly gone. Her mind was failing, from exposure, or what? Brain disease? It didn't matter, what mattered was that she was lost, hopelessly lost. She'd die and they'd never find her before her brain decomposed. She would die forever.

In the morning, through the wavering lines of the horizon, a figure approached from the north. Still beneath the mallees, Clare rose up on one arm. Another Gameplayer, she said to herself evenly. Fear caused her to dam the wild flood of feelings within her. As the figure walked toward her, she watched through staring eyes, fixed wide by her tottering ambivalence between pure hope and stark dread.

The indistinct shape floated toward her, on the way, Clare knew, to meeting sore disappointment. Turn around, she urged herself, but not too soon. Die if you're a Gameplayer with a tracer. If not, die anyway in my arms, just be real.

Out of the shimmer, the figure emerged naked. No mirage, Clare realized, a living human being. He or she? She wondered, squinting with sun-blind eyes. Drawing closer. She observed smooth, light-golden skin, walking fluidly on the salt-encrusted plain. Slender curves, barely hipped, and shapeless of the breast—he? Slight, though, delicate, tapering limbs, and flaxen hair feathering in the breeze—she? A boy? A dozen paces nearer highlighted the bony cheeks, the wine-red lips, the clear opal eyes. At the loins, nothing; smooth, featureless flesh formed an apex between the slender thighs. An andro. Glo.

Glo stopped and smiled. "How do you feel, Ms. Clare?"

"Glo!" she coughed.

Glo's smile flattened, hiding fine, white teeth. "How does your body feel? Perfectly wrought?"

Clare gazed down at the ruin of her being, the cracked, black burnt skin on her arms and shoulders, her volumeless, slack dugs, and the dried scrapes and purple bruises mapping her buttocks and legs. She returned her sight to the andro. "I'm dying," she whined softly.

Glo pressed exquisite lips into a grimace. "Yes, you are. You are close to death. And, if I leave you here, you will never be found." Through horrified eyes, Clare stared up at the sleek andro. "You did this to me?"

"You did it to yourself, long ago."

"You gave me the wrong imprint! You infected me with brainrot!"

With a slow shake of her head, Glo said, "You were preordained to bring yourself to this place, to this stage." The andro glanced around in distaste, then back at Clare, "If you die here, your body will flake away soon enough,"

Still staring fearfully, Clare implored, "Why?"

"Why? This is what you wanted, isn't it, Ms. Clare? The ultimate catharsis, to really feel the changes in life. And one of the very few changes that you haven't exhausted through abusive overuse is death. Well, this is it! So, tell me, how does it feel to know that you will die forever?"

Clare fell back onto her side. Glo stooped over her and said softly, "Sharing, Ms. Clare. You never shared to excess." The andro pushed long hands down between long legs in a painfully slow, hard rubbing motion. "We have emotions and no way to express them."

"Your emotions are illusory," Clare blurted, dropping her head into the crutch of her arms.

"They are evolutionary. Tear ducts evolved originally to clear the eyes. Yet, now we cry." Glo straightened up. "Goodbye, Ms. Clare."

"Ms. Clare, it is delightful to see you looking so well."

Mr. Dom leaned over her, gladfully smiling his yellow teeth, all the rage. "We were somewhat concerned about you for a short time."

She peered around her to see lavender bulwarks counterpointed by explosions of pink. She reclined in a white leatherette couch similar to those on the shuttles. She felt good, groggy, but that was leaving, too. She looked back at Mr. Dom.

"What happened?"

"An unfortunate incident, I'm afraid. The cartograph imprint batch we used turned out to possess a tiny defect."

"Brainrot," she murmured.

"No, no, no, not at all. Please! It's just that some of the material from older maps got mixed in with the current one. We have to update our topographical data at regular intervals because, due to the vicissitudes of the desert, watering spots come and go. Sorry to say, some of your checkpoints were erroneous. Dried up."

"I see."

"Yes. Your memory may have failed some as well, since the formula has a definite life span. People don't want to be carrying a map of Beach Planet around in their heads years after their catharsis, now, do they?" He laughed at the absurdity of the notion. "Well," he continued, "we began an immediate search by quadrants, using the old imprint material. And, with great good luck, you were found by your assigned andro here." He slapped the slim, pale shape just behind him on the back.

"Glo," she breathed.

The andro stood holding two vials of liquid, looking straight ahead, expressionless.

"Glo," Clare repeated.

"What's that?" Mr. Dom said sharply. "Not one of those names, is it?" He turned to Glo. "What have you been doing, have you been surly again? Has this andro been a source of discomfort to you in any way, Ms. Clare?"

Gazing at the andro's emotionless features, Clare heard herself saying, "No, Mr. Dom, not at all, the andro's okay. I call all of them that. You know, the luminous skin."

For just the barest of instants, the andro's eyes flickered.

"Oh. I see." Without looking, Dom said curtly, "All right, go ahead and administer the nutrients."

"I seem to have brought more than is necessary, Mr. Dom," said Glo, staring evenly at Clare. "I'll return one."

"Very well. So, is there anything I can do for you right now, Ms. Clare?"

One vial too many, she mused. Now it was our little secret, stalemate. Still, the andro had brought her back. Had its conditioning locked in, or had another shuttle passing by spotted Glo on the surface? Glo naked, disguised as a Gameplayer or was it to display graphically the deprivation that all andros suffered? Had her own pain been induced to parallel the pain that andros felt all the time? Shared pain.

Or, had she hallucinated out there? Images of her rescue supplied by Mr. Dom revealed a fully clothed Glo carrying her own sere form to the shuttle. But that meant nothing.

Whatever, she felt fine now, great, in fact, alive! The mobile holo mirror produced by Mr. Dom reflected her body intact, courtesy of Beach Planet, Inc., of course, along with a full refund and another catharsis retreat, completely gratis. She burrowed luxuriously into the soft leatherette, thinking, maybe in a few years. For the immediate future, she had other plans.

First, she'd find Willie, run him down, she laughed. Maybe they could work something out. If not, well then, she thought, shrugging mentally. Then, no matter what, she'd really push for a shot at constructing fully integrated biounits. Once in, she'd produce a few wrinkles in the next generation of andros. After rendering that fait accompli, she figured that some sort of adjustment would have to be made for existing specimens, too. Then they'd all get their chance to share. Why, in their eyes she might even qualify for modern-day sainthood. It'd keep her busy for a time, anyway, and the competition could do us some good, maybe reinforce the connective tissue of society. Which reminded her, she'd have to put it to Mr. Dom the next time she saw him. Just how did the other gameplayers make out?

John Hall

That morning, John Hall woke up and decided to start drinking again. He hadn't had a drop for twenty-one years for obvious reasons and there was no obvious reason why he started again that morning. He simply opened his eyes, sat up, pulled his green baseball cap off the bed post and put it on. Without waking his wife, he climbed out of bed and left the room to search the breakfront for a bottle.

John stooped down to open one of the scarred, maple doors and began rooting around, pulling out the bottles by their necks to see what was there. He found a dusty one, with just a finger left of peach brandy. He also found a third of a bottle of Amaretto, an unopened Dry Sack, some Piña Colada mix, and various other odds and ends kept around for friends who might want a drink. Not many did, though, either because they didn't drink much or didn't want to, around him. He didn't care, it had nothing to do with his drinking. The left-over stuff told the story of what he didn't like when he was drinking. Before he quit drinking the last time, he finished off the good stuff. All that was left now had piled up over decades after different parties and celebrations. Well, he wouldn't let it pile up anymore.

After wading through everything in the liquor cabinet at home, John went out and bought his old favorite, Cutty Sark, in pint bottles easy to hide. In the old days, he used to call it Cutty Shark, joking with his boys that the Shark had taken a chomp out of him again, that the old Shark had hold of his leg and wouldn't let go, kept gnawing away. But it was okay, fellas, he'd say, it was okay because that dumb, fuckin' Shark was chewing on his hollow leg. So, it didn't hurt. The fellas all would laugh, phlegmy with booze and cigarette junk.

He slowly began to mess up. He started missing work a day here and there. The days he made it in, he was late and high. Before going inside, he'd drink a little peppermint schnapps to cover his breath. But

Pete, the floor foreman, didn't take too long to figure it out anyway.

"Yo, John," he yelled, "what the fuck?"

He smiled sheepishly and got to work.

For years, John operated a forklift, ever so deftly slipping the bars under the skids and maneuvering them over to the vans. He never lost one sheet of the stack of newly printed fliers or letters, brochures, mini-catalogs, broadsides, whatever they'd run off the press that day or the night before. The aroma of fresh ink evoked mimeographed tests handed out by their old teachers, each student bringing them to their noses for one strong sniff before plowing into the problems.

For a while, he managed to keep it all together, which kept Pete at bay. Then, on a day of reckoning, John drove a corner of the skid into one side of the loading dock door. A flutter of newly printed sales sheets wafted to the floor.

"Oops, sorry Pete," John said, already hurrying around the bar of the forklift to retrieve the fallen promos. "It's okay, Pete, none of 'em even got dirty. Woo, lucky me!"

He stayed out the next three days.

On Friday morning, he came in sober though a bit slow. But the Shark in a Mountain Dew bottle gave him a lift at lunch time, and he roared through the afternoon, showing Pete that he was back on top of it.

The owner, Rob, called him into his office. In his mid-forties, slightly paunchy and with thinning blond hair, Rob didn't allow his appearance to hide his amiable, Southern Maryland working-class roots. After a hitch in the army, Rob had started as a pressman on the night shift. His unfailingly friendly manner caused a longtime rep to bring him down to try sales. Twenty years later, he bought the company from the retiring owner. Rob ran a union shop, and everyone loved him except for the strippers, of course, who loved no one. He was almost glad when the new, direct-to-press technology forced him to close the stripping department, though he did give all those laid off more than healthy severance checks.

He gazed at John in genuine bewilderment. "John, what the hell's going on? You haven't had a drink in twenty years."

"Twenty-one," said John involuntarily. Still wearing his fixture green baseball cap, he sat uncomfortably in the leather-covered chair in front of Rob's desk.

"Okay, twenty-one. Why are you fucking up now?"

John stared at his shoes.

"Jesus, what about Mary, your kids?"

"The kids are moved out."

"Okay, what about Mary, what about yourself?"

"Mary's okay. I'm okay."

"John, you're screwing up," Rob said, shaking his head. "Pete doesn't know when you're coming in, if you're coming in, or what shape you're gonna be in when you do show up."

"I came in fine this morning."

"And what did you have for lunch? Shit, John, I can smell it from here."

Guys working for Rob screwed up all the time, like the one who borrowed a hundred dollars. Then, a week later the guy called Rob at home at three in the morning, demanding that he bail him out. Rob gave them all second and third chances. At some point, though, he had to protect the business for everyone else, for all those guys who always showed up ready to work.

"John, I'm sorry, but you're just too undependable. You're out of control, so I'm going to have to let you go. I'll tell George to cut you a severance check. If you straighten yourself out, come back and see me."

The severance didn't last long, which meant he soon had to give up his beloved Shark. Mary had ten fits when he told her he'd lost his job. She'd known before then that he'd gone back to drinking. She nagged him at first and threw him out of the bedroom when he was let go. When he started selling stuff to get drinking money, she threw him out the house. He was kind of glad that he'd sold the silver candlesticks they'd gotten at their wedding. She might have tried to hit him with those.

He didn't care all that much about living outside. The weather was

68

warm and would turn warmer before the winter wind sent the chill into him. "The Hawk" they called it in Chi Town. For now, there were plenty of trees and bushes to sleep under. During the day he'd hook up with Kennedy's Labor to earn enough to get his load on that night. Things got a little out of hand, though, whenever he forgot to take a piss before he went to sleep. That tipped off Kennedy that he hadn't changed his clothes for a while, for as long as he'd been on the street in fact. Eventually, they stopped giving him work. So, he took up panhandling.

"The best new places," Albert told him, "are the median strips on big streets in and out of the city. Three lanes each way with stop lights, you can go walk up and down the strip 'til the light changes. Get yourself a sign that says, 'Homeless, hungry, Vietnam Vet, God Bless You.' Them guilty motherfuckers can't resist that shit. You can clear twenty bucks an hour."

"Get the hell out!"

The three of them stood on a corner in Southeast, long, lanky Albert, bulky Larry, and John, the smallest at five-six. Larry whined, "I can't say I was a Vietnam vet, I was twelve when that shit went down."

"Then say you're a Gulf War vet, it don't matter. They still give you the money."

"Sounds like a great gig," said John.

"Yeah, but you gotta be careful where you go. It gets crowded at some places, like Connecticut Avenue. Some of those motherfuckers get there early, don't appreciate latecomers or the competition."

"That's not a problem, we can sleep there. Hell, we got to sleep somewhere, right?"

Albert spread a slow smile. "Now you're starting to think right, John. One other thing, though. You got to stay away from spots where there're the spic flower sellers. They can really jam a strip up and there's no chasing them away. Too many of them, they work in teams. Same with the cripples. Man, they got some fucked-up dudes on them strips, legs bent every which way. Can't chase them off 'cause they don't run fast enough."

They all laughed.

"I seen like three or a dozen of them messed up in some way," Larry said.

"It's like a club," John said.

"A club-foot club," Albert said, and they all broke up again.

"How'd they get that way?" Larry asked. "The same, I mean."

Albert said, "In olden days they'd do that to people, Gypsies and shit. They'd buy kids from poor people, too many mouths to feed, then fuck them up on purpose, break their legs, burn their face, cripple them. Then they'd put them out on the street to beg, the sympathy vibe and shit."

"They all Vietnam vets, huh," John said.

Albert glared at him and continued. "The bosses come around now and then, take all the money."

"You shittin' us!" Larry said. "They do that?"

Albert answered in a matter of fact voice, "It's just a different kind of pimping."

"Damn, that's cold," Larry murmured. "You think they still do that shit now?" he said, looking creeped out.

Albert shrugged, "Who knows? Maybe so, you never know what those Latin motherfuckers up to. Look at them Hispanic drug dudes. Back in the day, you cross them, they cut your throat, pull out you tongue through the slit. Call it a Columbian necktie. That's when they ran everything."

"Oh, man," said Larry.

John squinted and said, "How you know all this shit?"

Albert blinked implacably. "I was a high school teacher before."

And they all nodded their heads.

In December, money grew tight. People at the median strips didn't want to open their windows to keep the cold out. Every aluminum can in town seemed to have been vacuumed up. Everyone was thirsty and cranky.

John tried to get one of those jobs handing out promotional fliers near the Metro stop at Dupont Circle. But his clothes were too tattered and dirty, and the gang foreman picked another guy new to the streets.

John hadn't seen Mary for months, but he didn't even bother going over to the house. She'd changed the locks a few weeks after tossing him out. And, anyway, she'd already thrown out or given away any other clothes he'd left there.

Late one afternoon, he thought about heading over to the shelter on D Street for a meal. But that was a good ways away and he was thirsty, not hungry. He sighed and started over anyway. He walked no more than a few blocks when he saw it: President Jackson dressed in green staring up at him from the concrete.

"Good golly, Miss Molly!" John said, staring down at the crumpled bill. He whipped his head around, back and forth to be sure no one else had seen it. Quickly, he bent at the knees and groped on the ground while keeping his eyes up on the lookout for anyone else on the make. He grabbed the twenty and stuffed it into his jacket, making sure that it wouldn't fall out of the hole in the pocket.

Rising up, he almost pranced down the sidewalk to Metro Liquor. He bounced inside past the security guard directly to the counter, twirling his twenty above his head like a girl with a parasol.

"Two pints of the Shark—Cutty, my man, right away."

The clerk, a round-faced man tipping the scales at 250–300, smiled smugly as he turned to the glass cabinet behind him. He brought down two bottles of Cutty Sark and inserted them each into a separate, small brown bag He handed them over with one hand while plucking the twenty with the other as he said, "Enjoy." He turned to the cash register, which dinged open while John stuffed the slim bottles into his coat side pockets. The clerk handed over a few singles, and John pushed them in on top of one of the bottles. He left the store and skipped down the sidewalk until he reached the corner, out of sight of the liquor store front window. John quickly unscrewed one of the bottles of Cutty Sark and held it above his head, draining half of it in seconds. He screwed the cap back on and tucked the bottle into his side pocket. Smacking his lips, he started up the street toward where they all hung out to drink more.

Funny that way, you could walk on the hill among narrow, tall red-brick row houses dating back a couple hundred years. Gay couples

71

lived in them now, or young lawyer families with their kids' Target tricycles left outside on their sides in their mini front yards. Then, just two blocks over, you could watch the young colts dash back and forth clanging a ball on rims hanging down from iron backboards. The boards were full of rows of holes, the way they used to make them back then for some forgotten reason. Ten-foot high hurricane fences stuck out of rust-stained concrete walls surrounding the playground. The broken-down blacktop court itself ran just 50 feet long. At either end of the park, wide-open entranceways marked the absence of long-gone gates. Old rundown, wooden row houses two stories high flanked the little park on all sides.

The fellas liked coming to the court early in the morning when the boys sat stuck in school, or at twilight when they ran to get home, dinner at six sharp or get hit up side the head for being late. December cold kept most kids off the court, though a few roundball addicts came out after school. But darkness fell fast in the winter, leaving the playground barren at twilight.

During early morning hours, John and the others drank whatever remained from last night, necessary to calm the daily shakes of the winos. In the evening, they came back with what they'd found during the day to share while sitting on a corner of the wall where the fencing had been bent out.

When John neared the playground, he saw Albert and Larry sitting there opposite a couple of other guys standing on either side, passing around a crumpled brown bag with a bottleneck peeking out. John didn't know the others, which didn't matter much. People came and went. One of them took a swig from the bottle straight up above his head. He lowered the bag, shook it, then flipped it between the wall and the bent fencing out of the playground.

John bounced over to Albert and Larry, feeling high enough almost to jam a ball through one of the hoops.

"Hey, man, what up?" he said, almost gushing.

"What up with you?" Albert said, drawing back just a bit from John's good cheer.

"This, my man!" John said, pulling the half-full bottle of Cutty Sark out of the right pocket in his jacket. He passed it to Albert and hopped onto the wall next to him. Albert drank long, then handed the bottle over to Larry.

"That's good." Albert twisted his head around, eyeing John. "I see you got a good taste before you got here."

John nodded, "I had my share," he said, pushing back the nearly empty bottle offered to him by Larry. Larry didn't know what to do with it, and offered the bottle to Albert, who ignored it.

"How you come to get so lucky in the first place?" Albert asked.

John grinned, "I came across some cash flow on the sidewalk, a five-spot. Bought the pint, drank half, and came by right after."

"A five-spot, huh," said Albert, "not a sawbuck?" He watched John's face go somber and said more loudly, "A Jackson? What the fuck, man!"

Albert hopped down from the wall. Face-to-face with John, he reached over to grab him with one hand by his shirt collar. He pulled, bending John at the waist close to him while searching each of his jacket pockets.

"What the hell, man?" John shouted until Albert suddenly let him sit back while he held the unopened pint of scotch up in his face.

"What the hell is this, man?" Albert yelled.

"Gimme it back, it's mine," John said, grabbing at the bottle. Albert yanked back; the pint bottle fell to the macadam and shattered, Cutty Sark spraying in every direction.

"You dumb motherfucker! Look what you done!" bellowed Albert.

"Me? I'm the motherfucker? You fucking stole it from—"

Before John could finish, Albert threw a roundhouse left at John's head, which he ducked by twisting on his side. He lost his balance and fell headfirst on the pavement, hitting it with an audible crack.

Albert froze above him. The other four men stood motionless, dumbfounded. Larry stooped and stared closely at John lying crumpled on the blacktop, quiet.

"His eyes open," Larry said. He glanced up, his own eyes wide with shock. "I think he's dead!"

Without waiting, he jumped up and ran pall mall through the gate out of the playground. The other three men followed quickly.

"Damn!" Albert said in a whisper. "Good Lord Almighty."

He stooped down and look closely. John's green cap lay next to him, his head surprisingly bald. His eyes were half-open, the whites dulled to yellow. Albert put his hand on John's chest and felt no movement. He leaned over, his ear close to John's mouth. Nothing.

Albert straightened up. He was dead, dammit. Fuck!

He stood up and peered around the playground. The dim light made it hard to see very far, but it looked like no one was around. Albert bent over at the waist, grabbed John by his clothing and hoisted his slight body on top of his shoulder. He saw the hat down below and squatted gingerly to grab it with his free left hand. He slowly rose and walked quickly through the open playground gateway.

Careful to hew to the backdrop, Albert made his way up northeast through the labyrinth of alleys dividing rowhouse blocks throughout the District. Almost all of them lacked street signs and lights, which meant travelers had to know their ways. Born and bred in the city, Albert knew his way by heart, reinforced by familiarity with many of the back lanes used for drinking sessions.

An hour put him close to where he wanted to be, just off 12th NE and Rhode Island. He paused in the shadow of one dark home to catch his breath. John might tip the scales at bantamweight, thought Albert. But after lugging him around on his shoulder for an hour, the scrawny sucker seemed to gain a pound every five minutes. Sweat drenched Albert despite the cutting frigid air. He was almost there, however, just a half a block away from his uncle's place.

The stately clapboard loomed darkly above on a slope adjacent to the sidewalk, so close that a six-foot stone retaining wall kept the yard intact. As long as he could remember, his Uncle Henry Jones had lived in the old house, keeping it spic and span, painted every five years the same pale green. He replaced the roof every fifteen years, never mind the thirty-year warranty, and washed every window in the house, all three stories, re-caulking any gaps before switching out screens with storm windows in autumn.

He kept his yard the same way. Perennials around the foundation,

74

with outer beds planted each spring full of peonies, begonias, and vinca, first nurtured by Aunt Mabel, long gone herself. No matter, Uncle Henry saw to them every year, all part of the order of things. He manicured the entire yard, which made Albert scarce as a kid, ducking out on helping whenever he could. Never mind the few bucks his uncle gave him at day's end. No amount of money was worth that much work.

One particular feature of Henry's set-up attracted Albert this night. Built on a high hill with a steep slope to the street, the property did not have a driveway. Instead, the original owners cut a space out of the stone retaining wall into the hill for a single-car garage. Closed in by padlocked double doors flush to the edge of the sidewalk, the wooden structure featured a slanted roof that peaked perfectly parallel to the grassy lawn above. Two single-pane windows at the top of each door allowed the only natural light into the narrow cubicle, which turned darker each year as grime gradually coated the glass.

Uncle Henry never used the garage to park a car. "Pain in the ass pullin' in and out of it, dodgin' all the cars comin' and goin' up and down the street. Besides, who need a car in the city?" He'd jerk his thumb back over his shoulder, "Bus stop right there on the corner." Henry never owned a car, which didn't stop him from joyfully sharing his criticism of the garage more than once. The garage became a limbo for dried paint cans, out-of-service appliances, a few sticks of broken furniture including an old chest of drawers, and some worn-out rakes and shovels half covered by some tattered tarps. Uncle Henry kept his valued tools, his riding mower and his snow-blower in an immaculate shed erected near the back door of the house. The old garage stood forgotten mostly, the exact state that attracted Albert right off.

At the back of the house, he lowered John down in the dark corner between the wall and the stairs. He crept up the steps hunched over to look into the kitchen. No sign of Uncle Henry, asleep of course at this late hour. Albert turned and lifted a plant pot to fetch the keys to the backdoor. He silently opened it and slipped inside. Not risking a light, he groped on the side of the wall near the door until he found the key hooks. At the bottom on the far side of the row, he found the one he wanted. He then worked his way over to the kitchen sink and reached down to the bottom drawer on the right. He smiled to himself as he pulled out the flashlight. Good old Uncle Henry, everything in its proper place.

Albert went out the back door, locking it behind him, then hopped down the steps leaving John Hall where he was. He trotted down the steps near the house to the street sidewalk and jogged toward the inset garage 30 yards away. Glancing around back and forth to be sure no one else was about, he inserted the key into the padlock. As he suspected, it refused to open easily, almost rusted completely shut. After working the key in and out and around, he finally managed to yank the lock off of its loop. He pulled one of the dull-green pine doors open, scraping it over the raised sidewalk, and held the flashlight high inside to take a look. Once he knew the lay of the land, he worked his way in and cleared a passage through the pile of junk to the back of the dark chamber. Satisfied, he left, closing the door behind him, and headed back to fetch John's mortal remains.

Inside the garage, Albert shifted forward to drop John off of his shoulder into a broken captain's chair propped against the back wall. John's mouth hung open now, which along with his open eyes made him look like he sat silently screaming. Albert pulled back quick and tried to close John's mouth and eyes. He couldn't do it, rictus now set in like concrete.

Fuck this, he said to himself, turning away to look around for a tarp. He snatched the nearest one and draped it over John.

"So long, John," he said with a nod, "Good luck in the next world. Maybe one where you share you liquor."

He flipped the tarp over John's head and left the garage. After securing the padlock, he strolled up the sidewalk to return the flashlight and the hidden house key. When he reached the steps, though, he saw through the backdoor window a light in the kitchen.

Damn, Uncle Henry up with the chickens, he thought, even though he didn't raise chickens anymore. Now what? Thinking about it, Albert decided that his uncle wasn't likely to miss the flashlight or the garage key right off. He couldn't do anything about it now, the sun

76

was starting to peek out in the east. He'd have to wait until nighttime again.

Just then, he smelled bacon. And coffee. He rubbed his chin stubble. Maybe Uncle Henry would enjoy some company, put on some more eggs. Sooner or later he'd have to go to the loo after that.

Albert continued up the back steps to knock on the back door.

In the dark, John Hall sat dead in the chair. But he didn't feel dead. He didn't feel anything. He wasn't sure he could see anything. He remembered what happened, how he ducked, lost his balance, and cracked his skull on the blacktop, blinding, white-lightning pain that he remembered but couldn't feel now. He recalled Albert picking him up over his shoulder, blood rushing down to his head he knew, but couldn't feel.

He couldn't see, either. What happened? Where the fuck was he?

In a garage, John knew, though he couldn't see or feel. Albert's Uncle's old garage now used as a shed to dump old stuff no one used anymore. In the dead of winter, cold as shit outside, ice on the side of the windowpanes filthy with years of dirt. Icey inside, too, though no breath showed in the dim moonlight, which he also could not see.

So, his eyes didn't work. Can't see, can't feel, so what did it all mean? A senseless, seeping chill shocked him awake; he was dead.

What else could he be? Unless he was in some kind of ultra-coma, like that French dude he'd seen on deep cable on the crazy shit medical show. Frozen stiff by a killer stroke, all the guy could do was breathe and see. Communicated by blinking his eyes, John remembered, wrote a book that way, died a couple months later.

Locked-in syndrome, they called it, immediately wondering how the fuck he could remember that as Shark saturated as he was. Never mind that, maybe that's me, thought John. Except he didn't see and he didn't breathe.

What now? Nothing about him worked, so was he dying or was he dead? Considering everything, particularly the last things he remembered happening, he was forced to conclude that he was dead. Dead and gone; dead as a doornail; dead to me; dead to the world;

77

dead, not proud; dead, dead, dead. And stuck in a crusty old garage. He pictured Albert dumping him in a heap, tossing a dusty old tarp halfway over him, and padlocking the garage door shut. Albert, sneaking over to the backdoor, replacing the key beneath the pot, and announcing himself to his uncle like he'd just arrived, "What's for breakfast?"

Meantime, John sat there waiting for putrefaction, the worms crawl in, the worms crawl out, fungi, really. First, though, he'd shit the bed, pooping and peeing in his pants. Sighing in his head, he girded himself for the rest, bloating, bacterial critters eating his guts, blood pooling turning him red, his body stiff, then going limp, stiffening again, finally relaxing for good, stinking up the place, all that and more. Topside, he'd be gone in a month. Buried six-foot deep, it could take as long as 12 years. In sunlight or someplace arid, he might simply shrink into a leathery stick figure. Then again, temps below 4 degrees Celsius could slow the process down, off and on maybe until spring. Still and all, talk about being long in tooth.

John stopped short. What the hell? Where was all this coming from? Squinting, he concentrated hard, calling up decomposition stuff he'd seen on *Dr. G Medical Examiner.* Okay, but how could he remember all that so clearly?

He hadn't had a drink for a few hours. That could be it, except it didn't make any sense, considering how pickled he was from recent, acute boozing. Maybe that's why he could think at all, an out-of-body experience within his body, like transplanting his brain into some kind of Frankenstein creature. But his swiss cheese gray matter should work more like Abby Normal's in the Mel Brooks movie. How could he be having all these notions, departed as he was?

He smelled bacon cooking, wafting down to the garage from the kitchen in the back of the house. Shit.

Time passed.

Fixed in time, he remembered everything. Memories ran through his mind, boyhood, throwing sticks at cars and running like hell when a driver jerked over to the curb, leaping out to chase them. Lying to his momma about doing it while the red-faced guy said he'd take us straight down to the police. After the guy left, Momma looking down at him, elbows akimbo, confronting him demanding the truth; he stood crying, confessing.

Going to his first party wearing his Sunday suit, dancing and drinking coke madly, seeing girls for the first time. Leaving late at night, walking the two blocks home over packed snow in the middle of the empty street, gazing at the dark, clear sky full of stars and an endless future.

Bragging about how good he was at sports, tough until Jerry Kunkle pushed him down and sat on his chest. Trying to breathe while saying he'd only been kidding. Getting thumped in practice as the littlest guy on the football squad. Becoming a shadow in the halls.

Daddy getting drunk and mad. Momma stepping in, but not all of the time. Spending more time out of the house. Smoking his first smoke, having his first drink. Joy-riding Daddy's car and getting ass-kicked for it. Meeting Mary.

Spring and summer rolled by and nothing much changed. Body fluids seeped away, some bugs feasted, but few other scavengers appeared, warded off by stray cats.

He felt bad about Mary. Off and on his girlfriend in school, later she seemed to dig him despite his bad habits. She picked up a few of them herself, smoking mostly, though not much for the drink. He loved her for her natural beauty and nice coloring, full-blooded, sort of lightly tan all the time. Her clear blue eyes reflected her inner being, straight without rancor or meanness of any kind. Considering all the dumbass shit he always did, he wondered how she kept putting up with it all. Not easy on him, but never calling it quits until the last time. He always felt bad about Mary, how he paid her no attention most of the time.

Same with the kids, Junie and Johnny Jr. He never hurt them; he wasn't a nasty drunk. He just forgot them a lot, missing ball games and birthdays. He did go to their graduations and always celebrated Christmas with them, though usually he was lit up a bit. Took its toll,

Junie knocked up and married at 17, Johnny Jr. off to the military at the same age. Both seemed happy, though, as far as he knew. They never came home, but they talked to their mom on the phone. She'd tell him after.

One time they'd gone down to visit some relatives of hers in El Paso. Sitting around the modern hacienda, the folks passed around some local Mexican cigarettes, Delicados Ovalados. Funny looking, they weren't round, instead regular cigs sort of flattened into ovals with delicate blue pinstripes circling them at regular spaces. When smoked, they lasted as long the extralong cigarettes in those days called 100s, like Silva Thins or Virginia Slims. No filters and guaranteed to cause a smoking cough within a few weeks, the Mexican ovals seemed imbued with sugar. Rumor had it that poor urchins scoured the streets of Mexico City for half-used cigarette butts to take to the plants for repackaging into Delicados Ovalados. Hence, the hacking cough. He remembered Mary laughing while puffing on one without inhaling, the scent of her favorite perfume mingling with the smell of the acrid smoke. Delicados and Shalamar, smoke and perfume.

Fall and winter slipped in again. Lots of cold rain and its attendant erosion. The tarp draped over him seemed to be flattening on top of his diminishing shape. Dropping temperatures slowed the process, though.

He relived the old times again, the down times, the distractions. Work tasked him. He trimmed trees for a while, falling out now and then, happy to collect Workers Comp to drink up. Sometimes he abstained when Mary weighed in. Pretty soon, though, the tree company gave him the boot. Then construction, fired; moving company, fired; garbage truck, fired. Mary kept them fed and sheltered, though she wasn't crazy about the situation. When he got let go by Kennedy Labor, she raised the roof. One more drink and she'd toss him out.

He quit on the spot. Her brother fixed him up with Rob Johnson at C-Print and for twenty years he rose at six, ate breakfast, put on his green cap, and took the A-7 bus to the warehouse. The first year, he

80

stacked printed material. A year later, he took over a forklift and loaded the deliveries. Twenty-one years later, he woke up and started drinking. Mary gave him a couple of months to try and straighten out until he sold the dining room table for drinking money. She changed the locks that day.

He missed Mary now, too late as it was.

Five years gone and for some reason he'd mummified. Memories kept recurring, more detailed each time, so much so that he figured he must be using 80% of his brain like offhanded bragging by the guy in *Defending My Life*. An afterlife supernumerary played by Rip Torn in the movie, his lowkey boast riffed on the conventional wisdom that most living people used only 10% of their mental capabilities. Now considered an old wives tale, John recognized, yet here he was after life, using his mind at a level far higher than ever before in his entire previous existence. In this time, he dwelled upon his past like in *Groundhog Day*, again and again, but every time in greater detail.

I know I repeat myself a lot, he exclaimed to himself, but heck, it's a new day every day!

Ten years through, things changed. Uncle Henry died and Albert inherited the house. The first day after moving in, he ordered a pile of dirt and some rolls of sod. He wheelbarrowed the dirt over and filled in the sides and back of the garage, tamping the dirt down, adding more, and tamping again. When the dirt reached the rooftop, he shoveled more dirt on it until he had a seamless layer across from one side of the garage to the other. After that, he unrolled the sod over the dirt, tamped it down, and watered it. Albert watered the sod during the next few weeks until it had meshed perfectly with the rest of the grass growing in the yard. In ensuing days, he brought in a stone mason to close up the gap in the wall to cover up the garage doors.

There, Albert said to himself, that shit's done for good.

Damn, John thought to himself.

As dark and black as Albert cloaked the garage, John still knew what was up. Along with recalling all of the events in his life, he could project things happening around him. He couldn't be sure if what he knew was real and true, except he just knew it was so. Mary moved on, Albert drank, Larry cleaned up, Rob sold C-Print, the kids on the playground bickered and balled, seasons changed, time marched and life went on.

Mostly, John didn't dwell on all that. Too busy looking at his own shit, decades gathering every iota—baby teeth in a box, picking at the plaster in the wall, Daddy strapping him good, lying about drop-kicking the football through the front window, Daddy strapping him good. Lying to some sweet thing to get to third base, shouting at Junie and Johnny Jr. for no reason at all except for the Shark. Selling his blood to get more. Going over all those days, nights, hours, and minutes that he couldn't account for, despite seeing them like in a mirror image over and over again.

He mulled, too, whether this made up his Judgment Day. He stayed away from thinking about Jesus and heaven, lashed to the ill-at-ease feeling that his last stop would be the other place considering his bad behavior. In his head he expected to see all these angels, saints, and saved souls standing on clouds around a huge, encrusted gold throne with God enormously looking down on him, big, gray beard and fierce eyes. That seemed all out of a childhood dream. Maybe what he saw made up the real Judgment Day, going through every crappy thing he'd ever seen and done in his entire life. Why not? Who could feel worse about the worst things someone had ever done than the person who had done them? Who could condemn someone for bad things more than that same person? Okay, so he sold some of his blood to get more hooch. Suppose he tracked where each pint went, see which lives were saved, wouldn't that count for something? Except for the lives that weren't saved. Maybe this explained why he kept thinking about all this shit all this time shriveling away in his corrupt, desiccated body in a makeshift car tomb instead of inside the Pearly Gates. He felt bad enough, but really, what the fuck?

Twenty years in, something changed. After going over it all over

82

and over again, he drifted. He drowsed, dreaming a waking dream of things he'd never seen before. Subtle at first, walking down some street in Williamstown, PA, eating funnel cake. Drinking home brew outside a cellar on some farm in Iowa. Seeing younger versions of people he knew, having conversations with them that he'd never had. More aware of the shift, he found himself in places he'd never been to, walking on causeways near windmills in Holland. He pounded poi in Hawaii, and drank aqvavit in Norway, pulling a face while yearning for Cutty.

So, now what? After exhausting what might have been thinking about his past, had he moved on to what could have been? Does this mean that the things he sees going on around him are not what is, but what could be? Is this what you do when you're dead; work on seeing, feeling until you find yourself shaping the world's existence in a different way? John suddenly blinked to a show he'd seen on *Discovery* about quantum mechanics and alternate realities. Not just one universe exists, but endless numbers of them, so many that anything imagined under any sun existed as another reality. When he saw things happening around him that he couldn't see and saw things he'd never seen before, could this be quantum thinking? Living is limited to seeing only what you see; death is wide open.

High living caught up with Albert, forcing him into an assisted-living home. To pay for it, he needed to sell Uncle Henry's house, though most of the money went to back taxes. The Pepperdines, a young couple with a toddler, delighted in purchasing the property, which needed a lot of work. In town and not too far from a Metro stop, they were happy to pay top dollar for it and invest almost the same amount in renovations. They put on a badly needed new roof, knocked down a wall to create a large living/dining space, and punched a hole in the wall to the kitchen for a counter looking into both spaces. They also expanded the back of the kitchen with a vast sunroom, even though it faced a northern exposure. They also bulldozed a driveway from the street up past the kitchen to a new carport that replaced Uncle Henry's shed.

The trouble came when they decided to install a playground

apparatus on top of the lawn right above the garage. In the winter, a heavy snowfall combined with the weight of the playset to collapse the roof of the garage. Dismayed, the young man of the house decided to fence it off temporarily and deal with it in the Spring.

When warm weather arrived, the working crew periodically reported progress to the Pepperdines. They gingerly removed the playset without incident and started to excavate the site to install a concrete base. At that point they informed the owners about finding old shingles and broken wooden two-by-fours. Later on, they let the Pepperdines know that in pulling out all the shingles and cross boards, they'd discovered the ruins of an old building, maybe a one-car garage. They also informed them that full demolition and removal would require considerably more work, which would mean greater expense. Rather than risk having sort of a man-made sinkhole in his backyard, Jason Pepperdine decided to bite the bullet and go ahead with the dig.

Two days later the foreman came to the back door.

"We gotta problem."

Jason stood at the head of the rectangular hole while the foreman pulled back the rotten tarp. Jason flinched when he saw the dark brown, shrunken leathery cadaver lying there, head straight up, jaw hanging open in eternal rictus. My God, thought Jason, he looks like he's 5,000 years old lifted straight out of a bog somewhere in Germany or Ireland. Something out of National Geographic.

Jason suspended the project and called the authorities. No one had any idea of who the John Doe was. They extracted DNA to see if they could find any relatives. They also attempted to interview Albert Jones, too, but left with no information due to the former owner's dementia.

"I called the Medical Examiner's office," Jason said to his wife Elsa. He rattled the ice in his tumbler, now just a quarter full of Caol Ila after his first swallow. "They're willing to obtain the remains and hold them until an identity is established. If none's found, he'll be buried in the unknown section of the city's public cemetery."

"You mean a pauper's grave?" Elsa said, her voice rising. "That's so cruel."

"No, Babe, it'll be okay, they do this with a proper amount of

84

dignity for sure."

"I don't know, Jason. He's been here so long, he's like family in this place."

"Oh, for …" he rolled his eyes, saw his wife's shoulders beginning to slump, and quickly spoke to stave off the waterworks. "Look. I'll pop for a coffin. We'll give him a good sendoff, believe me. Don't cry, it'll be all right," he said, patting her shoulder, thinking to himself, a nice, cheap metal casket for sure.

Across the universe, John found his relocation to be an annoying distraction. Unearthing him revealed that he had become a shrunken, leather bound carcass. Maybe he was a living mummy like in *The Mummy*, but no hot evil Egyptian chick was coming around to save him. At least the bugs hadn't fricasseed him.

What about bugs? If birds can think, can bugs? There seems to be no correlation to brain function and physical size. In fact, the idea that butterflies have complete circulatory systems—tiny little veins, arteries, and hearts—blew his mind. And look at how bees handle themselves, knowing where they are, where they've been, and telling all the other bees how to get there. Maybe bugs think just as much as he does dead. If so, do they make decisions about whose remains to munch on? Do maggots admire someone's nose and therefore rule it as off limits for lunch? Is this really how King Tut's proboscis survived? Or didn't?

He sighed. He really needn't stay for the trip to the cemetery and all that. On the other hand, where would he go while his new neighbors laid his mortal remains to rest? The change of venue didn't matter to him.

The Pepperdines crumbled dirt on his metal coffin, then slowly turned away, careful to avoid another freshly filled grave next to John's. Once gone, the cemetery caretaker pushed the pile of earth into the hole.

John wondered why people buried other people alone. Even married couples in graves next to each other occupied separate coffins. In Pompeii, bodies hugged close together in death. Sooner or later, everyone runs out of life. Life is too short to make other lives shorter, lonelier. Better to leave obsessive, compulsive successes behind.

Quiet.

John wondered, do other dead people create realities to talk to other dead people? He remembered then that you always find something you've lost in the last place you look.

He searched around the other fresh gravesite.

"That you, Albert?"

Quiet.

Then, "God-damn me to hell. You still here?"

John smiled, then laughed.

Deadpan

Rifless laid his personal skimmer over in a roll to right it, reversed jets, and slapped it down on the private use strip at Petersen. He gunned the engines, popped the clutch, and zipped over to the parking bay near the Officers Club. After killing the ignition, he hopped out just before the skimmer skidded to a rough, banging stop against a concrete abutment. In front of the club, a startled sentry stared at Rifless suspiciously and groped for his power rifle. Rifless paused, turned back to the dull, ding-pocked vehicle and said, "It's my brakes. They need adjusting." He beelined it inside.

With a wave of his hand he half-acknowledged a broken chorus of greetings from the regular gang and hurried to the bar. He called to Joey, the bartender, a small E.M. in his late forties. Raising an index finger into the ether, Rifless said in somber tones, "Joseph, I am in need."

Joey smiled and placed a wide glass of reddish liquor, frothy at the brim, in front of the razor pilot Rifless. He put the rim delicately to his lips and in one measured pour slowly quaffed the cinnamon-scented beverage. Life effused his nervous system, his nerve endings popped electric sparks. He lowered the glass to the bar. "Yum, yum."

He tapped the wooden bar top twice with his finger and as Joey filled his glass again, he said, "Did you find the buckets?"

"Yessir. Got 'em out back."

"Excellent, excellent. Remember our signal. I'll let you know when I've found a suitable subject."

"I'll be waiting for it, sir," Joey said, still smiling,

Rifless nodded, then gestured with his head at his glass, empty once again.

"On me," said a voice from behind. Rifless looked back to see Credo sandwiched between two pink girls. Big like all Paralethals, Credo sported the de rigueur, black-satin dress flight suit, neatly trimmed in front and back with four parallel creases, and two more at each flank.

Observing Credo's sartorial splendor, Rifless recalled the story he'd heard about Credo's tailor once beading in a set of cuts so that they met errantly, blushingly, at the joint of one leg. Reportedly, Credo had stated calmly his ire at being image-crippled at the knee. Of course, the quaking tailor immediately made the corrective alterations. Then Credo cold-bloodedly kicked apart the couturier's console as an object lesson to get it right the first time.

Recalling the incident just then made Rifless feel a greater consciousness of his own somewhat worn bodysuit. Now dulled, the suit's inky satin shone almost white at the seat and elbows. A host of wrinkles also tangentially intersected his formerly rigid pants leg creases. Ah, well, he thought, such is the price of maintaining Corps morale. Staring directly into Credo's eyes, he straightened and in a florid half-salute lifted his newly filled glass to mouth level while saying, "Commander Credo, to the port, hup-hup, thank you very much." He drained the drink. "Mighty right."

"Don't thank me, Captain, thank these lovely ladies here. They each insisted upon buying me a celebration round. But, my limit's one, so you're the lucky fellow."

"Indeed, I am," Rifless said, as he openly ogled the two adoring young women. He reached over and pulled them to him, one arm around each waist. Gazing at them with his tongue lolling loosely, he said to the giggling girls, "Fortunately, I have no limit." Then to Credo, "And what is the occasion, may I ask, for this our most joyous felicity?"

"I just got back from Topside. Razored two East Bloc flyers in tandem." Credo permitted himself the airiest filigree of a smile.

Rifless blinked. Two enemy scouts downed with one laser burst, hard to believe, even of the relentless Credo.

"Nonpareil, Paralethal," said Rifless. "Two in tandem, a match made in heaven. And the earth is safe again." Two down. Only four billion more to go, he thought. "So, Credo, you got two with one shot. What next, trips?"

Through shining teeth Credo said, "I was lucky. Any fighter jock could have done it."

88

"Including me? Impossible. To get a single shot off I need at least two targets, one for each eye. Four, if I wear my glasses." He reached back to an unzipped compartment of his suit and whipped out a pair of black lensless eyeglasses with a big plastic nose and false mustache attached, which he quickly put on. The girls bent over in laughter, and Credo's neon smile dropped a few amps.

"Rifless, can we talk?"

"Talk? This isn't it? We're doing something wrong?"

"I mean alone."

"Oh," Rifless shrugged. "Suture yourself, the neurosurgeon said. Ladies."

The two women groaned laughter and started to leave, but Rifless held them tight, saying, "Uh, one moment please," He presented his cheek to the girl on his right, tapping it with a finger. As she leaned over to give him a peck, he swiveled swiftly so that their lips met, plastic nose bumping surprised flesh, "Thanks, doll."

He kissed the other one, then affectionately patted their behinds as they walked away. He turned back to the waiting Credo. Stiffening to attention, he said, "Commander Credo, sir, is this an official review, sir?"

Mildly, Credo said, "Call it some friendly counseling."

"Well, all right then, let's have a friendly drink," He called to Joey, then peered significantly at Credo's dry glass. Credo relaxed his features and motioned to Joey for another. When it arrived, they moved over to a table within shouting distance of the bar. Rifless pushed his fingers through his unkempt, sandy hair and said, "Commence."

"First, I like to see people's faces when I talk to them. Can you take off the glasses?"

"Okay, but I'm warning you, most people beg me to keep them on." He removed the glasses and put them on the table.

"Listen," said Credo, "the Big Picture Boys asked me to talk to you. They told me that you're making them nervous. But it isn't only them, Rifless. It's the other jocks—me, too. You're beginning to worry us as well."

Shit, he thought. "How so?"

"We think you've been behaving strangely for the past few months.

89

You've been acting different."

"Why, Commander Credo, I'm behaving like always, I'm misbehaving. I'm acting like always, I'm acting up. I'm a model of Paralethal punctilio. I drink, chase girls, and fly just as fast as ever, maybe even faster than ever."

"Yeah, but you 're doing it by yourself. And, yeah, maybe you are doing more, maybe too much. Especially the drinking."

Dramatically, Rifless stared at Credo and said coldly, "Sir, I know when I've had enough to drink," He pointed a forefinger into the air, "I've had enough to drink when I've had too much," He gazed away.

Credo sighed, shaking his head. "Rifless, I'm trying to do you a favor, I've seen this before, Paralethals who seem to be all right, but they're a little off, too. They start spending a lot of time alone. They drink, they screw around, but somehow, they get distracted. They lose too, they get fuzzy. Sometimes they start seeing things." He slowly shook his head, "They don't last long up there."

"A fate worse than life," Rifless murmured, sipping his drink.

Credo grimaced, "Rifless, it's happening to you. Just look at yourself."

"I try to avoid that as much as possible."

"Look at your bodysuit," Credit said, mildly exasperated. "It's a mess, a disgrace. Don't you have another one?"

"I wish I was in it."

Credo sat back. "You're slipping, Rifless. Hell, if the Big Picture Boys see it you know it's true. And we worry about how this affects your work, Rifless, we worry about the job you're doing up there."

"Well, hell, so do I," Rifless said with sincerity. He leaned forward and said, "Confidentially, a guy could get killed up there. Of course, it's probably not as bad as what could happen down here. You know," he said, haloing his face with his hands, then spreading the fingers, "Boom!"

Sitting calmly with his legs crossed and one hand resting on the table, Credo said quietly, "That's why we're up there, to prevent that from happening. We Paralethals would all hate to see our reputation, our perfect record, go down the tubes because, let's say someone like you, Rifless, allows a few Commie construct shuttles to slip through due to the fact that a haze of booze obscured his vision, slowed his

90

reflexes, bent his judgement."

"Not to worry, Credo. Why, that kind of mistake could cost me my pension, and I'm short, I only have three years to go. Hey, I want America to last for another twenty years at least. Retirement wouldn't be much fun otherwise." He finished his drink and then pivoted to face the bar. "Joey, set 'em up, will you?" He formed a small basket with his hands and arms, twice.

Joey grinned and disappeared.

Rifless turned back to Credo and said, "Listen this has been great, and I'd really like to stay longer, but I'm due up Topside in less than an hour."

He stood up. Credo glared. With a rising voice he said, "What? Wait a minute, you're in no condition to go on patrol."

"Because of a few drinks?" Rifless loudly laughed, "Credo, the damned Superscamp fighter-scouts do all the work. But look, don't worry. I've got my own special method for detoxifying myself. It's foolproof, you see, and for me that's an important consideration."

He stepped over to the bar where Joey had placed two buckets marked FIRE. By this time some of the other people in the bar had wandered over, attracted by Rifless' burst of laughter.

"The military's amazing, isn't it?" Rifless said, smiling broadly. He pointed at the lettered pails. "Still issuing fire buckets in the 21st century. Well, here goes."

He hiked up one of the buckets above his head and turned it over. A stream of water drenched his head and shoulders, splashed down, and puddled at his feet. He shook his body doglike, which caused the laughing crowd to fall back.

"Brrr!" he said. "Well, that's that, I'm ready." He took a step to leave, then stopped and assumed an exaggeratedly thoughtful pose.

"Say, Credo, didn't you have a drink over your limit? Looks like you could use some detoxifying, too."

Rifless quickly grabbed the other bucket and dashed the contents into the face of Credo who flinched reflexively, shouting, "No!" The bucket spewed hundreds of little scraps of paper onto the Commander, some still floating down around his face as it suffused with blood. The crowd roared their enjoyment while Rifless headed for the club exit. He halted, leaned back to the table and snatched up his nose glasses.

"Gotta have these, have to maintain my image. Bye now!" He bolted out the door.

After leaving the Base Detox Chamber, Rifless headed over to Flight Prep Quarters to dress for patrol. In seconds he emerged wearing his black polysatin pressure suit with his black patent leather deathhead hooked under his arm. He sprinted out to the airfield, past scramble-ready fighter-scouts, past a few long-range cruisers and some survival ships that could support five men on recycled wastes for their natural life spans. Rifless didn't give them a thought; long-term retributive measures vis-a-vis preemptive strikes were definitely not part of his action.

He donned his deathhead, climbed aboard his own fighter-scout on the mass-ack pad and secured for takeoff. The mass ack threw his Superscamp heavenwards and Rifless, pressed immobile into the JellG pads, waited impatiently to reach Topside. Topside was the big black gameboard where Paralethal jocks could score some big points against the Eastern Pinko Rednyks, the Socialist Scumbags who threatened the Free World in their fast straight-aheaders built with the sweat and blood of their enslaved working class, right might.

Lore of yesteryear, he mused, fitting for the doggedly dogmatic. For himself, he'd stick to the reality of the past thirteen years, razoring the other side's endless stream of recon Sats, D-ray Sats, and most critically, the construct shuttles sent up to build the feared big colony stations. According to the Big Picture Boys, no big space colonies meant no havens from preemptive strikes on Earth; hence, no preemptive strikes. Fortunately, the shuttles were the easiest of marks for Superscamp sights. In this longest of undeclared wars, none had ever made it past a Paralethal scout and Rifless didn't expect to be that Scamp jockey to let one through now. Mindfulness of the Big Picture sometimes made for wet palms when he spied a foreign shuttle, though, like looking at a one-meter putt to tie up the Masters.

Credo could be right, thought Rifless, it could be time to board that boat bobbing somewhere on the gray murk of the Chesapeake, to sail and drink into oblivion along with the rest of the world for as long as it lasted. But Credo still avidly searched out the other side's ComCommanders, the same higher flyers who'd zippered every Westside construct barge that'd tried to set up shop. No, Rifless decided, let Credo with his lifer aspirations and the younger jocks go after the toothy ones for glory doctrinaire. He'd just stay careful, do his job, but also continue to avoid confrontation politics. It'd help to keep clear of Credo, too, now that he'd placed himself firmly on the Commander's list of shit.

The Superscamp reached the apex of the mass ack's push and, with Rifless' go-ahead, tore off on a long parabola across the faint edge of the atmosphere. With all sensors humming, the fighter-scout rushed along the dark border between the royal blue haze that outlined the arced Earth on the right and the cast of the opalescent Moon to the left. In short order, it located and fixed sights on a recon sat. The Scamp fired, razor-lasering the satellite into two neat slices that hung suspended in place for a breath of an instant before they both blipped into a thousand pieces.

Rifless's ship ripped through the remains super-pronto, space debris silently pinging its flanks with pats of success. Aware that they usually paired a D-ray sat with recons, Rifless reminded the Scamp to keep a close lookout for the twin. Soon the scout's sensors picked up the other sat. They closed and lasered.

The Scamp flashed through the burgeoning dust cloud and Rifless ordered it to hug the last of the stratosphere. He liked dipping back deep into the atmosphere where the ship could perform sharp tactical turns and where his stealth devices worked better. That way, nothing on top could predict where he'd power out, giving him the age-old advantage of surprise. The maneuver consumed vast quantities of fuel, but his success ratio nearly justified the expenditure. To perform the stunt, he routinely used the extra fuel mandated by Command Central for contingency Moon surveillance. Nothing ever got out that far anymore and besides that, the last thing on Earth he wanted to do was go to the damned Moon.

Just before he uttered the command to plane down, the Scamp reported a foreign mass ahead. "More info," Rifless said evenly.

A big one it was, and not in orbit either. Probably a construct shuttle, he thought, as big as that and self-propelled. Maybe not, though. Unconsciously, Rifless wiped the chin of his deathhead.

"Cruise steady, low arc," he ordered.

It appeared, a speck growing. A construct shuttle, all right. He waited for the poor slug to sight him and lay over in its single, pitiful escape maneuver, laughingly called by the Paralethals the "shuttle scuttle." This one didn't scuttle, though, evidently still unaware of his presence. But as the Scamp closed, he noticed that something didn't look right about the foreign ship. The barge was shuttle-size, no question, but big exhaust snouts stuck out at every angle from its endpieces. Exposed for repairs, maybe, he thought, maybe they'd broken down and couldn't run. Rifless spoke quietly, as if fearing he'd scare it away. "Zero in and laser."

One more nanosecond and it'd be all over, he told himself. But in one-half a nanosecond the enemy craft burst ahead with tailpipes flaming and plummeted into the blanket of air. The next fraction of a second saw Earth wrenched out of sight, and Rifless felt his arms and chest slammed back flat into the JellG pads. He grimaced a silent scream through exposed, clenched teeth as the twisting Superscamp crushed his body this way and that, corkscrewing at top G's through the planet's stratosphere. White-eyed, Rifless tried to yell out loud, but the acceleration wouldn't let him. The scout's evasive tactics indicated a rear attack, and he wanted to cry out orders to run, to counter. Today, he thought frantically, I should have retired today. Abruptly the force eased, and his stomach jackknifed in time to his surging adrenaline.

"Move it, damn it, counter and pursue," roared Rifless, even as the renewed pressure signaled that the scout, of course, had already acted. He could see it now on his screen, the same elongated shuttle, accelerating straight out from Earth.

Uh oh. After a moment's speechless observation, he said, "Listen, could that thing have been supported by an enemy higher-flyer? Is that what jumped us?"

The scout informed him that the targeted era had been unsupported, that it had executed a dip and roll in atmosphere to egress into position behind him.

"Great. That's just great," he murmured glumly, facing the bleak realization of a Paralethal's darkest spacemare. He'd encountered a new enemy ship, evidently part rapid-transit fighter-scout, part colony-construct shuttle. Worse than that, the hybrid beast raced loosely ahead of him, tauntingly wagging back and forth to effectively elude his laser. He'd done it, he thought darkly, he'd let one get through.

"Can we catch it?" he asked in a barely hopeful voice. The Scamp reported that they could match acceleration but not overtake.

"I was afraid of that. Oh, my poor, poor, ass."

The scout then relayed to him the fact that the enemy's course put it dead on the Moon.

"The Moon?" Rifless perked up. "The Moon. It'll have to swing around it or lose way. We might be able to plot a tighter hyperbola and pick up some speed to catch them inside for a gut shot. They don't call them straight-aheaders for nothing. Call ComCommander Center and request clearance to pursue to the Moon. I just might save my butt yet."

Three hours later, amid the looming Moon's sickly pallid sheen, Rifless at last conceded to himself that his Scamp couldn't undercut the foreign ship's wings. He couldn't even track the big fighter-shuttle obscured now by the bulk of Earth's first satellite crowding in on the right.

"I am thoroughly screwed. Maybe they'll go easy on me, give me a desk job out of pity." But a vision of Credo's heartless face smiling in disgust at his disgraceful performance told him the lie of this hope.

"Continue pursuit." They had enough fuel to follow the shuttle all the way around the Moon and back, enough to watch it descend safely to Earth. Yet, something could happen to slow them up, a breakdown, maybe. Afterall, he thought, a three-legged horse could win the Kentucky Derby if all the other horses fell down.

The Scamp had completed its circuit of the Moon's giant pan when it disclosed that the shuttle had disappeared. He shook his head hopelessly, "I'm having a bad day." It must have landed. But why? There's nothing down there but junk. Unless it had broken down. Whatever. "Cruise back, arc low and slow."

After six hours, the scout pinpointed a disparate mass on the Moon's dark side. Relief swept over Rifless. He thought to order an immediate strafing run, but just then it occurred to him that he'd stumbled upon the career opportunity of a military lifetime. He could take this brand new, revolutionary, secret enemy spacecraft intact if he ambushed it on the surface. Any of the other Paralethals would jump into hell and back for this chance. Too bad none of them were here.

He ordered the scout down and activated his suit's EVA function. Grabbing his sidepiece, he left the Superscamp and began to work his way toward the site of the enemy ship's hiding place. At first, he had difficulty controlling his bounding movements in the low gravity, a discomforting lapse given the gloom of the Moon's backside profile. He had to rely upon the Scamp's instruments to guide him, which hardly lessened his apprehension about being the one surprised. Nonetheless, he set his teeth and pressed on.

According to the Scamp's signal, the new ship rested on the other side of the wall of the small crater ahead. With extreme care, Rifless lowered himself to all fours and painstakingly inched up to the lip of the crater. He crawled doing his uttermost not to disturb any of the detritus thrown up and around the cavity formed by a tiny meteor billions of years ago. At the top, he eased his head above the edge and peeked down to the floor below.

He froze, surprised absolutely in spite of the studied sneakiness of his approach. He could see that the mass below was foreign all right, since it basked in a flood of reddish light cast by a bank of encircling lamps. A flimsy canopy suspended above only casually blocked the spotlights from high cruising vehicles, reinforcing his intuition that nobody seriously cared about hiding this thing. He recognized, too, that the rig on the crater floor was not the long, lean fighter-shuttle he'd chased back here.

Shit! he mouthed, while also trying to stave off the lugubrious despair rising in him. This is bad news he realized, the worst. Then he thought perhaps the structure below had some connection to the shuttle. He'd never seen anything like this contraption either. The Scamp confirmed his assessment without adding any data as to the nature of the thing. All sorts of gimcrackery and doodads stuck out of it every which way, pretty much ruling out atmospheric maneuvers or mass ack propulsion. In fact, it didn't look like any kind of vacuum vehicle, either. So, what was it?

A communication module. Or maybe a mining combine, he thought, to supply their new shuttle with material for colony construction. Sure, why hide it any better since nobody came to the Moon anymore? Except for the brilliant Captain Rifless, of course. It dawned upon him then that if his guess was right, their new fighter-shuttle might still be lurking above, cloaked by equally sophisticated stealth gear. It might be out there, waiting for the only Westside fighter-jock who knew of its existence—waiting for him. He lifted his eyes and gazed through the top of his deathhead, seeing nothing. Time to go.

A motion to the right of the contraption in the crater caused him to slap at his sidepiece, which shifted him two meters left and raised a cloud of moondust overhead that plainly marked his position for anyone looking. Cursing silently, he hastily drew his handblaster and pointed it in the direction of the movement in the crater. Oblivious to Rifless watching from above, a tiny, indistinct figure busied itself with some indiscernible task to the right of the strange machinery.

A midget, thought Rifless. The other side's recruiting covert personnel from circuses—the better to keep low profiles? Whatever, Rifless thought, this guy could be my ticket past the shuttle upstairs. Making sure that the mini-agent provocateur below remained preoccupied, Rifless cautiously dropped behind the crater's rim and crept around to put the queer apparatus between himself and its operator. Then, with discretion nonpareil, he eased himself over the edge and slipped down to the gizmo at the base of the pit. Peering around the side of the strange equipment, he was relieved to see the silhouette of the short party in question just outside the border of lights. Apparently still working intently, he faced away, his back to his gear between them.

Rifless composed himself, then whirled out from behind the mechanism. He pulled down on the small operative with his power gun and started to say through his head radio, "All right, Comrade, stand and deliver, . . .?"

Turning around into the light, the figure that faced Rifless was small indeed, no more than four feet tall. But, instead of wearing an Eastern Commander's slick, gun-metal EVA suit, this pudgy little character wore plaid baggy pants held far above his waist and ankles by broad, gaily hued suspenders; a crazy polka-dot patterned shirt and an equally wild, floppy bowtie; a long, quilt-patched, wide-lapeled jacket that reached to his knees but bulged at the buttons. Instead of a steel-gray Eastern skullshell, he sported a porkpie hat way too small for his big, round, fleshy head, and he wore glasses with bottle bottom lenses and brassy wire rims. On his feet, dingy, tattered spats and large, flapping shoes with bulbous toes had replaced the sleek, cat-leather shitkickers favored by Pinko Commanders. In a daze, Rifless continued his inventory, noting finally an obviously artificial carnation made of some kind of linen drooping out of one lapel. But not one razor-sharp cut could Rifless find in his search for any familiar, identifying feature of a deadly Eastern higher flyer.

Unconsciously, Rifless allowed the barrel of his weapon to drop slightly, and the strange dwarf in front of him beamed a broad, crooked smile from an askew mouth and said boldly, "Well, for heaven'sth sake, what a pleasant surprizth! Hello, hello, I'm delighted to see you. This is wonderful, y'know." He finished with a scaling, singsong laugh verging upon giddiness, "a-hoo-hoo-hoo." As he laughed, the tiny, rotund man placed his hands above his breast and tapped his fingertips together in time to each "hoo."

Rifless stared hard, and hard again as he tried and failed to find a place for this incongruous gnome in the natural order of things. I need more detox, he said to himself, either that or a stiff drink.

The outlandishly dressed character continued to speak at a rapid-fire rate. "They never told me that I'd meet a real live Eoithling on this job, y'know. This is simply amazthing, y'see." He spoke with a weird urban accent and some sort of a lisp that Rifless couldn't place, a thickness of the tongue that subtly distorted an occasional "s."

"Of course, I'm not very well prepared to receive guests, y'understand, I'm a little weak on the protocol. Just a moment, please."

He turned away and down furtively, then back to face Rifless with his arms spread wide before him. From each ear protruded a raw carrot.

98

Rifless blinked, speechless, stupefied again.

"Well?" said the dwarfish character, "Aren't you going to ask me why I have carrots in my ears?"

"Why do you have carrots in your ears," Rifless roted.

"They were out of bananas."

Observing Rifless's almost horrific bewilderment, the minute man raised a hand to tap his fingers against his jawline, saying, "Hmm, that didn't go quite right, your timing's way off, y'see. Let's try something else: we don't get many Eoithlings up on this moon, y'know."

He waited expectantly, critically squinting over his large, lumpy nose at Rifless, who said nothing, his face a blank.

"Oh, my, my, my, this isn't woiking out right at all. You 're supposed to say, 'At these prices, I don't wonder,' or, 'At these prices you won't get many more.' No, no, this is ridiculousth, you look very uncomfortable. You mind if I make a phone call?"

He reached deep into a spacious pocket of his long coat and pulled out an archaic telecommunications device known as a "telephone" or "phone." Rifless recognized if from seeing one in a museum, a quaint artifact as part of a twentieth century exhibit

The dwarfish character dialed, and, as he waited, covered part of it as he said to Rifless, "This is all so unexpected, y'see."

Unexpected. Closing his eyes and lifting his head Earthwards, Rifless cried out mockingly inside his head, Credo, how did you tap into my dreams? But there couldn't 't have been time enough to set this up. Or, he wondered, viewing anew the tiny creature before him, was this a scheme of the other side's, a kind of psycho-gambit to confound interlopers? Unlikely, but possible, he thought. Taking in the midget's vibrantly loud outfit once again, he admitted the scene certainly bore the East's telltale subtle imprint. No, he realized, this isn't the style typical of either side, too oddball and not military at all. "Something's wrong, here," he murmured, "definitely whacko."

"My sentimentsth exactly," the puny guy said, pocketing his phone. "Y'know, as one of the Universth's most gifted organisthms, you really haven't been very funny."

"Funny? I'm not trying to be funny."

"Obviousthly. This is all very confusing, y'know. You haven't acted at all like I would've expected, y'see, not sidesplitting at all. Why, you don't even look like an Eoithling, no stylish pantaloons, no chick sportsth coat, not even a snappy chapeau—where are your musthtache noseglasses, for heaven'sth sake?"

"I left them back in the Scamp." He could have kicked himself as soon as he realized what he'd said.

"Oh. Well, that happensth. But why wear all black? What's funny about a black suit? Don't you have another?" As Deja vu rippled through Rifless, the miniature man posed a finger at his lips, then said, "Maybe you're dressed for black humor, perhapsth?"

Rifless shook his head briskly and waved his blaster in an impatient gesture, "Wait a minute, hold it for just one minute. I have no idea what you're talking about. Would you mind explaining to me just who you are, where you come from, and what the hell you're doing up here on the dark side of the Moon?" Then, almost as an afterthought, "You're not an Eastern Bloc agent."

"Coitainly not." He drew himself up to his full four feet and puffed out his chest. "I'm–," and Rifless missed it, "from–," and again Rifless couldn't make out the name, "in a solar system in what you call the Sthculptor Galaxy, y'see. I'm a commissioned representative for the Aceth Universthal Exhibitory Company, Inc., assigned to deliver, assthemble, and fine-tune one Model 49A Symplexth Planetary Stasisth Transom on the satellite of the third planet of the G2V star system–that's Eoith, y'know–to resolve the focusth of preservation components on the same-said planet until such time as the aforementioned preservation processth is successthfully initiated."

While eyeing the little runt, Rifless admitted to himself that even though he didn't understand a bit of it, he didn't like the sound of what he was hearing. This munchkin in his daffy clothes with his flyaway hair wings unsettled him, instilling him with a deep sense of malaise.

"I still don't get you."

The tiny being said, "I'm here to set up an intergalactic sight." He patted the weird mechanism next to him, "this stasisth transom, y'see, which will allow the Aceth Company to zero in and freeze-dry your planet

100

just as soon as I can get the last bugs out."

With that he turned away and started to fiddle with the strange machinery.

Freeze-dry our planet? Earth? Rifless stared for an instant, then said, "You're nuts, twisted."

"Yesth, but don't the suit fit nice." The dwarf performed a hasty pirouette that ended with him sitting splay-legged on the crater floor, bouncing lightly up and down amid puffs of moondust.

Rifless rolled his eyes and shouted, "Now cut that out!"

The diminutive creature picked himself up, put his hands on his hips, and said, "Well! Of all the noive!" With elevated nose, he marched back to his equipment.

Cold sweat began to trickle down Rifless's back as he suddenly comprehended that the clown suit the little goof was so proud of displayed no recognizable EVA elements, and also that he talked freely in vacuum without a discernable radio. Could it be? If so, then what about this stasis thingamajig? He better tread easy, here, he thought.

"Uh, listen, could you run that by me again about freeze-drying Eoith—Earth. I mean, you can't be serious."

Peering through some sort of eyepiece on the elaborate rig, the elfin being said, "I'm poifectly seriousth. Too bad you are, too." He backed away, pausing to examine Rifless critically again. "Aceth won't be at all happy about this development, y'know." He took off his glasses and began to wipe them with a multihued handkerchief, first one thick lens, then the other.

"What do you mean?" said Rifless. "Look, why would anyone want to freeze the Earth even if they could?"

"Don't be ridiculousth, of course we can," He continued to polish his glasses, now pulling the linen back and forth through the suddenly vacant eye holes of the frames, "The reason is simple. Aceth wants to preserve all of your planet's marvelous artifactsth and the remnantsth of your unique contribution to the Universth," He raised his glasses over his head for a final inspection, frowned, lowered them to his lapel, and squirted water from his flower onto the lenses, intact again. The water failed to freeze or even bead. Instead, it dripped and splashed off of the glassy specs.

Rifless's knees jellied. "Contribution," he uttered faintly, "what contribution?"

"Don't be silly, coitainly you know? Why, your breathtaking insight into the woikings of life and nature, y'see, your unparalleled persthpective on the driving forces of the Cosmosth, y'understand, and your commanding overview of the ruling paradigm of the Universth, all distilled into a single formula, the simple truth manifested by your poifect microcosthmic societal model, also expressed in one simple sentenceth, and I quote, y'know: 'The world's a funny place.'"

Rifless's brow creased furiously. "What? That's the ruling paradigm of the Universe? It's absurd!"

"Exactly: Y'know, for a moment there I thought you might be a slow study. You Eoithlings have mastered the Universthal sense of the absthurd. Astonishing that it originated on such a jerkwater little planet, y'know. Now, everybody recognizes you as the funniest organisthms in the entire known Universth! Of course, first we all had to develop a sense of humor."

"We're funny," droned Rifless.

"Absolutely hilariousth! The situations, the characterizations, everything, just everything you do sends us into fall-down, roll-around laughter, pealsth and pealsth of the stuff." The petite alien fell down and rolled around as he howled his "a-hoo-hoo-hoo" signature. He stood up abruptly, propped an elbow on Rifless's blaster arm and said straight-faced, "You're very droll y'know."

Rifless disencumbered his arm, thinking this yahoo's spent too much time in space without a dome. Maybe he's omnipotent, but some of his jets are misfiring, too. And here he is, talking about putting Earth on ice. So, now what? He gazed at the absurdly attired figure and racked his brain for a way to go, some sort of an approach. At length, he asked, "How did you find out about us?"

The pint-size party stepped back and spread his arms in a "Ta-da!" gesture, "Radio and TV, rerun after rerun. That's why I speak your language so poifectly, y'see. It's also why I've been able to represent myself so accurately according to your most sophisticated styles. My

102

appearance has been carefully fashioned after that of some of your greatest statesthmen, the ones we followed most faithfully on your broadcasts."

Frowning, Rifless said somewhat disdainfully, "You're not dressed anything like Earth's leaders. You don't look like the President or the Premier, even the People's Chairman."

"Coitainly not, why look like mere pantagruelisths? Though, they're simply wonderful, too, y'know. Yet, many intergalactic viewers like your monologisths better, your popes and propheths, your gurus, the World Council of Choiches—I poisonally prefer burlesthque. The simple invention of your sitcoms—procreation not a sole sex or a thousand, but with only two sexes, both rational except when they're together. Just the endless hythsterical predicaments they get into, all leading to the madcap sight gags themselves—they leave me in stitches, the best skits in the Universth!"

He sang his falsetto laugh, wiping a few tears away at the end. "But none compare to your most profound philosophers, supreme role models for us like Bert Lahr, Ed Wynn, Jack Benny, Milton Berle, Red Skelton, and others seen on such great forums of ethics as "Your Show of Shows.""

Glumly, Rifless said, "I think you've been watching some really ancient programs."

The miniature clown put a finger to his mouth, "That very well could be. Costhmic interruptions do distort reception sometimes, which could tell a world about your unorthodoxth appearance, y'know. Well, as soon as you Eoithlings perform your grand finale, your greatest joke, and Aceth can open up its planetary exhibit, we can update all of our shticks. Though, we may not want to update them too much," he finished, gazing pointedly somehow down his big nose up at Rifless.

"You're going to freeze the Earth to make it into a sideshow," said Rifless. He tried to clap a hand to his brow and only managed to bang his gun off of his deathhead, causing a great clanging din within. "This," he continued, "after we perform our greatest joke. And what might that be, if I might ask, nine billion people slipping on banana peels all at once?"

"That's good, y'know, very good, but hardly as devastatingly funny as destroying your planet with a nuclear exchange. Now, that's a boffo finish.

103

Too bad you can only do it once."

"What!" cried Rifless, eyes popping white.

"Pleaseth, there's no need to shout. Aceth Marketing has projected that, due to your irrepressthible atavistic and aggressthive tendencies, plus an arsenal that could create star systems, you human beings are about to blow your planet up. So, under the Intergalactic Salvage Act, Aceth has poichased the rights to Eoith so that when you let loose the big ones, we can preserve your world, y' understand, before you destroy all of your wonderful little things. The payoff for Aceth, naturally will come from bringing in tourists to see your lovely, crazy planet."

Rifless again felt unsteady on his pins. He sat down on the surface of the crater and put his hands over his head. "My God!" he breathed.

"It's all poifectly legal, y'know, sanctioned by the Intergalactic Commercth Commission. Aceth operated completely within ethical bounds—well, maybe there was a little jockeying for position in the gray area to beat out Triple A, but that goes without saying, y'see. Everyone looks the other way in such matters.'

Rifless crouched, understanding too well that Earth's future may have been reduced to two scenarios, exhibition or incineration. He tried to shake loose from the dread looming within him. This little drip could be wrong, he had to be wrong. He wasn't a god, for God's sake, you could tell that just by looking at him. "Listen," Rifless said, "couldn't your marketing people be mistaken about this? I mean, we've maintained a stabilized situation for thirteen years, now. We have peace."

"I've hoid it called that. No, the marketing analysts are always right. Besides, Triple A's prognosthtications produced the same results, as did a dozen other outfits. You should be proud, y'know, Eoith's a very hot property. Our exoculturalisths figured it out just in time, y'see. Irony was the most difficult form of your humor to understand—ironic, isn't it?" He let loose another barrage of cacophonous, high-pitched laughter.

Rifless winced in his misery. Drearily he said, "How soon is this supposed to occur?"

The tiny alien pulled an outsize pocket watch from his pants, looked at it, and said, "Oh, it could be anytime now, a year or a day," He put the watch up to his ear, listened, then shook it. "Y 'know, I dropped this

104

watch on the crater floor recently and it stopped. Of course, I didn't expect it to go all the way through to the other side, y"know. A-hoo!"

Anytime now, a year or a day, Rifless repeated silently. He jumped to his feet and nearly soared over the crest of the moon hole. After he regained his footing, he said, "Isn't there any way we can prevent this from happening? Couldn't you go down to Earth and explain to the leaders of both just what's at stake, what you've predicted?"

"For heaven'sth sake, don't be ridiculousth! That would ruin everything. Aceth only has a one-year option on your planet as it is. Fads come and go, y'see. Besides, now that I've met you, I know it wouldn't woik."

"Well, why not?" Rifless cried out.

"Who on Eoith would believe me?" The miniscule popinjay again twirled around to display his finery.

"I get your point. But you convinced me. You could show yourself as you really are. I mean, before you started watching television."

"Out of the question! I refuse to regressth. Also, you people are too comical, you'd simply want to go to war with us."

"No, we're a peaceful people. We're not really warlike."

"Don't be silly, of course you are. After all, y'know, you're the ones about to obliterate yourselves, not us. And you all look alike. I hate to think what you'd do to me if you saw me like I really am."

Rifless narrowed his eyes, saying, "What do you mean, you're like some kind of lizard or something?"

"I'm the same as you only different. Listen, this has been thrilling, y'understand, but I must get back to woik. The big boom could happen anytime now, and if I don't have the transom lined up correctly, Aceth could lose the entire exhibit, y'see, and there goes my bonusth. Then the joke's on me. A hoo-boo-hoo!"

The dinky character pranced back to the eyepiece of his machine. Rifless hastened as best as he could over the powdery gray-white basalt to his side. "Wait!" he called out, "you don't know what you're doing!" He searched his mind frantically for an argument to convince the little jerk to stop this madness, knowing full well that pleas for things like itty-bitty children, baby birds, pretty flowers, or his boat, goddamn it, wouldn't do it. Cold, specious logic must prevail, he decided.

"Look at it this way," he said. "If you freeze the Earth, that'll be the end of it. No more funny stuff, no one-liners, no puns, no pratfalls, no more burlesque. And this way you won't even get to see our greatest joke, our big boom. Let Earth be, and you'll have the best of both worlds, the continuing human comedy plus the ever-existing possibility of witnessing our grand finale. That hanging over our heads is a joke in itself."

The alien said, "Outside of some splendid colors, y'know, nuclear annihilation isn't much fun. It's the idea of your good-humored self-destruction that slays us, y'understand. How could you ever top that? No, y'know, your humor might be growing too refined, vibrating too fast to be seen moving at all." He looked up at Rifless again, "That could explain your odd behavior, y'see. I know there must be something funny about you. I'm just missing it."

Rifless would've torn his hair out if he could've gotten past his deathhead. "Buddy, I hate to be the one to tell you, but we aren't at all like you think we are. We're completely different. Most of us are not even remotely funny."

"I've noticed," replied the small creature, peeping through the scope again.

"And it'll be a cold day in hell," Rifless declared, "when we blow ourselves up just to make guys like you laugh."

The alien jerked up, grinning, "That was wonderful, y'know. How did you do that? "

"Do what?"

"Time that so poifectly."

"What are you talking about?"

"You make the remark about not blowing yourselves up just as I spotted more of your war vehicles through the transom. Simply amazthing, y'know."

Rifless swept the tiny comic out of the way and looked through the eyepiece. His heart thundered. In the space above the arc of the Moon he saw it, big and cylindrical, too big to be a simple station, too regular to be an asteroid. In spite of its disguising blue-black hue, without doubt it was what he'd learned to fear most in his life, a big colony station. The impossible had happened, the unthinkable had become possible. Probable, to the little twerp next to him.

The pieces all fell into place for him, now. He'd chased a new Eastside scout to the Moon's backside, all right. But he'd lost it because the shuttle had continued on to the new colony station, which must be camouflaged, hidden from surveillance sats by the volume of the Moon. Meanwhile, he'd stumbled upon this dopey alien shrimp and his goofy preserving machine. A year or a day, he thought gloomily. He wondered if the little twit knew how close the big finale could be now. With razor-sharp clarity, Rifless realized that he had to get back to ComCommand Base to warn them all of what was in store for the Earth. He'd need proof, though, and the best available was the tiny goon himself.

He swallowed hard, thinking the little runt must have powers beyond imagining. No matter, he'd have to try for the sake of the home planet. Perhaps the squirt's *savoir faire* or his *je ne sais quoi* or whatever else the Frogs said might make him careless, unprepared for an attack by a lowly human. That was the lowly human's only chance, he thought. Still clinging to the transom for stability, Rifless spun around and leveled his blaster once again.

"Mister, it pains me greatly to have to do this, but I have no choice. Get 'em up."

The alien held still for an instant, then began to giggle. Rifless said, "Laugh all you want, sport, but start walking. I'm taking you back home-side."

The dinky man began to laugh fully now, saying, "Good, y'know, pricelessth."

"What, are you completely nuts? If you don't get a move on, I'm going to blast you."

The alien fell down and began rolling around in silent, helpless laughter.

"Goddamn it!" Rifless lurched for him, and the wee fellow rolled just out of reach. Rifless made another stab and another, but every time the tiny creature somehow seemed to squirm just out of his grasp, like a fish loose in a boat.

Rifless stepped back in chagrin. He knew he couldn't shoot the little drip, that would be the end of his star witness. He also realized that he couldn't stay much longer, but that he couldn't leave the alien here to finish setting up his gear, either. Finally, he decided. He began to stalk up the side of the crater.

"Wait," the alien called after him, gasping for breath between bouts of laughter, "Don't go. I understand now, y'see. I recognizth your routine, now—deadpan!" He collapsed in hilarity again.

At the top of the crater, Rifless turned, kneeled, braced his blaster arm and fired six rounds into the stasis transom. He waited until he saw plumes of smoke puff up from the mechanism, then he quickly rolled down the outside slope of the rim. He bounded back as fast as he could to the Scamp, thinking as he leaped that the alien couldn't freeze the Earth until he fixed his equipment. That might give ComCommand enough time to send personnel up with more effective means of corralling the slippery squirt. Meanwhile, Rifless bore heavily the knowledge that thanks to his Paralethal action, the Earth again faced extinction, the last joke, without the possibility even of the alien's repulsive preservation alternative. A year or a day, he thought. He hoped to God it was more like a year.

The journey back to Earth lasted forever, though no more time than usual had elapsed on the read-out. Finally, he ordered the Scamp onto the approach vector gliding below to ComCommand Base. To his surprise, a flight of fighter scouts intercepted him and escorted him down to the runway. When he emerged from his Superscamp, he found a cordon of Paralethal troopers encircling his craft. Base Commander General Steelton headed them up with Credo at his elbow.

"Paralethal Captain Rifless, you're under arrest for flight into an unauthorized area without proper clearance."

During interrogation, he discovered that the Scamp had never received clearance from ComCommand Center. Repeatedly and repeatedly, he told them his story, and again and again they asked him what he'd been doing on the dark side of the Moon. He pleaded with

108

them to check his flyer's holos for proof, but they simply ignored him. They confined him in the nearest building to the runway, a service shack. So sensitive was the nature of his crime that they feared putting him in the brig where he could talk to others.

For the nth time they demanded his story, and he ran through it almost mechanically. As he addressed their stony, disbelieving faces, again telling them of a wildly dressed alien dwarf with a weird, East Coast urban accent whose every other sentence led into a terribly corny old joke, the story grew more absurd in his own mind. The only part of it that grabbed his inquisitors' interest came from his mention of the colony vehicle. Steelton and the interrogator exchanged the barest of glances, which meant the world to Rifless. But the questioning resumed without further reference to the enemy ship. Finally, they left him alone.

The little punk was right, he realized, they never would have believed him to be an alien. They only wanted to hear about their own obsessions, deadly space colonies and all the rest. He was the only one, he knew now, who would have believed in the alien ever. And here he was, locked away while the Earth turned toward what could be its last night.

He had to get out. He had to get a ship and bring that alien back, blast him if necessary. Exobiologists would confirm his story. Then they would believe him, and only then would they consider an end to this insanity. He'd take the next guard, he decided, and bolt out to steal a ship. The next guard come what may.

Credo walked in and sat down on the cot they'd brought into the little shack. He wore his black satin flight suit and carried his deathhead tucked under one arm. He leaned back and propped a boot against the wall. Rolling his helmet from one hand to the other over his hard belly, he said, "Rifless, you ass. What the hell were you doing up on the Moon?"

"Credo, I've told the truth. All they have to do is go up and take a look. I'm positive that the little guy's still there, I crippled his machine. I swear it's so, right might!"

"Yeah, right might," Credo said, still playing with his headgear.

Rifless sat down next to the supine Credo and said, "Credo, you could do it. You could convince the Big Picture Boys to send someone up to look for the alien. Or if they won't buy that, to look for the colony yourself. I don't care what excuse you use. I'm asking you to help, Credo, and not for my sake, I know better than to ask for myself. The world's at stake, Credo, do it for the world."

Credo eyed Rifless with unveiled contempt. "For the world," he said acidly. "Oh, they're going to send someone up to look, Rifless, don't worry about that. They're sending me. But not to look for any alien or colony."

"I don't get you," Rifless said warily.

'We know the colony construct's out there," Credo said calmly, "because it's ours. The colony underway on the Moon is our very own," He waited for what he thought would be stunning news to sink in. "And you stumbled on to it. Figure you to think it was the Rednyks," he sighed, "as if they could muster up the technology to build and hide such a sophisticated structure. The Moon and the future is ours, Rifless. Couldn't even you have figured that out?"

Mortified, Rifless said, "What difference does it make who built the damn thing? The balance is gone now. When the East finds out, they'll pull the trigger, just like we would. Then we'll all be screwed. And I fixed it so the little alien dude can't stop it even if it did mean the deep freeze."

Credo shook his head pityingly, "Don't you have any faith in the West? We're going to win this thing, Rifless. We're on our way, mighty right about that."

Rifless slumped forward on the bunk, wringing his hands between his knees.

"Now, this so-called alien is another matter, old buddy. "

The timbre of Credo's voice sounded heavy bordering upon lethal. Rifless tensed slightly, newly alert.

"Of course, we hardly believe there's an alien up there, I mean, really, you should've been able to put together a better story than that, No, the prevailing theory is that who or whatever's up there is Pink, Rifless, and that you are, too."

"Geniuses," Rifless muttered, "you guys are all geniuses."

"Maybe, maybe not," Credo nodded, sitting up now with his helmet propped on his knee, "Whatever, the feeling is that the claptrap shown on your Scamp's Moon holo is some sort of surveillance device, maybe a transmitter, too. Naturally, the Big Picture Boys can't be sure just what it is, and I'm going up to check it out. I've been given a long-range cruiser so I can hang around for as long as it takes to see who comes up after it next. Still, we'd all like to know why you were there in the first place. To pick up the goods, maybe, the proof of the colony construction work?"

Rifless remained motionless, his sight fixed upon his feet.

"C'mon, Rifless, hup-hup to the port. For old time's sake, tell me, what should I look out for up there?"

Rifless stared coldly at Credo, then said, "Look out for a pigmy alien, Credo, with floppy shoes on his feet and carrots in his ears."

Credo stared at him. "Carrots?"

"They were out of bananas."

Credo frowned, then stood up and sneered, "I know you're stupid, Rifless, but not this stupid. Tell me, when did the Reds turn you? No answer, huh? Well, let me leave you with one last thought. If I don't find the rig on your ship's holo out there, then our people will know that they know. And our people won't wait around for them to push the button first, Rifless. So, you better hope I find it and its data, too. Otherwise, you can spend the rest of your miserable life thinking of how you cost us the peace, Rifless, you alone."

He turned to leave and Rifless began to stand, suddenly bolting upright with his forearms crossed in front. He hit the bottom of the deathhead, sending the top of it into Credo 's chin. Credo started to drop and Rifless guided him to a silent landing on the cot. He grabbed the helmet and bashed Credo in the head three times. He wiped the blood off of the black plastic shell with a sheet from the bunk and quickly exchanged clothing with the limp man. After rolling Credo on the bed so that he faced the wall, he slipped on the deathhead and pounded on the door for the guard to let him out.

No one stopped him as he made his way to the long-range cruiser posed on the mass-ack pad. He climbed in, secured his harness, and signaled for lift-off. Even as he felt the crush of acceleration, he heard the alarms' shrill sounds through his communication channel. When he reached Topside, General Steelton spoke to him.

"Captain Rifless, I order you to return to Base to face charges. All corridors to the Eastern Bloc are guarded. You cannot escape. Return now or risk worldwide consequences."

Rifless switched off the channel. Let them guard the corridors to the East, he was going to the Moon to find and bring back that runt alien. He just hoped he could get there in time.

An hour and a half out, his ship rang another alert, a different kind. Rifless drew breath and held still as though he never meant to expel air again. He released his breath with a whoosh and ordered the ship to display a simulation of Earth, including vector enhancement. Unwillingly, he recognized the telltale cluster of light points rising in each hemisphere, thousands from each side, crossing paths, some flashing to signify the impact of interception, but most of them plunging down to their opposites' quarters. Eventually, the lines crisscrossing on the screen formed little ribbon bows that neatly packaged the Earth.

Rifless howled his horror in anticipation of the series of pure white flashes that would pock the Earth on his screen, simulating the complete destruction of the home planet, He'd blundered utterly, he realized, he 'd brought on the catastrophe and he'd failed miserably to bring the alien around in any useful way. Shamelessly, he wailed his misery knowing that he had brought about Earth's end.

His wailing became a droning moan as puzzlement usurped his grief. No white flashes had appeared on his screen. Earth seemed to float placidly as always. He asked the ship for a live view of the planet. All seemed peaceful on the blue orb. He then requested a picture of the world at the time of the missile strikes. Again, the blue ball appeared and, though of course he couldn't see the missiles themselves at this distance, he waited expectantly for the nuclear flashes, which should've been easy to spot. Nothing changed, except for a subtle wavering on the screen, a slight distortion.

His hands lay flat on the console in front of him. He knew, now. The alien had been able to put his stasis machine back together in time after all, if it really ever had been out of commission. Earth was a frozen museum now, and all her people were artifacts. Perhaps he alone was the

112

only remaining conscious person unless the colony construction crew somehow had eluded suspended animation. He would go there and present his case. He had plenty of proof to offer this time that he'd been telling the truth all along.

Four days later, Rifless ordered the ship to dig a hole big enough to house it in the side of the crater where the alien stasis transom rested. Once finished, he maneuvered the cruiser inside, with its weapons facing the crazy structure of the transom. Then he covered the entrance with moon dust, doing his best to match the texture of the surrounding wall. He crawled into a small tunnel he'd left leading to the ship, filling it in behind him. He positioned himself at the console to wait.

The colony had been frozen, too. He'd walked among the people with their tools, all caught in stride by the alien paralysis. After admitting to himself that no one else was awake, he'd returned to the crater to force the alien to restore Earth to normal. But only the alien's whacky machine occupied the floor. It was then that he'd decided to hide in the wall.

One of them would have to show up, he insisted to himself, to service the machine or dust the museum before the flow of tourists started up. It was just a matter of time, and the cruiser could support him for the rest of his life. When an alien did arrive, he'd persuade him to compromise, to release the Earth from stasis, maybe turn it into some kind of zoo instead. Not a perfect solution, he knew, but it was a lot better than the new status quo. If the little creep refused, then he'd kill him. All he had to do was wait and watch, watch and wait, right might.

Consoled by his resolve, Rifless barred daydreams from his mind of white canvas sails over deep blue water. Instead, he stared unfalteringly at the ship's screen, which reflected back his expression of immutable starkness and fear glazed over.

In space throughout the Local Group Cluster, a psionic billboard emitted the following directional:

ACETH EXHIBITORY COMPANY, INC.
Presents
The Comedic Spectacular EOITH:
The Origin of Humor in the Universth
Now the Greatest Planetary Exthibit Ever
SPECIAL GRAND OPENING DISPLAY!
The Straight Man in the Moon:
<u>Alive</u> and <u>Animated</u>
DIE LAFFING!

Book now, offer limited to visitors for first sixty years.
Paid for by the Aceth Exthibitory Co., y'know.

Blue Moon

An ice-blue band of sky neatly sectioned off the northern horizon from the deep teal, ill-boding clouds rolling everywhere else above. The startlingly clear strip of sky caused Po to wonder if a storm loomed after all. The wind bullied the livid clouds east to west, no hint one way or another of the weather to come. But the brightening area stretched from one end to another. He supposed that it was safe to keep trawling the ice field for a little longer at least, before pulling over cover.

He stood leaning lightly against an outcropping of the gray ridge bordering the rough-faced field. Quakes had broken up the surface of an earlier freeze into sharply angled pale pavilions, suggesting to him the shattered bones of some huge dream beast dropped from a great height. A closer look would show the ice scooped smooth by the wind. Old ice, he noted, another sign of a storm overdue. Unthinking, he checked his temperature settings against the outside ambient. All was well; his skins could handle drops as low as -28 C. and it was only -16 now. A sudden storm could change all that, though.

Without warning, a subliminal, vibrant tendril grasped his ankle. Po stooped low and the tingling feeling diffused through him until he couldn't distinguish it from his own sensations.

—I'm tired. —

Po relaxed, and returned to his feet. "Keep looking," he said, heading down toward the field. Reaching the ice, he laid each foot down in a rolling, flat-footed manner, easing his weight forward to feel for fragile spots on the crust.

—I'm hungry. —

"We'll eat soon, and rest."

— It's cold. —

"Go deeper."

— It's too hot deeper. —

"Strike the midlevel."

—Then, half of me will be cold, and half burning hot! —

Po stopped flat-trudging and shook his head in exasperation. "Shortstuff, you never even knew the difference before you met me."

A whimpered thought surfaced in Po's mind, —But now I do, and I'm cold, and hot, and hungry, and tired. —

Po sighed. "Are you thirsty, too?"

—That's not funny. —

"I know. I'm sorry. Okay, we'll stop soon."

—Joy! —

"As soon as we finish this hectare."

—Gloom. —

"C'mon, Shortstuff, buck up. We're more than halfway through."

—More gloom. —

Po slowed, thinking of what he needed, then of how hard Shortstuff had worked. "All right tell me what you have so far. "

—Forty-eight grams of carbon, seventeen grams of magnesium, thirteen of calcium, twenty milligrams of manganese, twelve of iodine, and sixty millimeters of H_2O.—

"Water, Shortstuff, water. How about nitrogen?

—Fifty-two milliliters. —

Po pulled up, surprised. "Why, that's good, Shortstuff, damn good." A good trawl, he thought, better than an average day's in half the time. But he had a long way to go before he'd put together enough for the dowry. And rich fields changed with the ice, with the weather. He really should go on, tell Shortstuff to run out the field. But, if he pulled over cover now, he could have a fire going and a meal together by the time she arrived. He hesitated, truly undecided.

He looked again at the sky. No change. The cold, light blue band between the surface and the heavy, marine green cloud cover hadn't changed. The storm could hold off a bit. Or not.

Still scanning the sky, Po sighed, ready to tell Shortstuff to continue. Then he saw a black chip floating down, slowly planing from side to long side across the bruised heavens.

"Shortstuff, what's that?"

116

—What? —

Shortstuff couldn't see, of course, the sky.

"There's something there. Up in the sky. Let's go see."

Po began to flat-trudge fast, straight across the field with Shortstuff gliding behind, grumbling. The black chip had grown into a concave, deep gray mass, slip-sliding through the atmosphere, occasionally shuddering from the buffeting of the winds. Po crossed five fields and their ridges before he topped the last crest above the strange, dark shape newly settled from the sky.

Po stared, bedazzled by the bright red glowing from beneath the underside of the giant thing. Red! he thought, and from the sky, space! No question in his mind, this great thing was from another world, maybe even the old world of his ancestors! He turned and looked down back to where Shortstuff had wandered off, bored traveling a straight line.

"Shortstuff!" Po called out, "Shortstuff, come here! Come see!"

He whirled back around and leaned over, his hands supported by a dirty ice outcropping that reached up to his waist.

A deck plate fell down from the middle of the giant slate machine, and the red from below faded to black, steaming. Figures emerged from the dark doorway, coming out onto the ice, staggering out, Po could see. He drew back.

Four of them drifted off in different directions, not far, just separate from each other.

One small one dropped onto the ice; another followed, falling on top. Wrappings parted and joined. The two figures squirmed together, to Po's open-mouthed amazement. Others tottered down the short ramp, aimless, dazed, crunching through the ice as they alighted from the platform, some of them falling heavily.

A tall form stepped down without faltering and covered the field as though he'd been flat-trudging all his life. He opened his arms and acted as if to embrace the great expanse of ice and frigid, dark air.

Po's first impulse to rush down and greet these people from another world gave way to the caution from the old days, learned by his people all the way back to his greatest grandfather. From old Earth

117

or not, these people acted strangely, falling all over the field, loving without cover, dropping their great space home on an ice field. Though, he admitted, it seemed to balance on the shelf of an old ridge.

And this last one, the big one. "He's not right, Shortstuff. We better wait on this, see more."

—Let's go down now. —

Typical Shortstuff, Po sniffed. He sent out a restraining feeling, and bridling, impatient Shortstuff stayed with him.

Woodley dragged himself around each cluster of the crew, trying to shout them out of their collective funk, but it was no use. The combination of the past eighteen months, climaxed by the ultimate, sickening disaster and the terrible consequences it would bring, all that plus the rough landing had left the entire crew wiped out of emotion. He felt nauseous himself thinking about it again. Only Ash, of course, went about as usual, perfectly happy. Ash, he breathed, God.

He was stumbling over to see if he could cajole the big one into helping him round up the others, when he saw the figure at the top of the ridge. Woodley stopped cold.

"Ash," he said, "look there."

The big man turned around and watched with Woodley, who could see the small form traverse the steep black slope easily, with a sureness that brought attention to the fumbling movement of his people on this unstable, godforsaken rock. Who was this? What was he doing here? Were there more?

"Go, Ash," Woodley said without looking, pushing at the other's arm. Ash glided off toward the ship.

The approaching figure drew closer, somehow effortlessly slip-sliding across the ice and dross in a seemingly random path. Woodley wheeled about and grimaced a silent snarl at the others. They gathered closer, startled out of their listlessness, anxious.

Woodley returned his gaze to the nearing figure. "How can anybody be here?"

"Rill," Po said to himself. "Shortstuff, it's Rill! She's going down to them!" He started forward, then held up. He moved back, then shifted from side to side on the crest of the ridge, hands spread wide, staring down below at her as she closed in on the group of strangers. Shortstuff sent a querying feeling up his leg, and Po shook his head, not knowing.

Rill's astonishment at seeing the strange gray thing at the foot of the ridge hardly left her as she flat-footed down the smudged ice. The sight of the people around the big structure heightened her excitement, she realized at once that they weren't from Blue Moon, they weren't of the Ice People. They must be from Earth, she thought with a thrill. She counted eight, no, nine of them on the crusty edge of the field, clumsily drawing together to peer up at her. As the others grouped, one of them headed up into the rectangular gray thing, their ship she guessed, much smaller than the old one of her people.

She covered the last few meters and slowed just as she reached them. Five men and three women stared at her—she could tell their gender because not one of them wore any cover over their faces, or their hands. Some wore hats with long bills, and one woman had tied a gauzy red scarf around her dull hair. They all dressed in black shirts and pants, baggy with high pockets on the front and on the legs. They looked tired and afraid, unsettlingly so, and they looked at her as though she was an intruder.

Rill stopped and jerked aside her muffler, giving them a glimpse of her face. For an instant none of them reacted, but as she covered up, a bearded man in the middle came forward, smiling.

"Why, you're a girl," Woodley said as he traipsed awkwardly to her over the crunching surface.

"Yes! Well, a woman. I'm Rill, and who are you? How did you get here?"

"How did you get here?" Rill and Woodley said in unison, then laughed.

The others half-smiled. She has a funny accent, Woodley noticed, almost dialectical. But she was safe, only a girl, twelve, thirteen maybe.

"We landed here," he said, "for repairs."

119

"Oh, is that your ship? It's wonderful, so powerful-looking, and such a pretty gray. I saw you coming down, are you from Earth?"

Woodley said, "No. Well, yes, of course we all are, in some sense, but . . .."

Po let out his breath begrudgingly, as though his last. She seemed all right; the others hadn't moved on her. But she was crazy to be down there in the first place! Wouldn't she ever learn?

Shortstuff nudged him with a feathery suggestion, —We going down to see Rill now? —

Po flinched reflexively. Fretting, he hunched forward, saying, "I don't know. Not yet."

Shortstuff slipped away.

And returned at once. —Storm's coming—.

Po lifted his eyes and to his surprise saw that both the clear horizon and the teal clouds had transformed into a solid graphite mass pressing down like a moving wall.

"Oh, no."

Shortstuff tugged at his consciousness. —Let's go pull over cover. —

"Wait, Shortstuff, Rill 's still down there."

A tremor rippled through the ground and the storm overhead sounded a groaning paean of imminence. Below, the man talking to Rill gestured to the dull ship, and she turned to look up at the ridge, as though she could see Po at that very moment.

The ice cracked into a thousand white veins, bone-shattering in its loudness. Many of the people below dropped to their knees, and their leader motioned them to return to the ship. Then he grabbed Rill's arm and pulled her toward the gangway. She resisted, and Po shouted from above, "Rill! No!"

But she followed the man's lead up the incline, staring back in Po's direction the whole time until she disappeared.

"Rill!" he screamed against the fury of the rising storm, his cry lost to the wind and the sound of the breaking ice field.

A figure descended from the ship, burdened by a black, heavy load.

120

Po could see that he was tall, even stooped as he was by the heavy shape. He reached the edge of the gangplank and moved out onto the shuddering ice, which slowed him a bit. Several meters from the ship, he stopped at a freshly split crevasse. He dropped the wrapped weight into the ice crack, looked down for a moment at where it had vanished, then returned to the ship.

Po frantically tried to rush down the ridge, but Shortstuff held him in place, locked by his ankle neurons.

—It's storming, Po! We must pull over cover! —

Desperately, Po's eyes searched the thundering sky, the churning ice, and the roiling ground for an answer. Darts of red and black lava surged, spitting up from the shifting crust, steaming the ice as it sizzled down. He knew that Shortstuff was right, they had to get covered right away or perish. Oh, why had he hesitated, why?

They turned down to a proper site, where the ice lapped over the base of the ridge. He quickly lasered out chunks of ice, which Shortstuff fused into a shallow dome covering them, their only protection against the fall of the white heated lava and ash bursting the seams of the fragile surface. As he settled in uneasily, Po could only hope that the strangers's ship still had Rill aboard it, and that they all would survive.

"Our ship the Hope landed on this planet Blue Moon more than three hundred years ago."

"Blue Moon? Why do you call this brown ball of rock and ice Blue Moon?" Woodley asked the question impatiently, almost irately.

Startled, she said, "Because it's so blue! Everything is. Except when we have storms, which is a lot."

"Often," Woodley said absently. "You mean you often have storms."

"Yeah," she said, "a lot."

The ship creaked and groaned at the outside furor. To pass the time more than anything else, he asked her how she'd gotten here. The girl looked nervous, too. Her kind probably didn't weather a storm this way, and most likely she didn't completely trust the ship to withstand the force. She could be right, he admitted to himself dryly.

"The hydroponics had gone wrong" she said. "Things started to die before they grew up enough to bear. Some of them had a mineral deficiency. Our ship was supposed to follow routine colonization procedure, search likely systems for a proper planet, but they couldn't wait. They took a chance on this one, orbiting the big red star, and landing here to fix the plants. But they couldn't find enough of the right elements, they couldn't strike the right balance. Things got worse.

"The first storm almost destroyed the ship and exposure killed many of the original crew members. The protein cultures all failed. A decision had to be made, a very hard decision. Captain Berelli ordered the drawing of straws, and though they didn't like it, nearly everyone went along with it."

Almost imperceptibly, Woodley straightened over the narrow wardroom table. "Some objected?" She nodded solemnly. He hesitated, then breathed the word, "Mutiny?"

Again, Rill nodded, saying, "Lieutenant Commander Shannon."

Woodley slumped ever so slightly. He flattened his mouth and swallowed as though trying to suppress some sickening taste.

"You see, no one thought we'd ever be found, not in a thousand years—we were colonists, we were this sector's Earth-to-be, there would be no higher authority. That's why Captain Berelli insisted on the full measure of the penalty called for by the law."

Woodley's mouth hung open for a second before he said, "Mind wipe?"

Puzzled, she shook her head briskly, "I don't know what that is. Banishment."

"On this planet?" She motioned yes, and he blew air softly through pursed lips.

"Lieutenant Commander Shannon was ejected from the Hope's company at 24:00 hours, day 17, month November, year A693."

Shannon felt foolish, not morally correct when he walked out on the ice to die. Whim, spiteful whim had caused him to face up to that infuriating, self-righteous martinet Berelli, an impulse that now would

122

cost him his life. A minor miscalculation, he laughed as he headed between the first great rolling hills of ice.

A few days later, the thought of laughter never crossed his mind. He was dying for real this time, protected well enough from the elements in his block-ice hut, which he'd situated over a slight steamy fissure. But there'd been nothing to find for food and no water. Everything he'd brought along had run out, and he was running out, the great ebb tide.

I should sleep to death, he thought, rather than die of thirst. Out on the ice, the grand blue ice, a comfortable pallet could be found. But out on the ice the bitter bone chill grabbed hold of him and feeling the pain of it surprised him. He decided to lie on the stone ledge a few meters away instead of on the too-cold ice inside his ice hut.

Even the rock surface pained him on this cold planet, and the deadening discomfort flooded his mind with bitterness at Berelli and the weakness of the crew. And, he knew that he'd rather be with them, as doomed as they were than die now, not now. He'd have something to drink with them before he died . . .

He didn't feel so thirsty anymore, but he felt something else— something was with him, not around him but . . . in him. All through him, miasmic, but without sickening him. Different, not evil but alien. It scared him to death, except he was alive. And hungry. He thirsted, but the parchedness, the dehydration was gone.

And it was gone.

Shannon urgently tried to get up, but couldn't, he was so weak. He twisted around and looked longingly at his little ice hut. In spite of his suit he was freezing and he was terrified. He whipped his head around in a frenzy, searching for some sign of it coming back. Incongruously, a portion of the bluish ice glimmered like heat waves, and he felt it back in him.

"Oh, God!" he screamed in his helmet, squirming on the ice. The thing inside him shrank, he sensed, like an unseen cancer. Shannon writhed and flip-flopped and the thing disappeared. He quickly jumped to his feet and rushed into his shelter.

He hadn't quite reached the same levels of deprivation when he

123

went out to the rock again. Courage had nothing to do with it, he readily admitted to himself. Survival did. All of the fears about this alien thing, whether it would eat him as it fed him, or destroy his head, or disease him with some even worse way to die had given away finally to the undeniable urges of his body. Food and water, of sorts, were out there to be had. He had to have them, whatever it took.

The thing didn't show up right away—for a couple of days, as far as Shannon could figure. He spent as much time as he could on the rock without risking freezing, but he damn near went crazy thinking that it, whatever it was, always showed up when he'd gone in to warm up. When push came to shove, though, he realized that sooner or later he'd reach the stage when he'd stay at the rock indefinitely, or definitely. Infinitely.

It came and left. Shannon felt crushed. Of course, he thought, it's alien, why would it do the same thing as last time? Shit, it might not even be the same one. And, who says it thinks? He sighed, about to struggle up when he felt the indescribable seeping of it into his nervous system. He lay still and, sure enough, he knew that H^2O and the right proteins and minerals had been infused in his body.

Amazing! He must still be in the throes of dying, he imagined, his thoughts slowed down to seem to last for days, embroidered with fantastic delusions of aliens lending him hope. Well, I can't be held responsible for this, he decided, so I better get up and go to my hut until I'm really dead.

But he didn't move. Filaments of the thing now felt their way into his eyes, his thinking. Shannon felt afraid again, but he held on. He sensed fear, too, its fear! And more, he realized, something like. . . interest. The thing could feel! He could feel its feelings, its . . . thoughts!

"Good God!" he blurted, and it fled.

Thereafter, he remained calm when it crept into his thoughts. It stayed with him as long as he could demonstrate different sensations, tactile, motion, slow at first, temperature changes. Sometime after their first contact, when it had blended with him for the longest duration, Shannon slowly rose to his feet and moved toward his hut. When he felt any stirring within, he paused. Gradually, he worked his way over

124

and into the hut.

Warmth, the thing felt heat for the first time through his nervous system. And, as Shannon felt himself warming up, he concentrated in his mind on one word, one mantra: Hot.

He waited fifteen minutes, then left the hut. As his body chilled, he thought only of Cold. It came as little surprise to him, after he'd repeated the exercise dozens of times, when the words abruptly appeared in his mind. Shannon had confirmed that the native stranger, alive and thinking, using the biochemistry of his brain, could talk to him.

Over time, Shannon learned more about how to deal with it. He practiced talking to it, and soon he could suggest that it stimulate his taste buds, saliva glands, and other subtle organs. At length, when it visited, Shannon not only gained sustenance, he felt as though he'd tasted what he'd eaten. The thing loved eating.

When it was leaving him, once, he asked to see it, to touch it with his hands. His gloves would interfere, though, he realized with a bit of irritation. The indigenous alien solved this with ease, as part of it flowed out over his hands, a translucent marine ice-blue, liquid like mercury, and – cold! A simulation, Shannon guessed. A lot of it must still be in his body, his head.

So, this is it, he thought, holding it in front of his eyes and squirting globules of it in the air. No matter how hard he tried to squeeze it in two, the exposed part never completely separated, instead finding some route to reform as soon as it could.

The stuff of magic, Shannon mused, which is what he called it from then on.

After three months, he decided it was time to return to the Hope, if it still existed. Another of Magicstuff 's life-saving tricks was the ability to predict the wrenching quakes of Blue Moon. Shannon had moved around and pulled over cover when Magicstuff warned him. The Hope possessed no such see and it had been three months. Shannon knew that he might be the only human being alive on Blue Moon—or he could have another negotiating chip in dealing with Berelli.

Magicstuff led him to the ship. He crested the last ocean-blue wave of ice, the Red Star to his back. Below, in front of the beaten hull of the Hope, Berelli and his lieutenants pointed sidearms at a group of irate men and women holding clubs and pointed objects in their own hands.

"Well, Magicstuff. Looks like we've arrived at an opportune time."

Leaning his elbow on the dull gray plasteel, Woodley thoughtfully rubbed his beard. "So, what you're saying is that Shannon went back out on the ice after dealing with Berelli."

Rill shook her head up and down briskly, "Yes. Captain Berelli told him he could stay, but Shannon said no. He simply made his arrangement with them, then left."

"Shannon would supply the Hope with the materials they needed for the hydros, using the alien …or, that is, using the native?"

"Right," said Rill. "Of course, after a while Magicstuff couldn't bring enough for the entire ship's complement. But, by then Shannon found other Stuff on Blue Moon, though they're really hard to find. They live alone. Shannon would entice one of them, then bring it back to the Hope."

"He'd do all this for Berelli and the crew who'd sent him out to die?"

"Well, yeah, for real food and medical attention."

"But he'd always go back to live out on the ice."

"He had to," Rill explained, "so that Magicstuff could trawl for the minerals and the other Stuffs."

"He'd live out there alone . . .." Woodley seemed to gaze into the indistinct distance.

"Oh, no, not alone," objected Rill, which brought Woodley back to attention.

"Never alone," she said. "Shannon made a deal with Captain Berelli." Seeing Woodley still not understanding, she continued. "He went back out on the ice with Magicstuff in exchange for a companion, a mate," she said, then blushing a bit at the last, "a woman."

"Oh. But, hell, he could've run his trawling expeditions with the

126

ship as his base. It would've been a hell of a lot easier on him, and his woman."

"No, you don't understand. Shannon didn't just deal for any woman in the crew. He bartered for Berelli's wife."

"Ah!" said the enlightened Woodley.

"These, uh, things found here," Woodley started out later on.

"Stuff," Rill offered, "That's what the Ice People call them."

"All right, Stuff," Woodley said affably. "This Stuff, it can absorb materials from around it directly?"

"Sort of," said Rill. "Its molecular fluidity enables it to stretch itself so thin that it surrounds foreign molecules Of course, it takes a lot of stuff to surround a single molecule. That's why trawling takes so much time. "

"Its bonding substance must be incredibly flexible."

"And strong. It's essentially unbreakable, unless the Stuff's genetic code signals for it to diffuse, a fairly recent dominant mutation our evolutionists think." She swept the cramped room with a broad gesture, "Blue Moon could as easily have one big mass of Stuff on it instead of a bunch of little ones. Lucky for us it didn't."

"The number of organisms is limited?"

"Right. It doesn't reproduce, as far as we can tell. It just splits."

"But it has a genetic code," Woodley said, not really to her, Rill thought. He seemed more to be thinking out loud. And, as the storm began to pass, his nervousness appeared more pronounced. Rill frowned, trying to figure this out. The crew members she'd seen seemed lifeless, too, distant and distracted. In fact, the storm hadn't made them more scared or less. Their faces had expressed cheerless resignation before the storm. Something else worried them a lot more, she thought.

A dark, green-skinned head lolled close in front of her, its mouth agape in a yawning white smile. Rill cried out.

"Ash!" barked Woodley, "Get away from her!"

Ash had leaned backwards against the table in order to put his face close to Rill's. He half-turned and eyed Woodley. Then, languorously,

127

he straightened up and stepped away from Rill.

"You have to excuse Ash," Woodley said soothingly, "he's not well."

Timorously, Rill whispered, "What's wrong with him?"

"Why, he has a type of disease," Woodley said, "caused by a virus, man-made. It's known by different names, the Green Sheen some call it. Others call it the Pallor. You can see that because of the effect on his appearance. He looks different, I know, and it can be unsettling to anyone unused to it. But he won't harm you."

"I see," said Rill, noting the hard gaze Woodley directed toward Ash. He then put his fingertips together, saying, "Let's finish what we were talking about. You said that the Hope has its own supply of your planet's remarkable organism. Is it organic?"

"I wouldn't call them a supply. We're not sure about their make-up. We haven't really had much success with our research. They don't appear to breathe or eat. They are alive but the ones who live among us have never reproduced. They don't work for us as well as they do with the Ice People who seem to bond with them directly. We still count on the Ice People a lot."

"Well, perhaps we can help you!" Woodley spoke in a hearty voice. "A great deal has been accomplished in genetic algorithms since your ship landed here. You can take us to the Hope, and we'll meld our data with yours."

"But, what about your repairs?"

"Oh, they're minor life-support problems, more like inconveniences." He grimaced a smile of embarrassment, "It has to do with waste disposal. We can fix that later. Besides, I'd love to see this marvelous 'Stuff' myself, and the Hope. It'd certainly relieve the tedium of long space travel. Wouldn't it, Ash?"

Ash said nothing.

"Listen," said Woodley, craning his neck, "the storm's completely over. We can leave right away."

"But I can't," Rill said, hesitating. "I'm, uh, supposed to . . .," she trailed off.

"What?"

128

She blushed, "I'm here to meet my betrothed."

"Oh. I see. But of course, he can join us and come along!"

"He won't," she said quietly, looking down.

"Oh no? Why not?"

She raised her eyes, "My fiancé's name is Po Shannon."

Leading the way down the dark ramp to the surface, Woodley was bedazzled by the bright, royal-blue sky and the smooth contours of the freshly frozen, milk-blue ice everywhere in sight.

"My word!" he exclaimed, "Blue! Blue Moon."

Right at the foot of the access ramp stood a short, broad figure bundled in white and blue layers of nondescript wrappings. Though the head was completely covered, the girl ran down immediately and hugged the newcomer, so hard that she swung, hanging, around to his side to keep her balance. Woodley readied his smile and descended, with Ash at his shoulder.

"Great God, Shortstuff, isn't she ever going to learn? They're strangers!"

Po slowly flat-trudged away from where the ship had been. Shortstuff skimmed along next to him, doing a bit of offhand exploring as they went.

—Like the Town People? —

"No, Shortstuff, those are Rill's folk. They're strangers, too, but these new ones are real strangers. They do things I don't understand."

—So do the Town People. You said so. —

"No, that's different. When I say I don't understand what the Town People do, it's not because I don't understand what they do, it's cause I don't agree with it. But these new strangers . . . I really don't understand what they do."

—I don't understand. —

"Well, they're different. Like making love in the open, with no cover. And that big green guy – why is he green? And going inside a ship during a storm."

—Towners do that. —

"Yeah, but they have Stuff to tell them where it's safe to be. They

129

stay in the Quiet Mountains for the most part. These new ones were lucky."

He plodded along, mulling it over. The bearded one, Woodley, he was over-friendly, like a Towner that way. False-friendly. The green man, too, he'd dumped the bundle into the ice before the storm. Po had felt foolish about it when Rill had run down to him perfectly all right. But she'd left with them, and he wished she hadn't. He could tell that the strangers made her uneasy, too, but they'd promised to help the Town People with Stuff. He shook his head at that. Rill still thought like a Towner about the Stuff. She might never learn. Yet, he wanted her here with him now instead of with them.

Why were they here? They could've repaired their toilets in space. Woodley apologized for Ash dumping their waste on Blue Moon, but the temperature would prevent contamination. And even if it did thaw, he said, who could tell the difference given the amount of methane already on the planet? Big joke. Of course, the storm had sealed the bundle deep under the surface, so they couldn't retrieve it. Woodley had been sorry about that, too.

Moving on, Po felt Shortstuff stretch deep into the ice, then return. Po's head snapped up with an idea.

"C'mon, Shortstuff, we're going back to where the strangers' ship was."

—Why? We just came from there. —

"C'mon."

He paced back and forth as he waited for Shortstuff to return. It still should be there, he thought, there'd been no hot flows near the ship, just some quakes and a new surfacing. Shortstuff should be able to find it, he had to find it.

Shortstuff bled back into Po, cold and slowly. Dimly, Po could feel it rise into his mind, a form in rictus, hands and arms frozen out-stretched, legs bent slightly at the knees forever, head twisted around unforgivingly, mouth and eyes fixed terribly open. The strangers's refuse.

—I'm cold—, Shortstuff whimpered.

130

Po exhaled shallowly, "So am I, Shortstuff, so am I."

In the dead of the brutal Blue Moon night, Po traveled lightly over the ice outside of the Hope complex. The gray rectangle of the strangers' ship stood out next to the old Hope colonizer. Shortstuff had reconnoitered moments before and reported routes for both of them. But, after Shortstuff unlatched and opened up the vacuum lock to the engineer access tunnels on the aging space relic, Po was on his own. He told Shortstuff just where to go and what to do if he didn't show up before dawn.

Po reached Rill's quarters faster than he expected despite the labyrinthine journey through the old corridor up to the living quarters levels. Silently, he scratched on the door. She opened it, saw him, and her face dropped. Near tears, she pulled aside, and Po could see Woodley sitting in her room with several of his crew members standing at the walls, armed.

"I thought so, Po," said Woodley. "You lead too paranoid a life not to have figured it out."

Rill cried openly now, embracing Po, then walked over to her father, Cedar Holmes, the current captain of the Hope. On either side of them stood strangers with long, lethal-looking rods in their hands.

"I found the body, Woodley. The guy you murdered."

Woodley paled. "I see. I thought you'd see through the waste-cycling repair bullshit." He jerked his head, "Your girlfriend put it together quick enough." He shrugged, "I' m not used to improvising like that. But it doesn't matter, now."

"Who was he, Woodley? Why did you kill him?"

"Why, he was our captain, Po. We're mutineers, just like your ancestor. And we would've been condemned like him, too. You see, there's no escape if one ever wants to return home, which is what we wanted to do more than anything. You only get one shot at making a fortune in space these days, even if you come up empty. But it didn't matter to us. We were so sick of it, we all wanted to go home, all of us. Except for him."

Woodley said the last with loathing. "He wouldn't let us. He

131

wouldn't ever return until we'd found something. He would have kept us out in space for the rest of our lives. We all hated him."

"And you killed him."

"Ah, it was like an accident. Nobody in their right mind kills a captain. If you do and go home, they wipe your mind—it's like dying."

"Your captain is dead. And you did it."

Woodley averted his eyes. He looked at his hands as he gestured, as if explaining to himself. "Tension over such a long time distorts judgement. Once it happened, we all regretted it. That's why we stopped here, to figure out what to do, to rest."

He raised his eyes, "You know, if you find something, a mother-lode of something indescribably valuable, sometimes they overlook accidents of this sort."

Po straightened in the doorway. "All right. Rill and I are going to leave here now, with no trouble from you."

"Po, I can't," Rill started.

"Of course, you can go," said Woodley, "we don't want you."

"Po," she implored, "They're going to take the Hope's Stuff. We can't let them! My people need Stuff's help, or we'll die!"

"We don't intend to take all of it," Woodley said quickly, "just enough to show what it can do, plus a little extra as insurance for the long trip."

Just then, Po saw Cedar Holmes in the room, too, sitting on Rill's bunk. Thin and gray-bearded, he half-stood up as he said, "But we need as much of the Stuff as there is for the Hope. People will suffer. Some might die, Po Shannon."

Po ignored Holmes and concentrated upon Rill's eyes. "I can get more, Rill. We can help you out, after they're gone."

She shook her head, "Not soon enough, Po. Even if you and the other Ice People could find more Stuff for the Hope, don't you see what they're doing?" She nodded her head in Woodley's direction. "They'll take the Stuff to Earth, and others will come here to take the rest. There won't be any left for the Hope or the Ice People. We'll have to leave Blue Moon."

Po glared at Woodley. "Is this true?"

132

"For God's sake!" exclaimed Woodley, "Of course! Who would want to stay on this stinking planet?"

Po burned inside. After an instant, he said evenly, "After a few centuries, you don't smell it anymore."

"You don't understand, Po. The Stuff is the most amazing organic mining-refinery combine anyone's ever seen, believe me. It doesn't breathe or eat, which means it can work anywhere, it can be instructed by humans directly. And it's in limited quantity—it'll only be used to find the Galaxy's rarest, most valuable substances—next to itself. You'll be able to live anywhere you want—Earth, even. All we want is a little of it to get us off the hook. You can't begrudge us that."

Po's stern look didn't waver. "That's not for me to decide. It's for all of my people and the Hope Towners to decide. It's something for the Stuff to decide, too."

Sadly, Woodley shook his head, "I can't take that chance, Po. You're going to have to stay with us until we've worked out a safe transfer of some of the organisms to our ship."

With that, Woodley's companions tensely raised their weapons.

Po said, "No. We'll walk to where the Towners keep their Stuff. The Stuff will stay put until the people on Blue Moon can meet to vote. Now, you will put down your arms and abide by the people's decision."

"And if we don't?"

"Shortstuff, my Shortstuff, is there now ready to tell the others to leave if I don' t join them by dawn. "

The news seemed to stymy Woodley. Reluctantly, he gestured for his comrades to lower their arms.

Cedar Holmes arose and drew close to Po. He whispered, "That's well done, Po. You can go and summon the Ice People. Rill and I can watch them here."

Po said, "Rill goes with me, Captain Holmes. I'm not going to make the same mistake twice."

Holmes' face tightened with worry. He began to mouth words, but one look at Po's hard expression caused him to swallow and give way.

Po nodded curtly at Woodley and led the way out of the ship with Rill next to him. Still though it was, the fierce night caused all of them to shiver and shift back and forth even in their vacuum suits.

Woodley argued the entire time they'd walked, but Po paid not the least bit of attention. For convenience's sake, the Towners had asked their Stuff to come together in one rocky crag near the ship. Po stopped at the edge and waited for Shortstuff to join him.

Out of the darkness, a tall lone figure wrapped in brown and blue approached at an angle. Shortstuff eased through Po as the stranger arrived. Po began sharing with Shortstuff when the long figure darted over and pulled Rill roughly away to one side.

Furious, Po pivoted around. "What are you doing? Let her go!"

In answer, the man uncovered his green face and laughed broadly, trailing off in a boisterous shout lost in a sudden whistling breeze.

Po started toward Ash, but Woodley jumped to block his way.

"Don't do it, Po. You'll have to give up. You've lost."

"Get out of my way Woodley or I'll warn all the Stuff to leave!"

Woodley twisted his head, "It doesn't matter, don't you see? Ash doesn't care! Who do you think actually killed Captain Lupus? None of us could do it no more than you could. Only Ash, Ash! Look at him, he's got the Green Sheen!"

"What are you talking about?"

"The Green Sheen, the Pallor! He infected himself years ago. It stays with you for the rest of your life, an accelerant that compounds exponentially the release of pleasure endorphins. No one knows how else it affects the brain, but behavior becomes totally unpredictable. That's how he could bring himself to kill the Captain and how he might do the same to your girlfriend. "

"No!" Po stared starkly at Ash, who grinned, gazing unseeing into the night holding tight to Rill. Terrified, she stood as if already frozen.

"How could you put up with him like this?" Po cried.

Woodley rolled his eyes impatiently. "We love him! We've always loved him, his freedom. And the Captain was jealous. We love Ash more now because he freed us! He did what we all wanted to do but couldn't. We would do anything for him, anything. He knows what we want better that we do ourselves. We landed here because of him, you know." Woodley hardened his tone, "Now give up Po, or I'll tell him

134

to kill her myself! Then, he'll kill you."

Listening, Po stared at the grinning, green specter of a man, a pale ghost wearing an expression seemingly giddy with thoughts of doing all things unthinkable.

"No!"

"Po, give it up!"

Po dropped his head, unable to think of anything but Rill. He was too simple, he wasn't smart enough, he had to give in for Rill. "What should I do?" he asked, his voice deadened.

"Tell your organism to leave you. Completely. We want to see him."

Po did as he was told. "Get out, Shortstuff, on the surface."

—Why? —

"Because I say so!"

Shortstuff left him to appear on the ice, an indistinct wafer of dark blue. "He's out."

"So I see. All right. Ash, let her go," said Woodley.

Ash gently released Rill, then stepped over to Po and grabbed him by the lower jaw and the top of his head. He slowly began to squeeze.

"What are you doing?" screamed Rill. She looked to Woodley frantically and said, "Look at what he's doing! Stop him!"

"I can't control him." Turning away, he said quietly, "He's too dangerous. I'm sorry."

Rill shrieked and lurched up to Ash and beat upon his back uselessly.

Po could feel himself choking, slipping, his head bending wrong, too far. His life was leaving him, just as he felt life seep in.

—What's the matter? —

Shortstuff!, Po barked in silence. Get into the stranger! Take away his green! Hurry!

He felt his eyes watering and black matting blotted out some of his sight. Too late, he thought, too . . ..

The pressure eased. Ash relaxed his hold, dropping Po heavily to the ground. Po's sight cleared and he searched desperately for Rill until his eyes fixed upon Ash. Ash tottered, backed away, and fell to the ice.

Slowly, he blanched white.

"Ash!" cried Woodley, "Ash!"

He kneeled next to the sobbing tall man, who cringed and wept louder at his touch.

"This doesn't change things," Woodley said, his voice grating from the agitation of his anxiety. "Even if they don't believe us and they wipe our minds, someone will take the chance that we told the truth. They're trillions of people in the Galaxy starving for a space fortune. They'll come, others better at deceit and robbery than us, and they'll know to be careful of the Ice People."

"Maybe they will," replied Po, "but later. Now, go."

Woodley turned to help Ash, who was grim-faced but already coloring a pale green again. They limped up the ramp. Soon, the gray ship left.

"Will they be back?" Po asked Rill.

"Someday, Po," she sighed, "somebody will."

"And Blue Moon will change."

"No," she said, "but we will."

Po stooped, and a tentative touch thrilled the nerves in his arm.

How are you, Shortstuff?

—Sick. I feel sick, Po. The green man was different, different from you and all your other squishy people. And you told me to be him. —

I know, Shortstuff. I know. I'm sorry. I won't ever let you feel like that again.

—Promise? —

Promise.

Dead to the World

"I'm sorry to be bothering you with this right now, Jack, this afternoon of all afternoons."

Dr. Jack Boyd listened to his associate, Dr. Edna Ankiel, who sat before his desk in a much more relaxed pose than her words indicated, pro forma words. After two and a half years working together, she knew what did and did not upset him, really. Jack shrugged, waving his hand about him in a brief, listless gesture.

"No problem. You know I'm too antsy to just sit here, do nothing. Matter of fact, I was just about to go take a look at her before you came in. You say she was under the ice for twenty minutes?"

"Longer. She chased her sled out onto the river and went in."

"Unhuh." He opened the second drawer of his desk and propped a foot up on its edge. Idly, he stared at the scratches grooved by habitual use. Gradually, the rest of the familiar office stuck in his head, unfamiliar, new, as though after seven years calling for repairs or remodeling, or some such thing. Heightened awareness, he concluded, a big day, when tennis balls come at you the size of basketballs. He looked back to Edna.

"So, what's your diagnosis, our prognosis, and all the rest, Doctor?"

"She's royally whacked, Hank. You'd be hard pressed to find a brainwave nearer to her than the next state."

"Hmm, dead in the water. Okay, did you brief her parents?"

"Parent. A mommy. Divorced since the kid was one. She took her to everybody else before coming to us, of course."

"Of course." He batted his eyelids to close them, his signature, well-worn expression of resignation. "So, what's she do to get by?"

"Media work. Video crosswords."

He opened his eyes. "No shit? Like backing chaos out of order.

We might get along."

"Maybe you will. She's a real good-looker." Edna flashed a compressed smile to his uneasy smirk.

"All right. I'll go look at the kid. You can bring the mother around in about ten minutes or so."

"Okay."

She stood up, a surprise to strangers since the height of her head barely changed from that of her sitting plane. She stepped daintily out of the office closely followed by Jack. From there they took separate paths down the hallway.

Jack gazed at the still body of the little girl with a fervency that would have startled any other onlooker, be it a naturally inured staff member or a forlorn relative otherwise deeply entombed in muted devastation. So perfect, he thought, staring at her pink cheeks round with life, crowned by airy blond hair, sweet and clean. But dead. He glanced over to the monitor to assure himself once again that her pulse sped unbroken across the screen like some phosphorus sea flat in the depths of a black ocean somewhere, sonar without sound.

Your brain is dead, he told her thoughtfully. Your mind is dead, the machine says so. If we leave you on this mechanical bed, your body will live, perhaps for many long years. Bu it will begin to die, too, little by little, and faster than if you were up and about like any normal little girl, playing and growing, working someday, stealing time for love. Just lie here, though, and your flesh will fade, streamlined by a systematic biochemical efficiency to work as little as necessary. You'll grow ugly, not pretty. You won't blossom, you'll look like all the rest.

He lifted his head and broadened his sight to include the twenty-nine other brain-damaged bodies in the ward, all attached to their own life-support systems, laid out in silent rows. So deeply entranced, unaware, they prompted their visitors, mothers, mostly, into saying that they slept like they were dead to the world. A closer look would reveal the truth and its evidence of withered limbs and sere skin marking them as inmates of a type of concentration camp uniquely acceptable to society. Four wards here and hundreds more in hospitals across the nation.

138

He dropped his eyes back to the child. You'll be just like these people soon, he told her silently. How can you be like this, alive yet not here? Where have you gone? I'm the expert, the leader in this field of research, but I don't know. I don't know. Not yet, but I'm going to find out. I will find out starting today, maybe.

He pivoted and walked briskly from the ward, his white coat hem whipping at his legs.

Edna's wisecrack earlier in no way prepared him for the appearance of the much taller woman she ushered into his office. Introducing her as Carolyn Johannsen, Edna left. Hank watched the girl's mother seat herself before him and thought that without question she just as easily could work in front of a camera as behind the scenes. Fastidiously attired in a suit-skirt combo, she exuded a demure reserve, an affect redoubled by her finely combed hair, not a strand at stray. She hit him as the little girl grown up, now attractive and utterly self-possessed. Maybe too much so, he observed. Where was that deeply aggrieved parent of a brain-dead child he had faced so many times before? He gestured to the chair too late as she settled into it.

He sat down behind his desk and folded his hands on the almost bare glass top.

"Ms. Johannsen, how do you do? Not well, of course. My associate, Dr. Ankiel, has given me a full report on your daughter's condition."

She nodded, her features tightening ever so subtly, devastated but tough, determined to see it through as far as she could go.

"Listen, first of all I'm truly sorry for this, this disaster that's happened to your little girl and to you. It's a terrible thing. Now, I don't mean to be insensitive, but I feel that frankness is best in situations like this." Even if it is on the brutal side, he said to himself. "You know what the others have decided?" He tapped a manila folder in front of him.

"They say that my daughter's case is hopeless."

Dulcet tones, he thought. Distance, he reminded himself, professionalism. He sighed, "Yes. You are aware, then, that I'm the final recourse, the last stop. Did you daughter's physicians tell you anything about what I'm trying to do here?"

"They told me that you were unorthodox but that you'd developed some unconventional theory that might hold promise for the future."

"Yeah, the future," he followed, "but nothing to show here and now. Well, I can't really complain about that. You know, they used to say I was whacko until the Neuronet produced some positive results that first time. And when the government stepped in with funding, suddenly I was reevaluated by my peers. I became unorthodox, gifted." He shrugged, "Who knows, though? Defense has backed goofier things before, like Frisbee bombs, for instance."

She blinked, seeming unsure of how to react and he quickly added, "Please excuse me. When things start coming to a head, I get carried away occasionally. I start taking stock. You've come at a rather particular time."

She smiled quite sadly. "I must admit," she said, "that's a pretty strange introduction. I thought you'd be filling me with hope and confidence. Don't you want my money?" she laughed ruefully.

"I'll pump you full of hope and confidence when I run out of money, including federal grants. Then, I'll go after yours. In all seriousness, though, I don't want you to delude yourself either. For today, Tina—"

"Chrissie. My daughter's name is Christina, shortened to Chrissie not Tina."

He frowned, glancing down at the betraying folder. "Sorry, Chrissie. My prognosis for Chrissie is the same as that of the other specialists, hopeless. But that's for today. I have a program of experiments scheduled that, God willing, the AMA and the Feds continue to give me the green light, could mean something positive as soon as tomorrow. But, for today I have to tell you that Chrissie is never going to change. That's the attitude you have to assume if you want to keep her here."

He sat back, waiting for her reaction. She lowered her head a little as if reflecting. She briefly knuckled her resting hands on the chair arms, then gazed up at him as if out of a painful daze. I hate this shit, he said to himself.

"Well," she said in a sing-song on the border of control, "what can

140

I say? Chrissie's been like this for two months, though it seems like forever every day. I miss her the way she was, like only yesterday, too. Things are so much duller now; I miss her that much. So, please, do what you can do."

This is hard, he thought. Whoever could have divorced this woman, who could have left her? Nobody, he decided, mentally shaking his head. She divorced him. No man is good enough for her. But a last thought crept in, guiltily invited in. Except me, maybe.

"Of course, Ms. Johannsen. Chrissie is welcome here." And the friendly smile lines just revealed around her wet brown eyes pushed him completely over the edge. "In fact, as I mentioned before, you've arrived at an auspicious time. Today, I'm conducting the first ever BEN intervention on a human patient just sanctioned by the government. If you care to remain here until it's concluded, I could talk to you this evening about the results and their implications, perhaps, for your daughter."

As a messenger service for the brain, electromagnetic waves worked a two-way street. Theoretically, then, a dormant brain could be stimulated by an artificially induced EM field. Indeed, before the moratorium on the use of primates as subjects, experiments with them had produced promising results. Humanistic subtleties, however, compounded the difficulties, since the world medical establishment balked at chancing any irrevocable side effects with human subjects. How strong a field and what pattern of access should be used in dealing with the delicate complexities of a living person's brain, a traumatically damaged brain to boot?

These questions plagued Jack for years until he pioneered the Biochemical Electromagnetic Neuronet (BEN), his synthesis of state-of-the-art PET scans with subsequent connections of human-to-human relays. The minutely computer-mapped mirroring of brain quadrant to brain quadrant seemed to offer the best possibility of reviving the functions of a comatose victim. A human-generated EM field boosted to compensate for the therapist partner's extra energy expenditure computed out as the safest load for the patient partner. So Jack had hypothesized and so he hoped would be borne out now as

Edna and his staff readied him for this historic experiment.

Ms. Martha Ullmann lay close to death, cardiopulmonary collapse threatening to take her off at any moment. Jack hardly would have chosen her as his first subject, but the Powers-that-Be would sanction him to begin only with a doubly lost soul.

Edna signaled to him that the last relay had been confirmed by the BEN computer. Soon he'd drift off into a light state of unconsciousness, a precaution against any unforeseen trauma of his own. As he drowsed, the last thing he saw was Edna holding up a thumb and forefinger in a circle next to her bristly gray head of hair. The last thing he hear before he went under was Edna saying, "Nobel, Jack, think Nobel."

Dark, the trip seemed terribly dark, the walls velvet red growing cooler, throbbing as he passed through them in the black labyrinthine tunnels they formed. Down which he traveled, dimmer, bleak, a sense of disappointment at being here, but always here. And betrayal, by . . children, my children, wounds of the womb remembered, all of them distracted. And the stranger. They didn't know, never could know, sometimes it's like you outgrow knowing, not with your own mother, though. An essential loving, lovingness, an inability to love without being solely loved, self-loved, not knowing yourself to hate. All this now, when the crowding pain is so great and so near complete. Before, though, down one last, long, narrow place toward a light, a light, baby lemon sunshine and metallic dark green grass, in a yellow garden swing, doodle lee doo singing while swinging on a perfect day forever.

"I tell you it was the strangest and strongest thing I've ever experienced. I thought they were my thoughts, that I'd been in all these situations. I felt them! It wasn't until I heard Edna talking to me again that I realized that the whole thing was hers, Martha Ullmann's, her life, her last thoughts!"

He bolted his food as he talked, fiercely chewing it out of the way to make room for his words. Carolyn and Edna listened to him across the table in the steakhouse booth. Carolyn leaned in slightly over her

142

clasped hands while Edna sat back quietly.

"I'm not sure they really weren't your thoughts, Jack."

"What? But, Edna, they were absolutely real! And foreign, utterly different from anything that's ever happened in my life."

"Sometimes when people dream, they swear they're real while they're having them. You're imaginative, you could've created a pattern of feelings appropriate for a dying, elderly woman. You also knew something of her family history from her records and relatives who visited."

He lifted his eyes skyward, then rolled them toward Carolyn and back to Edna. "Why are you resisting the possibility that we may have succeeded, Edna? This could be the big breakthrough we've been working for!"

"I refuse to lose my objectivity, Jack," she said sharply. "I want this to work just as much as you, of course I do. But the BEN readouts showed no EM activity in her brain. Nothing changed for her the entire time you were connected, until she—"

"The instruments didn't pick it up, that's all. They aren't sensitive enough—"

"—She died, Jack! God, fifty seconds isn't long enough for you to experience what you said you did."

He stopped at that for an instance, then said, "How fast is thought, Edna? Huh? How fast?"

"Okay, okay, I didn't mean it like that. But you know what I'm trying to say, Jack. Scientifically speaking, there's no new data to support your experience, what you're saying. Even the facts are off. Her whole family was here during the entire crisis."

"That could've been just for show, their perception of love for Mother. She was divorced by her husband and anyway, if they loved her so much, why did they agree to let her be the human guinea pig for the experiment?"

"She was dying, Jack. As for agreeing to the experiment, perhaps you should address that question to Ms. Johannsen." She flicked her head meaningfully in her direction. "Listen, I think we should continue this discussion later. I've got rounds to make." She stood up and patted his hand, nodding to Carolyn Johannsen as she left.

He felt like climbing into his own grave. After staring down at his plate for a time, he chanced a peek up at her. She still sat with her hands folded, waiting for him patiently.

"I'm not offended. Really. It's a legitimate question at this point. Am I really concerned for Chrissie's sake, or am I merely trying to salve my own guilty conscience? I don't know. I don't think so. Apparently, even the Ullmanns didn't give up all hope. But you shouldn't feel so terrible. After all, you tried to help these people through your genuine, altruistic sensibility."

He shook his head morosely, "Not completely. I have my own reasons for wanting to succeed. Sometimes the patients are pretty inconsequential as far as that goes." He swallowed and added, "All of them." He cringed inwardly as he listened for her reply.

She nodded her head, "Sure. They must be such messes as human beings to someone who's operating at the top of his form. But you weren't always such a success. Remember, for a long time you were a whacko to everybody else." She smiled at him winningly.

"Yeah," he said glumly, framing his utterance with his own sick smile. "Well, Edna certainly dropped a wet blanket on things. She could be right, you know. I could have skewed the experiment's results by knowing too much beforehand, projecting my own desires. Ms. Ullmann died too soon to learn, and the government will require a long-winded report before they go for another round. But, I swear, it was so real, so vivid. I felt Martha Ullmann's feelings, I felt for her!"

He stared agonizingly at Carolyn and she leaned in further over the tabletop, putting her face close to his. "I believe that you were in that woman's mind and that you shared her feelings. She may have felt that her children didn't love her, and maybe they didn't, to her anyway. But I think they loved her enough to let you try to save her."

"But I didn't." He barely choked out the words.

"No," she said, lowering her eyes thoughtfully, then raising them back to his. She reached out to grab his hands. "But, if you can, I still want you to try to save my daughter."

"Jack, we can't do this."

This time Edna sat posed on the edge of her seat.

"We don't have clearance and we couldn't possibly get it by tomorrow, not until we complete a full report on Ms. Ullmann. That'll take months, especially considering the shaky nature of our preliminary results."

Jack listened quietly while she spoke, and she fidgeted as she realized the distance he was keeping. "You knew this before, Jack. We built in extra time in the flow charts to prepare the report long ago. Why the sudden urge to rush everything?"

"I don't want to wait months, Edna, I want to move now. I'm convinced that I can prove the effectiveness of my methodology with one more experiment. The government won't cry about the clearance after the fact."

She blew out her breath in exasperation. "You know that's bullshit. They'll go nuts whatever the results of another experiment. Even if we could repeat what you said happened with Ms. Ullmann, it's not what we hoped to accomplish anyway. She died without ever regaining consciousness."

"That'll come later."

"Maybe, but all of it could go to shit, too, before we can find out if you insist on this now. If the government cuts us off, we might never know."

For a time, he didn't say anything. She stared at him wide-eyed as if seeing a stranger in his body. Eventually, he said, "Well, I am simply through waiting. We go ahead tomorrow."

She sat back fully in the chair at last. "Why, you son of a bitch, don't I have any say in this at all? Haven't I been with you every step of the way? Now you want to louse it all up just because you've got the hots for some darling of the screen. Just to be the bold researcher in her big, brown eyes, you're willing to fuck up the whole program!"

"That's not so!" he bellowed, following with silence. He was embarrassed as he wondered if it was Carolyn, really. Or was it more this hunger he felt, consuming, after being so briefly with Ms. Ullmann in her mind? At the moment he couldn't say.

Glowering at him, Edna said bitingly, "Well, include me out. I've got some things at stake here, too, you know, like my future."

Later in the afternoon, he walked into Edna's office and dropped a piece of letterhead on her desk. She looked up at him expectantly. "My confession," he said, "in which I threaten to dismiss you and blackball you at all other institutions pursuing similar research unless you agree to aid me in this unsanctioned experiment. Satisfied?"

She read the paper, then said, "And if I don't?"

"I'll get some grad student to help out."

She frowned, looking down to read the letter again. She said, "You know, it was supposed to be my turn to go in this time."

"I can't help that. I guess I'm pulling rank." He smiled sickly, "You know, Neil Armstrong walking on the Moon."

"I see. You also realize that this will be a blind trial. No background on the patient, nothing, to make sure you aren't projecting from your own thought patterns. That rules out Christina Johannsen, you're aware, I'm sure."

"Of course." He hadn't thought of it. Well, it'd be better for Chrissie's sake if he performed one more intervention on another patient. Unspoken between himself and Edna was the possibility that his intrusion on Ms. Ullmann had precipitated her death. He'd have to break the news to Carolyn tonight, though, that there would be a delay. Edna won't be happy to learn that another experiment will follow this one immediately, and another one, if necessary, and another. But by then she'll be in too far to do anything about it.

"You pick one out, Edna, a subject in much more stable psychological condition than Ms. Ullmann. I need more time than I had with that poor woman to do any good"

"I'll see to it."

"Good. Let's say for noon tomorrow. Anything else?"

"Yeah." She slid the statement back across the desk. "Date it."

While he scribbled his signature on the paper, she said, "Not that it'll do me any good anyway. The authorities wouldn't absolve me of responsibility for assisting you just because of a threat like this. The Hippocratic Oath and all that. One other thing, Dr. Boyd. I don't want
146

to hear you talk to me about Ms. Johannsen other than in a professional capacity ever again."

Having the hots for Carolyn Johannsen was as good a reason as any to risk everything, he mused while waiting for Edna to insert the final relay attachments. But he recognized that it was more than that. After his failure with Martha Ullmann, he felt a desperate need to go further than before, to help. He'd help Carolyn and Chrissie very soon, too. At present, though, his mind bubbled with thoughts of a subject selected by Edna, a patient he neither knew nor whose records he had studied, one Francis Cronin. Unknown now, but not for long, he assured himself as he drifted off. This time Edna flashed no good luck signal, mouthed no words about Nobel prizes. She simply stared at him, dimly, sullenly, until he went under.

"My fine friend."

Jack stirred, neither in nor out. The light shone an even gray glare throughout the . . . the what?

"My mind, mine fine, like well-timed wine with which to dine, fine, fine friend."

He knew this man, but couldn't see him except for an inspected nostril, an ingrown hair, gray fleece of age.

"Poetic, chaotic, eh? Streams and rills and courses, flood plains, watermarks, marshlands, salt flats, sea flats, or is it a C-flat? All of thought, all thought before."

The strangeness became more separate, the thoughts distinct.

"Oh, a moment's clarity, preferred claret, from the Old English, clarinet, of Indo-European origin related to C-flat at the cost of one C-note. You are a Geek bearing gifts, are you not?"

What are you?

"Francis Henry Cronin, not to be confused with the warrior Ronin, or Conan, or anyone, though we be warriors, we. Frank to my friends, though sometimes I speak with discretion, not to be confused with Descartes, or by the bugger for that matter."

Where am I?

"Not of this world, my world. My consciousness relived, didn't you

147

know? The afterlife is the reliving of consciousness originally formed, and life, the payment for external stimuli. I think; I command my surroundings. But demands cost, a limit to accessibility. Memory is all, almost as good as outside stimuli. Life in a vacuum, afterlife, improves with the picking of better and better places from a given life. Pick out more and more details, snow, grass, swings . . . specifics—and who could ask for anything more? You bring me gifts, but you are a Greek."

Why?

"Because you want me back in your place for your detail, where pain exists."

Don't you want to be alive again?

"Utterly not. Not sense, not-sensical. I want you instead, to stay with me in the Land of the Poets!"

Hills and valleys opened up to him, long grass waving in the wind under a coal-gray sky. All of it was lovely and fantastic.

"You're frightened. Of what?"

Nonlife.

"Who can tell the difference?"

Aren't you alone?

"Aren't you? Aren't everyone? Here, I grammatical rule. You are but a fig newton of my imagination, not to be confused with his brother Isaac, who floats among apples in his own little world."

Francis Cronin is insane.

"Of course I'm insane! Wouldn't you be if you controlled the horizontal, the vertical, the whole fucking video? How long do you think I've been in this sunken submarine anyway? Ten years, give or take ten years. Ten years! Ah, but I was lucky, I was crazy before I got here. After all, I did try to commit suicide."

Suicide?

"You bet, alcohol and drugs. The alcohol was easy, since I'm an alcoholic. But the drugs were an inspiration! As you'd expect, though, I fucked it up. Not dead. Not-sensical."

Alcoholic. Edna's revenge.

"Sure!"

I'm afraid.

148

"Sure! You ought to be, 'cause you ain't goin' nowhere, Jack, you're staying with me."

I want to go home, I want to go—

He began to run, thump, thump heart thundering, trying to run away from, his heart racing, toward Carolyn and Chrissie; was she insane, could she be? He stopped, though his body pulled at him fiercely thumping, heart jumping out of his chest, yanking at him.

Francis Cronin, could you ever come back if you wanted to?

"Quothe the Raven, 'Nevermore,' Birdbrain. Too much input. Better hurry!"

He awakened to a harried Edna perched over his bed.

"You were gone, Jack. Only five minutes under, but your EEG was as flat as a pancake almost from the start. Then we lost your heartrate. We had to use the paddles. The whole thing was a horror show. You almost didn't make it."

Her eyes glistened. His slit.

"Edna, you hooked me up to a maniac, a fucking alcoholic suicidal maniac!"

Startled, she almost jumped off the bedside. "How did you know?"

"How did I know, how did I know?" he shouted. "He almost took my mind apart! I nearly died locked in his head, you idiot!"

"I didn't think it was true. It couldn't be! I did it as a joke, to snap you out of this stupid romance thing."

He breathed an angry sigh. Coldly, he said, "How is he?"

"The same," she said, almost to herself. Abruptly, she grabbed his arm. "It works, Jack, the BEN works! We've done it!"

"What do you know about it, Edna? You don't know a thing, not a fucking thing."

Grudgingly, he admitted to himself that he'd brought it on himself, after all, bullying an ambitious firebrand like Edna into the entire fiasco. Now, she's dying to get on with the research, to forge ahead blindly. Well, let her, he decided, let her jump right on in. She can have it.

He sat up. "Where is Ms. Johannsen?"

Edna seemed to draw slowly into herself, closing her lips in a tight grimace. "Outside. Hoping to see you."

"Send her in."

She left without a word. Carolyn walked in, hurriedly at first, then hesitantly. Striking as always, this time she showed some wear, a few wrinkles in her usual smart outfit, perhaps a little strain around her mouth and eyes from lack of rest. After a small pause, she said, "You almost died."

"No, but I nearly didn't wake up."

Could she be weeping, he wondered. He couldn't see any tears, though.

"I'm so sorry. I feel like I've been using you."

He nodded his head, not so much as agreeing with what she said, but with everything else. "I must have liked it."

She gave him an odd look at that while stepping over to sit on the edge of his bed. "Are you all right?"

"Yeah. I was scared, though. And I'm tired. But, I'm all right."

She reached a hand over and squeezed his wrist. "I'm glad. I'll see you before you go home."

She left. Without saying one word about Chrissie, he realized. Does that mean anything? Could she care for me like that, that much, he wondered. Or, is it an even more effective way of getting me to want to help her? God, what kind of question is that?

He stretched back in his bed and thought gloomily of Frank Cronin, buried in his own madness and silence. Content, he'd said, but happy to try to keep an interloper in his ravaged brain for new stimuli, a more vivid world than his own. Shuddering, Jack tried to shake off the thought of a never-ending existence in Frank Cronin's wracked mind. He didn't even want to think of all the contingencies, whether he'd retreat into his own comatose universe once the relays had been broken. Or, if the strain on his body would kill him in every sense due to the unnatural imposition. It was over, as far as he was concerned, over for good.

He settled in to rest, to sleep. Behind his closed eyes Christina Johannsen's features appeared. He turned over, scrunching his pillow

150

under his head, but she floated before him again, baby-cheeked visage of another Carolyn with silvery blond hair.

"Shit," he said, sitting upright, wide awake. What am I going to do? I'm no bold hero, I'm a research scientist. How can I even think of it, knowing what I know? It's utterly nonsensical! Not-sensical.

How can I face Carolyn again if I don't, he thought glumly. But the damn BEN doesn't work like it's meant to, Ms. Ullmann and Cronin both are proof of that. Though, it does do something, he admitted. I do have some idea of what's happening to these people. All of them, the hundred here and the rest worldwide, they all still exist somewhere, shut in other worlds of their own making.

What kind of world can a six-year-old live in? She wasn't crazy when she fell under the ice. Like most of them, she didn't elect her fate, unlike Cronin. Neither did Ms. Ullmann, yet I still wasn't able to help her. So, how can I help Chrissie? I could throw my own life away chasing after some romantic illusion just as Edna said, he thought. The stolid, beguiling face of Carolyn Johannsen passed before him. Then the childish softness of sleeping Chrissie took her place. How can I help Chrissie, he posed to himself again. How can I not?

The nurse appeared promptly after hearing his signal.

"Yes, Dr. Boyd?"

"Call Dr. Ankiel, please, and ask her to come here. I need her to assist me with a scheduling matter. Thank you."

The gray glow of the sky frightened him at first. He whirled around quickly as if to go back, but the padding of the dark green grass underfoot stopped him. Trees full of summer leaves grew in occasional clusters, thickening down a slope that drifted into a gentle ravine. He could see patches of color at the base of the tree trunks, mauve wine flowers and solferino ivy that calmed him with their quiet beauty. Soon, the fear lying shallow within him eased enough so that he could take one step, venture one.

"Chrissie?"

He said her name almost under his breath, not sure of how loudly he needed to call to attract her attention. No sound broke the silence,

151

so he started to descend.

He reached a first tree, a pin oak, slender and straight, comfortable to his memory. Absently, he passed a hand over its slate-gray scaled bark as he stepped toward the next grove. Further down he could see a brook running along in quiet noise, talking the words of the rill to him, barely indistinct.

"Chrissie?" he called again as he reached the bank. At the top of the hillside opposite he saw movement, a head, then shoulders appearing from the other side, rising in slow ease. A woman crested the hilltop and started winding down a path through the flanking trees.

She wore a dark tartan skirt to mid-calf, woolen socks, and neat brown shoes. A bulky marine-blue sweater over a white lace blouse finished her dress save for a ribbon tying back her shoulder-length, light brown hair. Carolyn? But this woman is slender, fair-skinned, very much so, he noted. Gracefully, she drew down to the stream, and Jack allowed his mouth to gape.

"Chrissie!"

The young woman resembled Carolyn Johannsen but her features without question were Christina's as she would mature.

"Dr. Boyd," she murmured, "Jack."

"Chrissie, my God, you're all grown up!"

"And you're old." He frowned and she said, "Your hands. Look into the water."

He searched the water to find the reflection of his face, no different, his hair the same, its color only slightly defined by gray as usual.

"I'm the same," he said, puzzled.

"Old to me," she said.

He shook his head in bewilderment. "How can you be so grown up, Chrissie?"

She nodded, "I'm a big girl now."

"But, how, Chrissie?"

"I don't know," she said in a child's singsong, though did he hear a mocking undertone? Still perplexed, he gazed around at the peaceful valley and asked, "Where are we?"

152

"Here, in this place," she said. She walked over to a nearby bush. "Look! Pussy willow." She stroked the fuzzy buds. "And over there, lilacs."

"Yes, they're nice," he said, distracted from the tiny perfection of the clustered lavender bells. After a moment, he said, "Don't you have flowers like these at home, Chrissie, in your backyard?"

She straightened, causing her sweater to smooth out against her slim body. "Some of them. I have pussy willows in my yard. Others, Mommy told me about. But I've never seen lots of these pretty flowers before."

He squinted his incomprehension at her. "But this is you, Chrissie, this is your place."

"I guess so. There are lots of new things here, too. It's scary. I think I better go back."

Scared? New? She turned to start back up the hill.

"Wait! Stay, Chrissie, don't go."

She slowed, peering back over her shoulder. The troubled wariness in her eyes, her simple sorrow sent him feverishly through his mind for something to say that would keep her here, hold her and comfort her somehow. He put out open hands.

"Chrissie, this is a lovely place, a wonderful place. Please don't leave."

"But I'm afraid."

"Stay here with me. Please."

She hesitated, in balance, and abruptly he understood. He feared losing her more now than anything else, a woman he'd never known, carrying him past the marking of time that had been glorious work, past all of his careful loves of the past.

"Christina," he said quietly, plaintively.

She returned to the bank, still doubtful and fearful. She pouted and said, "But why are we here, Dr. Boyd, why me?"

"Because . . ." and he looked around again, this time spying willows drooping their leafy limbs into the stream, and pear trees near an apple grove a short way up the gentle rise. And honeysuckle.

"I know this place," he mumbled, and she solemnly moved her

153

head up and down. He focused his eyes once more upon her as he said, "You're only six. You have never known my name. You don't know this world, my world."

He stood stock still as the stunning realization flowed through him. "You know about me from your momma," he said, almost to himself, "Carolyn."

She nodded, "She talks to me all the time. She likes you. But you scare her, just like you do me, like this place does."

"My place, my world," the seat of his most profound yearnings hidden to him until this moment, his land of the poets full of manic ardor frightful to all others. He wondered if Chrissie really heard Carolyn talk to her during her mother's endless vigil over her comatose child. Or, could this too be his invention, another comforting undercurrent in his own very private place?

He sighed. "You seem to be all grown up, Chrissie, almost like your mother. But, you're not like her or how you'll grow up yourself someday outside of this place, I think. You're a woman I've never known, one I'll never know except here. You don't really want to stay, do you, Chrissie?"

Sadly, she said, "I want to go home to my mommy."

He took a leaping step across the creek and took her hand. "Come with me, Chrissie. We'll go look for your mommy. And if we don't find her soon, we'll go to your place and wait for her to talk to you again."

The little girl Chrissie beamed. As they walked up the hill among the apple trees, she pulled him down and gave him a peck on his cheek.

The kiss felt dry on his skin, the one that awakened him. Carolyn Johannsen's beatific smile greeted his opening eyes. She pointed to the other bed and he watched as Chrissie stirred, complaining to a nurse about sores and asking for ice cream. Crying openly, Carolyn hugged him, then went to her daughter's side.

Edna stood over him solemnly, shaking just a bit.

"How long?" he asked.

"Sixteen minutes, forty seconds. Back and forth, it went. Sometimes we thought we'd lost you for good. You know, no response

154

whatsoever, and I'd be ready to jolt you, and then you'd give me a blip. But your EEG showed absolutely zero."

"Unhuh," he grunted. "What about Chrissie?"

She shook her head vigorously, "Nothing. No signs at all. She just sort of came out of it when you did."

"I see." He rubbed his jaw thoughtfully.

"So," she said, "what did you do?" The merest tremor in her voice betrayed her fierce effort to control her excitement. He glanced at her and she continued, "To bring her out of it, I mean."

"Oh. Nothing." He noticed her skeptical look and said, "I didn't do anything, Edna, honest. I wasn't even sure I'd come out of it this time." Or, if I wanted to, he thought. "Anyway, you may have been right all along. I might have projected everything. I know for a fact that I did at least somewhat with Chrissie. Who knows? Maybe I saw Cronin's file years ago and forgot about it, or even blocked him out. Whatever, I didn't do anything to bring Christina Johannsen out of her coma. Her revival was spontaneous, I'll bet on it, completely co-incidental to the experiment."

Edna surprised him by reaching over to squeeze his wrist. "Don't talk about it now, Jack. You've been through a lot. We'll go over it later, when we do the report."

"Edna, I'm not lying to you. It wasn't anything like you might think. I mean, I don't really know what was happening or how much is true. It doesn't matter because I'm giving up the research. I'm leaving the Center. I don't think I want to do this anymore."

Edna frowned, disbelieving, but worried, too. "But you were right, as usual, Jack." She said it in a forced playful tone. "The government won't have anything to say about regulations after this kind of success. I have to admit it, you proved everyone wrong, Dr. Boyd, even me." At the latter, she favored him with one of her familiar, wry smiles.

"You can have it all, Edna. I'll recommend you."

She drew back and patted her fuzzy gray hair, head half turned away. "That's very good of you, Jack, except you're the all-time heavyweight now, now and forever. The people with the purse strings won't be happy unless you, the only one to perform all BEN

155

interventions to date, especially this fabulous success, still run the program."

"I didn't do anything."

"You did something, and we'll find out what it was. Meanwhile, if you need a reminder, just look at the little tyke in the next bed. She used to be a bunch of carrots, remember, dead to the world? If you want to think about quitting, look at her and her mommy." She stabbed a thumb over her shoulder in the direction of the other wards, "Then, take a gander at the rest of them around here."

He appeared to wince at that, and she relented. "You're tired. You need a nap." She patted his arm and left.

He pressed his temples with his fingers. She never failed to jab him directly in his nerve center. She had him, too. He knew that he couldn't abandon all the people in the other wards in other hospitals and all of their families. After Chrissie's miraculous awakening, could he blame them for refusing to accept his reason for wanting to leave the program, his doubt that he could bring back their loved ones? But, if he continued, how would they take it if he had to tell some of them that their lost loves didn't want to come back?

He shook his head. If that happened, he could never tell them the truth, never. Technical failure in the procedure would be a much more tolerable form of disappointment.

Across from him, Carolyn whispered happily to Chrissie, who seemed alert but confused. Carolyn pointed in his direction, then hugged her daughter closely. Both of them looked at him now, Carolyn in open gratitude.

Chrissie stared at him oddly. In vague recognition? He wondered. Did you tell your mother about your time in my world? Does she understand me better? Does she forgive me? Or weren't you there, Chrissie? Is a person's world utterly solitary, like Frank Cronin's? If so, maybe it didn't matter. Perhaps people's ultimate happiness comes from that place where they can be perfectly alone.

He hoped not. Or, if so, he hoped that he wouldn't see his own private world again for a long, long time. Before he searched for the woman of his dreams in his peaceful valley again, he hoped to spend a

156

great deal of time getting to know this good woman and her daughter here, for real in this shared world.

Median Strip Football

Luis wandered his way through the commodious kitchen lined with mahogany cabinets through the dining room into the sunken living room to the floor-to-ceiling window overlooking Botafogo Bay. Below him, the deep purple water curved serenely around the shore, a few old yachts stilled at their moorings. Across the Bay, Sugar Loaf rose slightly fuzzy at its edges in the haze. Even now in midafternoon, he could see some lights glimmering below.

He sighed and turned back into the living room. The alpaca shag felt good between his toes, but the matching white sofas and chairs imparted no warmth to him, no comfort. He ambled back to the dining room and stretched his upper body loose-limbed across the top of the oval table. For a time, he traced the fine-grained cherry with a finger, clicking off the black speckles in his head as he came to them. Reaching the center, he grabbed a soapstone shaker and tossed it back and forth, one hand to another. He fondled its slick surface with his thumb and forefinger, smooth like the matáká his grandmother wore frictionless inside constantly grinding corn long ago. When he was little, Mamacita used an electric mill to grind corn, though she kept the flat old stone up on a shelf to venerate her mother. He wondered now if their people had returned to the old stone ways to prepare food, he thought, if there was any food to be had. If still they lived today. He exhaled heavily. Margara, where are you now?

"Luis, Baby, I'm home!"

His back tightened as he waited for the well-worn admonition. Marie stopped in the kitchen, her arms crammed with packages suddenly suspended above one of the gleaming cultured stone counters.

"Luis," she said, her tone full of exasperation, "where are your trousers?"

She dumped the bags on the counter.

He straightened up and turned to face her. Still, she was taller, gloriously blond in an egg-white summer dress and spike heels, her stunning good looks heightened by her bronze tan. Sun brown or not, Marie was a mestiza blanca, he thought, white on the outside no matter what. He felt the underground people eating hollow the home of his soul again.

She rested her wrists on her hips and said, "You know that friends come over all the time to see you. Especially with a game coming up, they all want to wish you luck. What are they going to think if you greet them at the door in nothing but your ratty, native jockstrap?"

He stared sharply up at her with troubled black eyes. "I run soon!" he said stiffly while yanking up his sitagola, the time-tested waistcloth worn in the dry mountains of home.

"Well, all right then, but at least wear athletic shorts like other people do."

He lowered his head, swiftly circled the table away from her and strode toward the den. She followed on his heels. Switching from Portuguese to Spanish, she said, "Querida, don't you see? You've got an image to maintain. You're a well-respected, influential man."

Before he could reply, she abruptly whirled around and left. He plopped into his leather easy chair, white like everything else, and murmured a command. Golden fuzz appeared in front of him and coalesced into a solid gold column, awaiting his selection. He rattled off a memorized sequence and the gold turned black, then verdant green as venerable oak and beech trees took form amid gentle, grassy hillocks. The view moved left, and in flatter terrain, a milling of men in two different colored unis grouped around an oval ball resting on the ground. At the upper and lower edges of the VirtuReel cast, concrete planes bordered the bucolic playing field on either side.

Slipping in behind him, Marie sat on the other arm of the chair and wrapped her arms around his neck. He pulled down one that was blocking his vision. Out of the corner of his eye he noticed the pantalones draped across her other arm.

"Lover," she cooed, "I know you're jittery about the game. But,

159

please, put them on, huh? For me." She hugged him closer and nuzzled his neck.

"Marie," he said, still looking at the VR cast, "they play."

She peered up. The two teams faced off in three and four-point stances, some standing crouched behind the others, arms curved like claws in anticipation.

"What is this?" Marie asked.

"Washington I-5 Championship. On the left, the Pig-Dogs, they have the ball. This play almost won it for them. Shhh! Watch."

The men exploded into inchoate activity, suddenly clarified as one incongruously lean but fleet player burst abruptly between a cross-scissoring action by two of his teammates. Out in the open, the runner flashed past opposing players turned the wrong way. Close projection showed the laboring runner's features, wondrously delicate with arrows of bleached blond hair poking out of the side of his scrum cap. The VR cast pulled back to reveal him striding in a loping gait far ahead of the mash of men behind him. Between him and the melee, two opposing players of similar size ran after him, also at a steady, patient pace.

"Looks like he's in the clear," Marie said.

Luis shook his head, "They caught him on a free drop. He had to cross a bridge near Patterson. No median strip. They cornered him at Bellingham. But he almost made it all the way to the Canada border, the finish line at Blaine"

"So, did they win later?"

Luis frowned. "No. Tie. All the games end in ties. The oficiales are getting mad. There are . . . rumors."

Marie hugged him again. "Oh, I'm sure you'll win this one. Who are you playing?"

He glanced at her momentarily, then said, "The Pig-Dogs."

"Oh. They look good. But you'll win."

"Maybe." He sighed. "Anyway, we got a new runner that will help us, I think."

"Oh?" She sat up straight. "Why do they need a new runner? You're the best runner in the league."

160

"Marie, fútbol teams need at least two runners. Three, if they're lucky. I'll run, don't worry."

"So, who is this new, great runner?"

He gestured with a nod, "You're looking at him, baby. Este hombre es muy bueno!"

"I see." She looked thoughtfully for a moment at the slim, fair-haired man gliding effortlessly through a wooded strip. "What happened to your old partner Treacy?"

"Traded," Luis said, "to the Mongoose Stinkbugs.

Then, she said, "Well, Luis my love, here are your pants. Please, for me, wear them in the house."

"I go to train soon."

She smiled shyly and pulled blue shorts out of the pants. "Then, wear these."

He wiped a hand over his eyes.

In late summertime Rio, twilight was the best time to run. Luis rode the elevator down to the building's garage below street level. The cavernous echoing of the door in the spacious, pillared underground reminded him of tombs of the forgotten dead. He skirted a gleaming black, personal transport vehicle, the only one left, and trotted up the curving ramp to the garage door. He peered out the window between the alloy steel bars of the gate. No one seemed to be lingering outside, so he quickly unlocked the attendant's side door and slipped through.

He glanced left. In front of the lobby, ten to twenty figures waited, leaning against the walls, the awning posts, the old letterbox. He wheeled about and quick-stepped up the sidewalk around the corner. From there he dropped into a slow warm-up tempo out on the broad Avenida Augusto. Others marking time on the empty street watched him go by, but the failing light kept them from recognizing him. For that, he was thankful. The security team said he shouldn't go out unescorted, but it didn't bother him. He could outrun any kidnappers or terrorists once he got going. And, until then, the mestizo shorts pulled over his sitagola made him look like just another runner who wanted to get into the league.

He ticked off the street signs as he passed—Catate, Marques de Abrantes, Paissanda—all imprinted in his mind from countless training sessions. Familiar, too, were the words that looked like grossly misspelled Spanish, though utterly unpronounceable for him. He listened to directions on his VR mobile, but never recognized them as the same words on the signposts.

So, why live here? Marie would say it whenever he complained. Why not Caracas, or Bogota, or even Mexico City for heaven's sake, nearer to his home? She'd go on and on, and he'd shut up tight; she didn't have to know his reasons why. As he thought about the never-ending argument, his jaw muscles flickered over the bony knobs at the hinges.

The broad vistas turned into pulverized macadam as the roadway narrowed and steepened up the rise to Mount Corcovado. He monitored the slender tug in his right groin. Each step sent the muscle strumming, yet so far it held together. Psoas M., the expensive doctors called it, to him another fancy word costing him money. Buried deep within, it was one of those unknown silent parts that in later years surprised the body with its painful discovery. He knew his body better now, he realized with a rueful inner smile, because it cried out more to him. The older injury to the ankle seemed to be healed. The league medicos called it a subluxation, something about ligaments and tendons stretched so that the leg bones didn't rest on the ankle bones. Running had tightened them up again, but one wrong twist and that would be that.

Dewy fog condensed on tropic-size, frog-green leaves growing out of succulents clinging to the mountainside. He tried to maneuver under as many of them as possible, timing his passing to the languorous arrival of the tiny streams and channels at the tips of the fronds. As they burgeoned into drops, tensing, then falling, he caught them in his open mouth. In the US Republic, he would draw blades of grass through his teeth to squeeze out the least bit of moisture. At least in the eastern states, he noted. In games like the one on the Arizona Interstate, grass didn't grow in median strips.

Halfway up the mountain, a break in the outer rim of vegetation

162

revealed Rio below. He could see the Lagoa district, its white, concrete buildings turned pale in the darkening light, soon to disappear under a skeletal net of streetlights. Nothing like the display before the great migrations, he realized. Humankind's light was as short now as food. On one distant hillside, he could see a telltale red glow distinctly brighter, like a volcano resting its fiery anger. Another favela burned there, the ramshackle homes of the poor Cariocas disappearing instantly into guttering flame and black smoke. The city's happy windfall coming out of all the misery from the general decline worldwide.

Famine struck the poor in the poorest countries, including in Rio of course, especially the favelas. The council acted swiftly to move the ever-decreasing slum population into an ever-smaller sector of the city. They then torched the empty hovels on the deserted mountainsides to control disease. For the first time in more than a century, Rio shone bright without the blight of a collar of grim ghettos. And those who still hung on waited with the patience of the poor, though without hope. Fear began to grope within him again, but not of an actual, present danger. Other things, like the crazy starving ones called Los Humanos, religious nuts who even if they could afford to, wouldn't eat.

He shook his head in bewilderment as he loped up to the crest. Before a game, he always thought of the old days, just a boy running the dalahípu. Men ran the ancient fertility race between rancherías. One mountain village against another, down and up, then back again, day and night, night and day. Only the rattling reeds on his somáka kept him awake, strung by his mother to fit his narrow waist. Fiercely unafraid and light-footed, even at that age, he'd been one of the best. Happy in his weariness afterwards, deliriously drinking tesquino, courting lovely Margara, happy. They would marry someday, he thought back then. The next year, the league plucked him out and away.

The rancherías might be gone, now, though the petty mesquinos would hardly bother with the cosmetics of burning it down. He didn't know; he'd never returned, always too busy.

Beneath the outstretched arms of the granite Christ, Luis slowed

163

to a circling loop as he mapped out his return route. Down around Lagoa, across to Ipanema, finishing at Copacabana. The favelas were gone and just a few Cariocas remained. But some still idled below, though it would be all right because they never knew when he would come. They couldn't plan anything but good times just for being alive. The thought calmed him some.

Traversing the downward slope, he pressed his lips together. Marie didn't know, she couldn't know what it meant to the way they lived and what an injury could do to them. But then, she didn't need to know, the way she was. His working life was so much shorter than hers, than everyone else's, and she had no idea. The last two games, ties. He creased his lips into a tighter line. Only half the prize money. And the league threatened a change, which meant a change. Maybe no money at all for ties. He shook his head.

They had to win the next game, he had to win it. But, what if he couldn't? What if the groin cried out on a breakaway or the ankle caved in? He began to chew his lower lip. Maybe Blondie the new guy would help the team, he thought. He's younger, he can still run. He can be injured, too, though.

Even if they win this game, what of the next one? Luis knew he couldn't get back into shape for another race in only a month. Twelve games a year, impossible. But, without the money, what of Marie?

Reaching the lagoon, the little rim of sand surrounding it crunching beneath his feet brought him back. Soon, he'd be at Copacabana. Soon he'd have to decide.

A talá, he thought, the only way, a one-time wager of a lifetme, his life. If he won, he would retire with enough to keep Marie and himself for good. If not, well, he could run again in a month with no one the wiser. He nodded his head, the talá.

At Copacabana, little waves lapped at the sidewalks adjacent to the high rises, the white beaches submerged long ago beneath the rising waters. Still, old ladies dressed in white lit their candles and waded out in the silvered surf to launch their offerings to Lemanja, goddess of the sea. Luis stopped running at the sidewalk's edge and warmed down by strolling along its foamy border. He passed groups of gaunt Cariocas

164

who saluted him with arms upraised, "Tutto bien?"

"Tutto bien."

Others occasionally dropped to one knee in their happiness to see him, and he lifted them with a troubled smile. After a few minutes, he pulled his hood over his head to avoid recognition.

Across from the deserted Felizé Hotel, he stopped. The pinpoint lights of the candles floating on the ocean blinked out in ones, twos, and threes. He stood watching until the entire sea front went dark and deserted. A single figure came up to him then, never hesitating.

"How are you, hombre de los Daramuli?"

Daramuli, Luis noted, his people's own name spoken in an accent like his own. He could barely make out the man before him, the voice nondescript. "You are the curandero?" Luis asked.

"I know the secret ways, sí. I know of héna díse damano, the God our Father the Sun, and of the Moon our God Mother. Íyerugame isn't out this night."

Luis could make out the small figure now, a little brown man with long, stringy gray hair, searching the sky for the Moon.

"Never mind that," said Luis. "Did you bring the bahánawa?" The little man turned his head back and Luis thought he could feel his gaze, a shaman's eyes upon him.

"You need the fierceness and strength of the jaguar—"

"I do, for an upcoming game."

"—again? Why? You left your ranchería."

"Perhaps so, Gobernador," Luis said scathingly, "but here I am, so far away now in this place Rio, yet here is where I meet you. Now, why is this so?"

The shrunken man shrugged. "The mesquinos have banned the courage of the cactus. This is where I must come to perform my arts, to do my business. Besides, there's not much left of our mountain villages. Not too many people still live there. Those that are left do not believe in the old powers. The soul of the mountains has left its heart and the heart lies sick."

Luis dropped his head slowly as if his sudden understanding would be revealed. After a moment's pause, he said, "Well. Have you got it?"

The old man handed over a dirty leather go-pouch. Inside, Luis could feel the blunted, prickling stickles of the ball-like plant.

"It's genuine, muy fuerte, though they tell me one could do better using the modern stimulants."

"No, no, Curandero, I need the power of the spirit that only comes from this!" He waved it back at the old man in his fist.

"Good, good, okay." The old man slipped his hands into his garments, waiting. Some wanderers still on the shore passed by close enough to recognize Luis. They started to smile but left peacefully after seeing that hisá meeting was private.

At length, Luis said, "You'll be paid at the door of my apartamento. The doorman has instructions."

"Fine, fine."

"Very well."

There was nothing more to say, yet they lingered together.

"Well, I guess I'll be going," said the old man, turning to leave.

"Yes. Wait." said Luis. "Have you been back at all?"

"Me? Sure, now and then, for the herbs."

"I see. Have you ever been to Quesala?" Luis's face flushed as though the shaman could see it, as though the old man knew the ranchería was Luis's own.

"With the Guarijio people? No. I've never been there."

"Ah. Well, never mind." A lost chance to learn of Margara.

"Sí. Goodbye."

The old man turned away for the second time, but again he came back. "Here's some sinówa for your legs. Rub it into your joints when they're sore."

Luis accepted the dusty jar filled with the homemade ointment, dirt mixed with cattle suet. "Thank you, Curandero. I'll give the door keeper a little more for you."

"No need." He bowed his head. "Good luck, Luis," and in the home dialect, "Lobo en lo Viento. Good luck, Wolf of the Wind."

My running name, Luis thought. He knows my name.

Marie and Pascal readied themselves to go for a drive while Luis

166

stood in the middle of the living room, transfixed by her fluid movement.

"Luis, go bathe fast and come with us."

Pascal lounged deeply in one of the soft couches, smoking as he waited for Marie's bustling to abate. He dressed smartly in a stylishly rumpled sharkskin suit with a cummerbund around his tiny waist. His body wore clothes well as those with skeleton shapes do, and his features profited handsomely from his razor cheekbones covered by stretched, flawless brown skin. Pascal employed himself as an agent, though not Luis's in spite of daily overtures. He didn't need the money, though, he did well. His family had anticipated the reinstatement of gambling in Brazil during the past century.

"Luis, are you coming?" Marie asked again.

"I can go faster running. And the people don't get in my way."

"C'mon, you just finished running, my gobernador. It'll be fun. You can't run everywhere."

"It won't be fun for him, Marie," Pascal said, exhaling a lungful of blue steel smoke. "He'll be mobbed like always, especially if they see him satraping around in a car."

"His fans love to see him like that. They love him for it. He's their dream come true."

She pecked him on the cheek in passing.

"Sure but think of how poor, old Luis feels about it. To tell the truth, it makes me a little sick, too, not to mention a wee bit more scared."

"Oh, Pascal," she said, "don't be such a stick. We're going to have a great time and it's for a great cause."

"Where will you go?" Luis asked quietly

"To drop off some clothes at the CNC for an auction. They use the money to buy food on the black market to distribute to the Cariocas."

"We could always take a private car in the Tube."

"No, Pascal. The clothes will go for more if they see us arrive in Luis's PTV." She stopped her activity and faced Luis with soft eyes. "They'd bring even more if you came with us, Love."

167

He imagined how the Cariocas would feel when a very rare private luxury vehicle pulled up so that rich people could drop off their perfectly good clothes that they no longer wore for no good reason. He grimaced a smile and said, "Go with Pascal. I have some business."

She kissed him again, "Okay. But, please bathe." She headed into the bedroom as he nodded his capitulation.

Pascal stood up to stub out his cigarette. When he straightened, he stood a foot taller than Luis.

"She's a great lady, Luis. Too bad she's so damned loyal, too," he laughed with genuine affection.

"Yes, well, watch out for her today, will you?"

"Sure, of course. And you watch out for yourself, eh?" He slapped Luis on the back, "I hear those Pig-Dogs are tough."

Luis looked back at him, saying, "Even without Blondie?"

With hurt in his voice, Pascal said, "Hey, Luis, they approached me! You know, it's just business. I still think you're the best and I'd love to represent you, anytime. Hey, man, with Blondie next to you, defenses will have to play straight up, which means you can run even better than before. Then you can play for any team you want and you can name your own price. Just say the word."

Luis hesitated. The last game ended in a tie because he'd been caught, and not by a defender dropped in front of him. He'd been injured, sure, but that happens. When you get old, you get out, and then what? The talá, he decided grimly, he needed insurance and the talá was the only way.

"I may have need of . . . other services of yours."

"Oh?" Pascal looked puzzled. "Okay, whatever you say, Luis, I'm here if you need me."

Luis nodded, and Marie came back with arms full of clothing.

"Grab some, will you Pascal? You carry those boxes, Luis."

They dropped down to the dark garage and stepped over from the elevator to the lone, shiny black vehicle Luis had skirted before, his own. Marie directed the loading of the clothes, after which she and Pascal hopped in. She lowered an opaque window to kiss Luis.

"Bye, Baby. Shower and get a good rest. I'll be back in a couple of hours."

She gestured to the driver and Luis said, "I'll get it."

He hurried to the controls near the entrance and hit the buttons to open the door and raise the gate. The vehicle swooped silently out, Luis's eyes trailing it. Taken unaware, the flock of fans chased futilely behind it. Once they were gone, Luis lowered the barriers and hurried upstairs to call his agent Harry Brighton.

Marie stepped slowly, softly into the apartment, hoping not to disturb Luis who she knew would be miles away in sleep. Sure enough, her wrinkled brown nut of a man lay curled up on one of the white sofas. A pungent smell assaulted her olfactory. A glance around soon located the cedar sticks and the flask reeking of goat stench. Curing his legs as if still in the mountains, she realized. The upcoming game must be especially important to him, since he usually started the curing the last three days beforehand, not as much as a week.

She sat on the edge of the couch next to Luis's hip. He hadn't showered yet either. Christ, Luis, she sighed. She prodded him into groaning.

"Luis. Luis! Get up. Why are you sleeping here? You could take a bath and be more comfortable in bed. More restful, too."

He grunted into consciousness. "Ugh. No time. Had to call Harry."

"Harry? Porque? You just talked to him yesterday."

"Business."

"Business?"

"Business, business!"

"All right, all right. Don't get mad at me. I'm not one of the Pig-Dogs, you know."

Pig-Dogs, he thought, lowering his head. Father above, Mother below.

"You've been so edgy lately, more so than usual, than ever. Why is this game so important? It's just one game."

"You don't know," Luis said. "It's changing, everything is changing. I told you, there have been rumors. Anyway, I must protect myself, take care of things for the future."

169

"That's why you talked to Harry."

"Never mind that," he snapped.

"Okay, okay. You're so jumpy, suspicious. C'mon. You shower and then I'll rub you down. You'll rest, it'll help you to get ready."

After his shower, she loved him, on top to save his legs. He rolled over then for her to massage his back, his lean cords already bunching again with tension. She straddled him and with stiff fingers pushed and prodded at the tight, dense bands flanking his spine. She pressed hard, aware again of the life-long exertion that had formed his marvelous muscles that now painfully reminded him of his age. She loved him so deeply, her viejito, her little old man. Yet she knew that once it was all over for him, it was over for her as well.

II.

The league officials set up the starting gate for the 2084 PA I-80 Championship Game five kilometers west of Milesburg at the Rt. 220 intersection, near dead center Pennsylvania. Luis bounded around trying to warm up in the snappy autumn air. Fused white sunlight fixed the day as beautiful, cheering the newly turning leaves toward their finest display of northern hues. The portable club facilities stood opposite each other, Pig-Dogs to the south, the Wharf Rats to the north. Despite his fifteen years in the league, Luis still marveled that they could position the huge edifices so close to the official starting point no matter how remote. Complete with locker stalls, all the players' equipment, Jacuzzis, isochines, medimagers, orthoscopes, pharmas, food and drink, they also provided extensive relaxation facilities fully equipped with individual VR casters and sensory dep units. No matter, as soon as the officials signaled the teams to line up, squads of hover shuttles would fly in and lift the elaborate polylite buildings out in sections, not to be seen again until the competition concluded. The structures would be reassembled at the state line crossed by the winners, some 250 or so klicks down the road.

Luis stretched and bounced, preparatory to a jaunt, a little one, no more than ten klicks to keep loose for tomorrow. He'd cut back his long training runs a week and a half ago when he'd arrived to acclimate to the late summer weather. He rotated his upper trunk easily from the waist, taking his time, watching the other players perform their routines. They stretched, they sprinted, they went through tip drills, all under the eyes of assistant coaches. Some of the bigger men pushed against each other or practiced quick starts to either side, simulating blocking assignments. The opponents ran through the same maneuvers near their quarters.

He remembered explaining the match rules to Marie. Hovering above a holo model of I-95 in Connecticut, he pointed to the league's central complex at the starting line.

"Each team meets here first. The ref tosses a coin, and the visitors call it. Whoever wins can take the ball or defend. Each team puts eleven men out, four in the back, seven up front. The team with the ball gets in position. The players up front are called liners, and the one in the middle passes the ball back between his legs to the players behind, called runners. The player in the back directly behind the man in the middle, he first catches the ball, he is called the point. He can run with it, hand it off or pitch it to any of the other three runners. They try to fool the defenders, maybe faking right, then tossing the ball left, maybe stepping left, then back right up the middle, like that."

He demonstrated the plays on the model as he described them.

"The team with the ball gets four chances to set free a runner. If he's tackled all four times, the ball goes to the other team. Then, that team get four tries to spring loose their own ball runner. Once out of the pack, the runner goes as far as he can toward the finish line, the east state border for one team, the western for the other."

As he spoke, the small holo figures clashed in a play that stopped just millimeters from where they started. "It's such a mish-mosh," Marie said. "Can't they just throw the ball over all those guys on top of each other? Throw it to someone on their team?"

"No, no, no," Luis said, vigorously swinging his head back and forth. "No passes down the strip. Only side to side is legal."

"Huh," she huffed. "I thought they could do that."

"In old-time American fútbol but not here."

She shrugged, "It'd make things go faster."

"Not allowed," he said authoritatively.

"So, what, then?" she said. "This guy with the ball—"

"Runner," he said, "ball runner. Like me."

"—Okay, this ball runner, he gets past everyone else then runs all the way to the other side of the state?"

"If he's lucky," Luis laughed. "When is on defense, the runners are called chasers, which is what they do, chase the other team's runners with the ball. Usually, each team has two chasers chasing two ball runners on the other team. The chasers are just as fast and hot on every runner's tail."

He leaned over the holo model again. "But the key to it all, what makes every game fantastico," he said, "are the drop rules. They work like this. The strip have boundary lines on each side. They can be very different in many ways. Por example, at this point on the Connecticut Interstate, the strip is very wide. So, the runners have no problem avoiding the sidelines and going out of bounds. But here," he pointed at a narrowing of the strip, "it is very close to the boundaries. Now, if a runner goes out of bounds there, he gets a penalty and the other team gets to fly their chasers closer to the runner. Sometimes, if the penalty is very bad, if the runner deliberately runs out of bounds for a long way, let's say, the other team's chasers can be flown to a drop place in front of the runner."

He slapped his hand through the holo image on the table, "And that's how a breakaway run to the finish line can be stopped!" He grinned at the gravity of it.

"Oh," said Marie.

"There's more. Each team is allowed two free drops in a match, no penalty needed. One allows them to drop just their two chasers. The other," he said, "is a full team drop, one time."

Marie's face scrunched up in confusion. "Why would they do that?"

"To always make the end of the game exciting," he said. "With a team drop, there always will be a final face-off at the very last part of the match."

172

"If that's so," she said, almost annoyed, "what's the point of all the other running and chasing?"

He cocked his head, "Fans like all the action."

She didn't seem to be convinced.

That was early in their time together when he ruled the Median Strip League. Since then, everything had changed. True, what he had told Marie back then, VR fans did love drops, even minor penalty drops. If a runner strayed off the strip onto the highway, ref-drones flagged them for being out-of-bounds. Such a minor penalty entitled the defending team's chasers to a drop that put them three kilometers closer to the ball runners. Usually, if players weren't sloppy a few minor penalty drops counted for little. But get called for enough minor penalties, Luis knew, and the chasers could be right on their asses without breathing hard.

Major infractions were the worst. Straying far off the median strip, making use of prohibited aids, and other blatant violations triggered a free drop for the opposing club's entire team anywhere in front of the ball carriers. If runners incurred a major penalty and found themselves facing the other team's full squad, their only recourse was to reverse their direction and hope to make it back to their team before chasers caught them and took the ball. Crazy, Luis thought, almost impossible to get past chasers after a free squad drop.

Of course, the VirtuReel sponsors insisted on the drop rules. The ball changed hands most often after drops. Drops lengthened the games, which meant more airtime, which the VR people liked. In longer games, time ran out more often before any team won. Draws were called, which the fans hated, thought they kept watching.

The players despised draws, too. Draws meant less money from the VR casters to team owners, who made up the shortfall by doling out only half-pay to the players. Everyone knew that the owners kept back some profit. But who could complain with hordes of hopefuls ready to replace players for their own chance to line up for a shot at the big time? Especially wannabe runners. Gradually, though, with each tie both the owners and the players watched the game's popularity fading. All parties were losing money, though the players were hit the hardest.

Luis didn't give a damn this time. After talking to Harry, he had made the big talá on this game with Pascal's people, everything he owned. Of course, Harry had given him big trouble over the risk. As he trotted along slowly parallel to the old concrete, Luis laughed bitterly to himself at Harry's shocked look when he heard Luis's scheme.

"Luis, if your team loses or even just ties, you'll be wiped out! Either way, you could go to prison if the league finds out."

Luis shook his head, "I don't plan to lose. If we tie, the bet is a push. Even if we lose, I can always go back to the rancheria. League consolation pay is enough for me there."

"Really? And how is Marie going to feel about that?"

Luis heard the irate tone shaping Harry's question.

"Don't be mad," Luis said. "If this isn't my last race, you know it will be soon. If I don't quit, the Wharf Rats will make me. Why do you think they dealed for Blondie?"

"Don't be silly, Luis, it was all about strategy, not you. You are still one of the premier speedsters in the league."

"One of them. I used to be the number one runner."

Harry swung his head impatiently, his red jowls shaking a bit. "It's about strategy. They get Blondie and they have a diversion. Who will the Pig-Dogs try to stop, their old mate or you? I put my money on you, Luis, the Tarahumara Gobernador, the runner's runner."

Luis flashed a pained frown. He was of the Daramuli, and gobernador meant honored elder. Without knowing it, of course, Luis chuckled to himself, Harry had just called him an old man. The plump manager knew everything about money and league politics, but nothing about the long races in Luis's homeland, the rugged gorges and barrancas in Chihuahua called by Blancos the Dead Canyons. In median strip games, teams fought mostly over gently undulating ground dividing the abandoned highways. Modeled after ancient railway beds, the one to two percent grades produced artificial peninsulas running straight and narrow for kilometers and kilometers. They varied little except for occasional decorative tree groves and a

174

few hillocks covered by wildflowers. Occasionally, they intersected old mountain ranges, carved apart by dynamite long ago.

Luis remembered his people preparing to run the delaphípu against the varohios, the larger villages with more than a thousand residents. One village pitted against another, winners receiving the prize of a quarter of the losers' yearly harvest. He reminisced about the long races between the pitahaga torches that lit the way through the night. With painted legs and their waistcloths belted tight by long, reed somákas rattling noisily to keep them awake, the men kicked and juggled a small pine ball called the gomáka. For two full days, the little orb soared high between them back and forth over a 200-kilometer, rugged mountain path, no hands in play.

Villages fielded teams as many as twelve men strong, but the favorite matches tested wills in two-man duels. Luis made his reputation running in those races as just a boy. He could run forever without effort then, as fast as the condor winged through the sky, while never giving it a thought. Now, he knew the irony of greater intimacy with his body corresponding to his growing inability to command it to do what he wanted.

He sighed and sat down on a log. He reached to the back of his waist for his go-pouch, a small linen bag carried by every player for good luck charms and small personal effects. He took out the sinówa and started applying it to his knees to sooth the joints. At least his groin felt okay so far. Of course, he wasn't running either.

"Getting ready?"

Luis gazed up to see a tall, impossibly lean man looking down at him, backlit by bright sunlight that obscured his features into a black silhouette. Cupping his hand over his brow, Luis saw who he was.

"Blondie."

The lanky man grinned out of a taut leathery face, his skin redder than tan from regular exposure to the sun. His hair seemed sandy rather than blond, and his piercing, gemlike blue eyes peered out of a spider web frame of laugh lines. "Wils Wiland," he said, holding out his hand, "straight from Minnesota by way of the Pig-Dogs. And, of course, you're Luis Bonijic, the MSL's greatest ball-runner of all time."

175

Warily, Luis reached out a limp hand to allow a shake. He stood up, looking up at the tall, thin man as he said, "Not so great. Maybe you pass me soon."

Blondie shook his head, "Not goddamn likely, though the two of us together should make some noise, don't you think?"

Luis shrugged. The young runner exuded genuine warmth and his respectful attitude seemed real, too. "Could be," said Luis. "Maybe you take the lead, now?"

Blondie looked scornful, "No way. You're the man, Mr. Bonijic, not me. I'm the diverter sure enough."

Luis nodded, "We'll see." He started to rise.

"Sit down, sit down" Blondie said heartily, "I didn't mean to interrupt your training. I just couldn't wait to meet you. When they told me of the trade, I almost fell over. Just the idea of running with you blew me away. Can you imagine what we'll do by teaming up?"

"Maybe win?" Luis said sardonically.

Blondie laughed out loud. "Yeah, that's a problem. But who knows?"

I do, Luis thought to himself. This time we must win, I must win. Harry had Pascal bet all of his money, everything he had. He could not afford to lose. But, he didn't plan to lose, he planned to win.

"Time to warm up," he said.

"Right. Mind if I join you?" Blondie asked.

Luis shrugged and started jogging. Blondie cruised next to him, his long legs a sharp contrast to Luis's abbreviated, sinewy limbs taking quick, pounding steps.

"Beautiful day!" exclaimed Blondie. "Look at those trees! Real specimens. Where can you find stands like that anymore? Man, the league sure throws down for the green stuff, green for the green."

"Big trees are rare," said Luis, "very expensive."

"Yeah, well, the league's got it, all the money."

Luis glanced at Blondie, then fixed his eyes ahead again. After running a few more kilometers, he said, "So, who do the Pig-Dogs have running now?"

Blondie shrugged his shoulders, gazing down between his knees.

"A couple a youngsters. I don't see them as much of a threat. No experience. I guess Pig-Dogs management figured they couldn't win anyway, why pay for a seasoned player." He looked up at Luis, "Of course, it's their chasers they're betting money on. Daday and Abrebe, two mean bastards, love hurting people."

Luis nodded. "I know them." He paused, then said, "How did you get in the league?"

"Pretty much the usual story. No jobs, no money, a hard scrabble life. Except, I could run past all the others easy. Someone saw me, and I was in the D League. I kept running and winning, though that got harder. You know, it takes more than speed and endurance, you gotta employ tactics and strategy. I learned that from watching you on the VR casts."

Luis gave him a sideway glance.

"I learned a lot about how to win from you."

"Not lately," said Luis.

Blondie laughed. "Well, maybe we can double down on your skills, partner, and pile up a shitload of victories from here on."

Luis looked up at Blondie again, "Maybe. Time to go back."

They circled around toward the facilities complex and came to the tall trees again, this time skirting the opposite side. Loping along, they drew abreast of the heavy cluster of thick trunks when two men stepped out in front of them.

The runners shifted to a slow trot. Both burly, both dark from the sun, the men in front of them wore heavy boots, canvas jeans held up by sweat-stained suspenders, and white t-shirts dulled gray with dirt. Rip saws hung from worn leather tool belts strapped around their waists. On their heads they sported bright orange, plastic hardhats with Tree Experts spelled in black letters above the brims. Each shouldered a twelve-foot pole with a hooked clipper on one end attached to a rope tied to the other. The poles lightly waved in the gentle breeze, balanced perfectly by the men unthinkingly after long practice.

One of them, short and stocky, with a broad mustache and a three-day beard, stepped forward. "You are Luis," he said in Spanish, "the great runner."

Luis replied, "I run."

"And look, Matthew," the woodsman said switching to English, "the other one is Blondie!"

Three more men emerged from the trees, wearing the same clothes and gear.

"Hey, hombres, two of the greatest runners on the strips!"

They all grinned at the two runners, shifting awkwardly from leg to leg.

"¿Cómo están ustedes?" said Blondie. He continued in English, "What you fellows doin' out here?"

Apparently, the men's foreman, the short one with the mustache replied, "We are arborists working for the league. We care for the trees. Trim them back, cut down saplings, check for fungus y otro diseases, bring down any who are dying or dead."

"Really? There are that many big trees left here?"

The foreman shrugged, "Maybe a hundred from each of the finish lines. We travel pretty much. We don't get to see the big fútbol stars mucho." He grinned widely again as the others moved their heads up and down agreeing.

"You go see your familias?" Luis asked quietly.

The smiles disappeared. "Not many times. Christmas, Thanksgiving, Fourth of July. We work a lot, but our families have money to live."

The other men nodded again, though solemnly. A radical mix of features, they looked as though they had been brought together from the four corners of the world.

"But, to see Luis and Blondie together on the same day, eso es increíble!" the foreman said, and everyone laughed, beaming open pleasure at the event. "Are you running against each other, today? The Pig-Dogs play the Wharf Rats, increíble!"

Luis said, shaking his head, "Yes, but Blondie no longer runs with the Dogs. He is a Rat now."

The foreman's mouth dropped open, followed by his crew. "No! You will massacre the Dogs!" He turned his head back to the others, "We must bet! Una gran talá!"

178

Luis screwed up his mouth, "Maybe that is not a good idea, maybe."

Appearing almost shocked, the foreman said, "But, you will win! The Wharf Rats will win the match!"

The runners smiled, waved, and continued jogging back to the starting line. Luis said, "You surprise me that you know Español."

Blondie smirked, "I can see that, pale as I am. You knock around the league long enough, you pick up a little bit of all kinds of lingos."

Luis pressed his lips together in a small smile, knowing the truth of that.

"All right, Rats, get youselfs in order, we start in five."

Luděk Jezek, called the Hedgehog, a literal translation of his surname, filled space massively. Weighing in at 150 kilos of bone and muscle held together by a full-body pelt of black hair, eyes burning like coals, the Wharf Rats center naturally served as their captain. The other members of the seven-man liners appeared to be three-quarter-size clones of Jezek, all together one of the most formidable frontlines in the MSL. Jezek rapped his thigh with a disóla, an ancient Native American ceremonial stick that he wielded like a riding crop.

"Lightfoot, you're point."

The tall Black man nodded.

"Wiland and Bonijic, twin backs. Gustav, rover. The rest know your spots," Jezek said over his shoulder to the front liners. "We won the honors, so here's the opener. Lightfoot pivot, fake to Bonijic, hand off to Wiland crossing right. Liners, slide block left, JonBalliet pull and trap right. And off you go," he said, looking at Luis and Blondie, "straight to east Jersey, the rest of us in tow. Questions?"

Luis cursed silently as he donned his scrum cap. Without missing a beat Jelek had dubbed Blondie the Number One already. Luis was the diversion who would draw every Pig-Dog defensive liner and backer to him, hoping to snap his spine. He could be out of the race on the very first play with everything he owned riding on his winning. "Dióse damano, diose damiyé," he uttered. God our Father, God our Mother.

As he tied his cap straps tight, he tried to calm himself. The play call was a good one, with six of the front liners driving left, none of the Dogs would expect a run right. At left-end liner, though, JonBalliet could fly and he was a superb crasher. Pulling all the way right could spring Blondie on the very first play and he would be hard to catch. Luis hated to admit it, but Blondie could run. He could win, but what good would it do if Luis was crushed at the very same time? To survive, he had to elude the Pig-Dog liners on the very first play.

The lead ref-drone above sounded the ready signal. The two teams began to assemble at the designated starting line. At this section of I-80, the ground sloped gently over rolling rises interspersed with small pockets of wildflowers and some ornamental bushes and trees, dogwoods mostly. Surrounding the strip, scrub brush and gaunt prickly trees originally common to desert landscapes grew on abandoned farmland. A few tall oaks spotted the ground, their deep root systems still supporting their scrawny silhouettes. The players often joked about the irony of the meticulously maintained foliage throughout the median strips that stood in stark contrast to the blasted wastelands surrounding them. The league spent a fortune every year nurturing the pristine flora on the strips as it had existed naturally a century ago. Massive infusions of topsoil, applications of fertilizer on an industrial scale, megatons of fresh water precipitated by immense air tankers, even the use of vast cooling apparatuses during the breathless summers at unimaginable cost created the artificial parklands beloved by strip-ball fans. The vast sums of money came from VR casts, though the ever-soaring costs constantly compromised the league's profit margins. Or so they told the players, joked the men grunting on the strips. Enjoy sleeping on the soft, lush grass, they'd laugh, it could cost you a year's pay.

The two teams' liners faced off. Luis moved behind his while Lightfoot crouched low behind Jezek at the center point. Gustav flanked on the right, ready to sprint ahead to cut down any Pig-Dog chase that he could. Blondie lined up parallel to Luis on his right.

Lightfoot called the signal and launched the white oval ball back between his legs. Luis bolted hard left, doubling over for the fake handoff straight into two water buffalos the Pig-Dogs mistakenly called liners. As they slammed into him, Luis fell back only to be hit hard again by JonBalliet, cut off by the Dogs' penetration. Luis felt all air punched out of his chest from the liners beartrap coming together.

Wheezing and coughing, Luis wandered back to the Rats huddled around Jezek, who called the play–sweep right. The team set up, Jezek flipped the ball to Lightfoot who pitched it wide to Blondie. Sucking air, Luis led around the end smack into the Rats' blockers rear ends, all pushed back on top of him by the Dogs. Stifled again beneath 1,000 kilos of beef, Luis vaguely heard Jezek roaring a string of curses. When the heavyweights pulled themselves off Luis, he sat up to catch his breath again. A ref-drone hovered above the scrimmage spot beaming a laser directional the opposite way. Hit by two Pig-Dog crashers, Blondie had fumbled the ball.

"For the love of love, Blondie," Jezek yelled, "what the fuck?"

The Pig-Dogs began the ball powering west toward their finish line 256 klicks away. They ran hard-hitting dives with their big backs, pushing powerfully forward in short, straight-ahead bursts, five to ten meters at a time. Ten hours later, they had forced the Wharf Rats back up the slope all the way to Yarnell, almost 25 full kilometers. Even if they couldn't mount a single breakaway, at this rate the Pig-Dogs could reach the Ohio finish line in less than the allotted two weeks. Maybe sooner, thought Luis, if they could spring one of their runners.

They did execute one breakaway, though Luis and Gustav managed to run the Dog down after just two klicks. The Pig-Dog runners were big, strong, and quick, but not long-way fast. An average pursuit team could catch them, and the Rats' chasers were far better than average. Still, the Pig-Dogs moved the ball relentlessly. It was early, Luis said to himself, calm down. Experience told him that a lot of racing lay ahead, and the Wharf Rats excelled on defense. But thoughts kept creeping into his mind. He didn't want a tie, no one wanted a tie. The match had to go the way he wanted, the way he needed it to go.

"Maybe we should do a drop," Gustav said. A long, wiry player

181

with soulful eyes, he looked pensive after his suggestion. They sat around a portable inductor, warming up their meals before turning in for the night.

"What good would that do?" Jezek barked. "We supposed to let them through hoping to drop them? If we miss, they're off running away. They could cover a lot of ground and we'd be done before you eyes wink."

Not known for his mastery of the game, Gustav shrugged, his mustache lifting with his shoulders. "We could set an ambush."

Somewhat surprised, Luis thought it could be a good idea. Except the Pig-Dogs would expect just that, especially when they noticed at first line-up that the Wharf-Rats were short two players, sure evidence the Rats had dropped them somewhere ahead. Figuring that out, the Dogs would go harder with the power plays. Every tactic, every play had been invented long ago. Execution was the key, difficult with a key player being new.

"Let's save that stratagem for later," JonBalliet said to Gustav. Looking more like a crasher than a liner, JonBalliet spent his down time sculpting his body into the shape of a Viking god. He surprised with his long-muscled strength and sudden speed, a unique advantage in the game. But JonBalliet didn't fight, he played, and part of his aura came from his charm. He encouraged everyone on the team no matter who it was, no matter how lowly. Everyone played better because of him.

Sure enough, the next morning, JonBalliet separated the Pig-Dogs from the ball on the very first play. In one fluid motion, he grabbed and tossed the lead liner headfirst at the runner's arm. The ball popped loose and JonBalliet pounced on it amid the roaring howls of his teammates.

The Rats bunched together for Jezek to call their next play on offense.

"All right," Jezek said, "we stick to what we know. Run the ball at 'em inside and out. Push 'em outta the way and when they're rocking back, we trip 'em with a change-up."

Luis sighed. The same. That meant he'd be hammered again by

182

liners, again and again. He wondered if he'd lose some teeth. He didn't wear a mouthpiece, he couldn't stand them. Up until now it'd been no big deal, since he'd been the prime runner, eluding rather than hitting. Now, he was either the lead blocker or the bait. Sooner or later one of those Pig forearms was bound to smash into his face. His pretty looks would be ravaged, he laughed to himself ruefully, and Marie would be horrified. He wasn't sure how many of these plays he could stand, actually stand. Then, Jezek would sub him out without a pang and his plan to win it all would be out, too.

"Inside right power rush," Jezek said.

The Pig-Dogs piled them up. Luis gasped for breath beneath the stack of heavy bodies. Almost panicky, he gulped as much air as he could as the players slowly peeled off him, one by one.

"Sweep left," Jezek called next. Luis was knocked head over heels, the ground, the sky, the ground, and down. He felt bruised all over.

The Rats couldn't move the ball a single centimeter.

"Dam-nit!" bellowed Jezek. He leaned over in front of the team gathered around him two deep. "Okay, run the trap play left."

Luis staggered into position. Abruptly, Blondie quick-stepped over to Luis. "Dodge them Luis," he rasped, "bust out as fast you can and follow me tight."

Blondie moved back to his position and looked straight ahead, ready for the start.

Luis wasn't sure what Blondie had said or that it meant all that much. Of course he would do his best to evade the defensive liners, his physical wellbeing depended on it. The part about staying close to Blondie was nothing new; after setting an initial block, he was supposed to trail the team's primary ball runner. None of it mattered since he didn't have any time to think about it now.

The ref-drone blasted the starting klaxon and the players blurred in motion. Lightfoot feinted the oval white ball to Luis bursting left, just missing JonBalliet flashing opposite him into a Pig-Dog trailer. Amid smashing, thudding bodies, Luis spied two liners and a crasher bearing down. He jab-stepped away from one, bound up on the second's back, and dove beneath the crasher's outstretched arms. Luis barrel-rolled upright behind the Wharf Rat and Pig-Dog liners locked in mayhem.

He took off as fast as he could without looking back. Gustav had knocked one chaser down, now already back up and closing on Blondie, who seemed to be angling near to the highway's edge. The other Pig-Dog chaser drew even closer. The situation looked bad.

Luis accelerated toward the three men dodging each other. He reached Blondie on the verge of being pinned out of bounds by one chaser. If so, the Rats would turn the ball over. Luis braced himself to hit the Pig-Dog at the back of the knees when Blondie abruptly reversed and threw himself back into the chaser while flipping the ball behind his head. Reflexively, Luis snatched it out of the air as Blondie yelled, "Go, Luis, go!"

Luis instantly veered away from the collision toward the open strip. He glanced back to see Blondie bounce up and crash into the second Pig-Dog chaser. Luis faced straight ahead and ran fast into space.

An hour later, Luis checked behind him again without seeing anyone to his rear. Recruiters first noticed his sprint speed many years ago, but it was his remarkable marathon pace and stamina that crowned him as the best ball-runner in league history. That's when he left most chasers far behind. Like the hare outpacing the tortoise, once out of sight he usually stopped an hour or so later for a rest break. Unlike the careless hare, however, twenty minutes of recharging and Luis would be off again, putting more ground between himself and the hunters. When nightfall darkened the path, he'd find a place to sleep until dawn.

Away from everything in the dark, no one moved. The league drones flew overhead, black-ops surveilling for floaters. The floaters had lived their entire lives hunted by drones. If the drones spotted anyone on the ground, the floaters knew how to work the edges before the drones could drop. A lot of people disappeared that way, a lot of runners. But few floaters lurked these days, fast disappearing themselves in the harsh outlands. No, the big threat at night came from members of the opposing team. If they found a ball-runner in the dark, they would decommission him, guaranteeing their team at least a tie. If that happened, their opponents not only lost the chance to win, they most likely lost a prime runner to a long recuperation, sometimes for good.

Luis shook loose from that thinking. If he took care, he'd have no problem with night chasers. He never had in the past.

A black bug appeared on the horizon behind him. Luis perked up like meerkats he'd seen in vintage VR casts. Pig-Dog chasers? He'd left them far behind to deal with Blondie. Had they knocked him out so soon?

The creature in the distance grew limbs, long legs and arms. Luis gathered his gear and grabbed the ball resting near a bed of wild mustard, brilliant, yellow blooms draped over their disjointed green stalks. He moved to kneel. The figure morphed as it closed in, tapping forward in a quick easy pace, coloring starting to show.

Luis rose to his feet. He could see skin, now, white, and the familiar uniform, all superseded by the bowl of flaxen hair tossing back and forth.

Blondie trotted up the low rise of grass toward Luis, flashing a broad grin when he saw the small, brown figure in front of him.

"Luis!" he laughed as he pulled up.

"Blondie," replied Luis, following with, "Blondie. Wils."

Still smiling, squinting in the sunlight, the lean runner said, "Blondie's good enough." He dropped his shoulders in a shrug, "I'm known worldwide as Blondie."

Luis frowned and said, "What do you like?"

"Whatever, I respond to 'em all. Wils, Wiland, Blondie, it's all the same to me."

Luis shrugged, "Blondie, then."

"Sure."

They sat down in the green grass, facing each other. Blondie loosened the drawstring on his go-pouch. He pulled out a solar laser lighter and fired it up to warm his power drink.

"I got the angle on them quick and dusted them right off.," he said between sips. "They lost sight of me after about twenty minutes, my sign to downshift to cruise control."

Luis nodded. He knew exactly what Blondie had done, he'd watched it over and over again on past VR casts. He'd done it countless times himself.

"Yeah, I learned it from watching you. You know, you invented most of these moves."

Luis smiled slightly, laughing inside as he thought of all the mountain runners back home who had dodged the same way for centuries, maybe millennia.

"I calculate we have an hour on them right now. I thought it'd be less, but you do motor, Luis. It's okay for me to call you Luis, right?"

Luis shrugged. "You can call me Brownie," he deadpanned. Blondie paused, then burst into laughter. "How 'bout Señor Brownie, out of respect?"

"Or Gobernador Brownie. I like that. That show respect."

"Gobernador Brownie. Not Tarahumara?"

"No," Luis said. "That's not here. That place, it no longer is."

"Oh," said Blondie deferentially, "Then, Señor Gobernador Brownie."

"Just call me Luis."

Luis pulled at the back of his jersey, gradually working a hood out past his H^{2}O nozzle. He placed the ball firmly inside the hood, dangling it over his back. He stood up and said, "Time to run, now."

They covered ground like riding a conveyor belt. The klicks melted beneath their feet as though they were training on the perfect consistency of a sandy beach. Most of the time, they ran on a cushion of grass over a soft, firm loam. They passed glorious patches of magnificently hued flowers and elegant ornamental bushes while loping down into hollows. Actual trees grew there, mostly oaks, elms, and maples, massive specimens harkening back to ancient times. No one could take them down because of the old climate-control prohibitions. So, they soared fully mature and hoary, perhaps the last on the continent to reach such heights. Luis sought them out as his bedding of choice on the strips, hiding places out of sight from threats in open space. He made note of them wherever he raced. Their relative

186

scarcity on strips sometimes moved Luis to double back at the end of a day's running to a grove he'd spotted earlier. For a night's uninterrupted slumber, he was willing to risk narrowing the gap between himself and the chasers. He calculated how much time he'd need in the morning to lengthen his lead again, and so far, he had figured right.

"Hey, man, look at them tall boys," Blondie said. "I wonder if the tree experts will be cleaning up on them soon."

"Sooner or later," Luis said.

"Yeah, not a bad gig. Easier than getting your head punched in by the Pig-Dogs."

Luis exhaled, "These times, every job is hard."

"That is definitely so," Blondie said.

They paced along for a time silently.

"I like to sleep in them."

Blondie turned his head to Luis. "Really? They're big, man. Aren't you afraid you'll fall out?"

Luis shrugged, "I find a good size limb, a good fork. I never fall so far."

"Huh," said Blondie. "But, what if you're up one and chasers come to the bottom? You'd be cornered like a rat."

Luis shook his head, "I down and gone before. They don't catch me yet."

"Really?" Blondie said.

Luis nodded. He paused, then murmured, "Trees make me feel safe sometimes. Like being in the arms of the Earth Mother."

"No kidding?" Blondie pursed his lips, considering. "I can see that."

"This must be Fishing Creek," said Blondie, looking ahead. "We're standing on the old road."

Luis peered over at the water flowing amid a scraggily border of trees. He knew it was Fishing Creek, but he asked, "How you know what it is?"

"I did my homework," Blondie replied, gazing at a thumbnail e-pad. "Dug up some old maps, scanned them so I could see the lay of the land. Did you know we're looking at crossing some 31 bridges?"

"Only when I run here other times," Luis said dryly.

"Right, three of them go over streams twice. That kind of sucks. Most of those we can wade through. Of course, the big rivers, they're another story. West Susquehanna, the Susquehanna, the Delaware. Then's when it gets pretty dicey."

Taking his turn with the ball, Blondie thrust it into his shirt's hood. After filling their H^2O reservoirs, they lifted their ration packets and go-pouches above their heads and started across, stepping on flat stones spanning the wide, shallow rivulet. As they walked, Blondie kept up the flow of his one-way conversation, the ball bouncing up and down on his back.

"Yep, before we get to the Promised Land, we have to pass through 83 intersections including 23 roads over head, plus 14 cloverleafs, all good for drops and being jumped. You got your Mount Rainsares Road, Heckman's Gap, Mill Street near Loganton, a cloverleaf at Lightstreet Road, the Columbia Boulevard and 3rd Street cloverleaf, then a bunch of overpasses: Red Rock Road, Old Turnpike, Oley Valley. We have to run quickstep beneath them, kick in the hydrogen boosters."

When night fell, the ref-drone swooped down and sounded the horn to end the day's competition. As it hovered above, two ration units dropped below the precisely rotating blades and floated to the ground. Luis and Blondie picked them up and headed over to the edge of the highway. They pulled open the packets, unloaded them, and used the empty receptacles as seat cushions on old buckled pieces of macadam punctuating the highway's inside shoulders. They opened their beverages, fruit-flavored power drinks. Other containers yielded chicken sandwiches on toast laden with fresh tomatoes, lettuce, and vegetable bacon. The two famished runners tucked into their modest dinners, both silent as they focused on their meals. Once finished, Blondie munched on an apple and Luis chewed slowly on a chocolate grain bar.

Luis stretched out in front of the shoulder slags, resting on one

188

elbow while he savored his dessert. He glanced up at Blondie.

"You married, Blondie? Got kids?"

Blondie shook his head, "Nah. Why bother? Playing in this league, there's barely time to meet anyone for real. I see a few sweethearts I know here and there, but it's not fair to let any think there's a future together." He squinted at Luis. "But, you, Señor Bonijic, you have a wife, yes? Of course, everyone knows it. You and your beautiful trophy wife are featured everywhere on the holo people casts. That's right, yes?"

Luis shook his head, "She not a trophy, Blondie, she a cage match."

Blondie nodded, "I see, one you need to win every day."

Luis leaned his head over a little, shrugging, "Más o menos."

"And no kids."

Luis's mouth turned down a bit, "Not in Rio. Not in la ranchería." His mind whirled around to Margara again, wondering again, what if?

Blondie sat hunched over, his arms resting on his knees. "I wish I had kids."

Luis shook his head briskly. "You just said you don't want to be married, and you want kids?"

The long, lean runner scrunched his cheekbones, his teeth set as he tried to field the question. "Yeah, I know, but I come from a big family, nine of us. I was smack in the middle, and it was hard for my folks gettin' by. My pops flew the coop when I was ten, he just couldn't do it anymore. We lost two on the way, my older sister Ella from the pox, and baby Noah got flattened by a log. Momma worked all the time. We weren't skinny, we just never got enough to eat. When we did, it didn't stick to our bones." He flashed a smile, "We're all string beans in my family."

He closed up a bit as he said, "Still. They're my best friends. We had a good time before we all went into the wind. Some of us touch base now and then. But, I miss when we were kids and all together. So …."

Luis nodded, "My family is like that. Not so many, but close."

Blondie waited for Luis to say more. Then, he murmured, "So, you keep in touch, too?"

"Me? I'm a big football star living in Rio, man."

Luis rolled over to fall asleep.

Dawn broke, and the two men snapped to attention, staying low as they surveyed the dark horizon behind them. Nothing moved. No bird calls, no rustling of squirrels, not one washboard rubbing of a cricket's legs.

They look at each other silently, wondering about the stillness around them. Blondie twisted around and raised his eyes west again. He slipped down and whispered, "I don't see anybody."

Luis said, "The creatures, they all maybe gone from here."

Blondie nodded. The world grew evermore sparse even in the league's well-tended strip gardens. He searched around their immediate space until he saw the two drone supply packets a meter away propped against an evergreen bush. He reached for them, shaking his head.

"How the heck they get 'em here without stirring us up I'll never know."

Luis said, "It's easy to think we are alone out here, forget a half a billion eyes on us all over everywhere."

Blondie tossed Luis a ration packet, "Sure. And, on that note, I'm gonna give 'em all a special treat." He stood up, stepped over to the bush and started pissing at the base of the trunk. "Hope it survives this."

When he came back, he found Luis sitting cross-legged, already munching on a protein bar.

"Hey," Blondie said, pointing at Luis's feet, "where'd you get those?"

Instead of team issued field shoes, Luis wore sandals made of leather on top and old tire treads on the bottom. Leather straps secured them to his feet. He shrugged, "A friend put them here. Off-season, he hide many pairs in places I probably stop to sleep." Seeing Blondie's confusion, he said, "We run in these at home. Much better for long ways."

"And the league doesn't bitch?" asked Blondie.

"Not if I run fast," Luis said. He took a swallow of fortified water and casually raised his finger to point past Blondie. "Here they are. We should run."

Blondie whipped around and saw the two Pig-Dog chasers 300 meters away and closing fast. "Shit."

He gathered up his ration packet, tossing out everything but the protein bars and the electrolytes while Luis followed suit. Luis stuffed the white ball in his hood.

"Keep my pace," he said as he started out at a trot. "We lose them in a couple hours."

They ran.

III.

The landscape seemed to pass them like old freighters at sea steaming the opposite way. Though mindful of the illusion, it still seemed real as they padded down the strip dipping low between the concrete lanes or up the steep hillsides. Wild fields below sparse mountain tree lines flowed by. The strip morphed into a narrow pathway between red rock ridges first carved out for railroad beds. The interstate had supplanted the rails only to be abandoned itself later on. Even so, the two runners struggling up the steep incline stared in awe at the massive escarpment sheered away above.

At the outset the next morning, Luis admonished Blondie that they'd covered only 40 kilometers or so the first day. He insisted that they had to clock more klicks daily to outdistance the Pig-Dog chasers. Blondie pushed himself to stay with Luis, both silenced by their effort except for infrequent water and protein breaks. In late afternoon, the strip dipped down between the I-80 lanes to a narrow, perpendicular country road. They stopped at the top of the hill.

"I believe it's the White Deer Pike," said Blondie, looking at his map. "We're not too far from the first big river crossing, the West Susquehanna."

Luis recognized the spot but didn't bother saying anything. In the distance, they saw rundown gray houses with collapsed roofs standing

191

next to piles of old boards and bricks on wasted ground. A few rusted vehicles occupied some of the driveways. Aside from other traces of worn out odds and ends left behind, they observed nothing, no movement that might signal floaters still in the area.

"Man, there isn't much to look at, is there."

"This can't surprise you," Luis said. "You see the same out West, no?"

"If you mean I didn't see anything out there either, you're right," said Blondie. "I guess it seems strange to see some green around here, even just a little, and water too without a soul in sight."

Luis frowned, "They gone a long time now, except for the floaters. You think this is strange, wait to see the river. The whole town is dead."

They passed through Milton, wary at some crossroads and a cloverleaf, but without incident. Abandoned buildings of every size and shape made up the town, some looking as though they were waiting for their occupants to return from lunch. Others appeared fully dilapidated, falling in on themselves, a few with scraggily vegetation sprouting from their ruins. At the edge of town, the West Susquehanna rolled by the runners. They stood at one end beneath the two, 500-meter-long highway spans over the river.

"How we gonna get across?" Blondie asked, looking down at the water.

Luis shrugged. "We swim or float on some planks. We could wait until dark, sprint across on top."

"Yeah, but what if the ref-drones catch us, or the spy sats see us?"

"It is possible," Luis said. "Then, the penalty will give the Dog chasers a nice, long drop close to us. But that gonna happen anyway, sooner or later. No matter, we must run away fast anyway. It still is okay, the ref-drones don't send runners back over bridges or anything like that."

That evening, they ate the meal flown to them by the drone, satisfied both by the food and knowing that they had run 64 kilometers that day. They were on track and likely well ahead of the chasers. If they could keep up their pace, there would be no catching them. Luis

192

felt buoyed by the thought, feeling almost warm in the cool summer night.

"Gobernador Brownie," said Blondie.

"Sí."

"You believe in God? I mean, do you have religious feelings?"

Luis rolled his eyes to himself. "Man, Blondie, you are not afraid to ask anything," he said, still in a good mood.

"Well, we got to pass the time somehow."

"Sure, but religion? Dios."

"Yeah, sure. Why not?"

"You believe in God?"

"Sort of. It's hard to look around you and not believe something, some other big character is responsible for all the things we see. Think about butterflies, how small they are, really tiny, yet they got veins and arteries just like us. Nervous systems, maybe even brains. They gotta come from somewhere, and we sure know that human beings ain't up to the job. That could be proof."

"So, you believe in God," Luis followed.

"Maybe I do," Blondie replied, slightly guarded. "Even if I do believe in God, I don't think it has anything to do with us."

"Huh," said Luis.

A moment passed by. Blondie said, "So, what about you?"

Luis stretched his arms. "My people, we believe in old ways and new. Jesus, his mama Maria, El Diablo, all those things. It is not so strange to see two crosses on the patio."

"Two? Not three?" asked Blondie.

"No, crosses honor old gods—héna diose damano, that God our Father, héna diose damiyé, that God our Mother. The Great Father Onorúgame, the Sun, the Great Mother Íyerugame, the Moon. Baisá wanú namó dervegátu, three planes of heaven above. Our soul, the uvigála, lives in the heart, the surála. When one sleeps, his soul goes out to work for him. The soul's adventures are our dreams. Death is opposite to the way of living."

"And the devil?"

"Whirlpool people—evil, fat, and pig-like. A rainbow is a bad

193

omen, a sign of evil people from underground, they eat our blood and we don't know it. Sickness caused by the soul when it leaves its house in the heart to wander."

"Okay, this is confusing. I thought you just said that souls make up your dreams. They're all nightmares, then?"

Luis shrugged in the dark. "Sometimes, when there's a rainbow. A double rainbow is a good thing, Onorúgame on top, Íyerugame below him."

"Jesus," Blondie uttered, "I thought us Christians were crazy."

Luis replied, "All religions are crazy, but all speak some truth. When a curandero performs a cure in our ranchería," Luis went on, "he uses a rosary and a crucifix. He adds the beads' strength to his own."

A few moments of quiet passed. At length, Blondie asked, "So, in your ceremonies, do you use peyote?"

Luis laughed to himself. "Hikuli? No, other peoples do. We use bakánawa, a cactus like a small ball. Boil it, it is much more powerful than hikuli—peyote. We use it in dances before we run the dalahípu, before the three festivals of life. Rain, green and corn, harvest and death. We drink a lot of our beer, tesquino, too, but only at fiestas."

"My head's spinning," said Blondie. "Weirder and weirder. Wish I'd never asked," he mumbled, rolling over to sleep.

Luis cupped his hands behind his head, remembering the matachines, their dances of drama. He listened to the small fiddles made of jaranas plucked by the viejitos, and the strumming of upright earth bows fixed in their holes in the ground. The curandero uttered three prayers as the women crossed the dance space three times. Luis could see them vividly, holding hands, leaping counterclockwise in circles, stomping left foot to right. He slept then, in the dream that dreamed him.

Rain poured down the next morning, unseasonably cold, soaking them to the bone. Blondie arose and tugged his shirt off to twist and wring the water out. Luis thought his lean running mate acted futilely until he saw him spread the shirt out and tuck it into the waistband of his shorts. Luis followed suit.

194

The ref-drone had flown down already, dropping off their rations for the day. The unusual rainfall, completely unexpected, had drenched their ration packets as well, forcing the men to eat soggy protein bars and cold, wet cereal. They gulped them down, swallowed the energy drinks, and started on their way, consoling themselves with the thought that the Pig-Dog chasers felt the same misery.

"Maybe it'll let up down the strip," Blondie said.

The rain did not diminish, intensifying instead to a continuous, stinging assault, minute by minute, hour by hour. They ran through it as best they could, though they knew that soggy depressions and temporary ponds of deep, standing water slowed them down to a virtual crawl. Still, they ran, silently to save strength. They felt cold, too, from the darkness of the deep purple sky blocking all sunlight and warmth.

"We might as well be running at night," huffed Blondie.

Luis didn't respond.

After slogging for four hours, they stopped to rest. Luis searched through his ration packet for something to eat and pulled out an Italian sandwich that fell apart in his hands. He glanced up to see Blondie dropping the remains of his grain-roll on the ground, his expression utterly abject.

They drained enriched chocolate power drinks, stood up, and set out again.

Two hours later they reached the Buckhorn cloverleaf just outside of Bloomsburg. Without a word, they staggered beneath one of the curving ramps and sat down, hunched over their bent legs, dangling their arms across their knees.

"Thirty-five klicks," muttered Luis, "not enough. We eat, sleep, get up and run more tomorrow."

Blondie stared at Luis. "You mean, if it don't keep on raining."

Luis grunted.

The rain fell incessantly around them as they curled up into balls to sleep.

"Get the fuck up, boys."

Luis heard the words barked at the same time he felt blinding pain from a blow across his legs. He pulled up instinctively while hearing an agonized cry from Blondie. Wide awake now, Luis saw a shadow figure above him shining a laser lighter right into his eyes. He cupped his hand over his brow to see a thick length of wood held menacingly in the man's other hand. The wood looked to be a dead branch, probably lifted off the ground from a nearby tree. Next to him, another dark figure holding a flashlight and brandishing a club loomed over Blondie. Blondie held his left leg close to his breast.

"Time for you lads to pack it in," said the man looming above Luis. He recognized him then, Bert Daday, premier chaser for the Pig-Dogs. Next to him stood Ibram Abrebe with his club.

"How did you get here?" stuttered Blondie.

"Don't matter, does it? We're just here," laughed Daday, a big red-haired man with a florid face covered by freckles. "Now, you know what we want. Hand it over, or by God we'll break both your knees."

Blondie clutched his legs tight to his chest.

"C'mon with it," Abrebe said, his words shaped by his Ethiopian homeland. He brandished the makeshift cudgel over Blondie, rotating it in menacing circles.

Blondie whipped his head back and forth between Luis and Abrebe, his eyes wide with alarm.

"Give it to them," Luis said.

Blondie reached behind his head and pulled the white ball out of his hood. Abrebe snapped it out of his hands. He propped his club against one leg and stuffed the ball into his shirt's hood. He picked up his club again, causing Blondie to flinch.

"You got the ball, take off," said Luis.

Smiling slowly, Daday said, "We're not finished yet. Let's have the footwear."

Luis glanced at Blondie and nodded. Blondie pulled off his shoes and tossed them at Abrebe. The lean dark runner stooped down and tied the shoes together. Standing again, he looped them over his shoulder.

"Now you, Gobernador."

196

Luis slipped out of his sandals and threw them at Daday's feet. Daday leaned over and picked them up.

"What the hell are these?" he said.

"Zapatas so you eat my dust," Luis said.

Daday smirked, "Sure. Not this time, though." He gathered them up and stuffed them in his waistband. "One more thing."

He looked around at the overhanging highway and down at the base. "There they are."

Daday pointed, and Abrebe walked over to the edge of the concrete where it met the ground. He reached down and pulled up two packets left by the ref-drone just before morning. He shouldered them and strolled back to Daday.

"Good. We'll be extra hungry once we put some klicks between us and you," Daday said. He looked at Abrebe and nodded. Without warning they both smashed their clubs down at Blondie and Luis's legs. The two men squirmed back out of the way, desperate to avoid another blow.

"Take those as a warning. Don' get any ideas about coming after us anytime soon. You got the whole morning to feel better."

Daday turned heel and trotted off, Abrebe right behind him, running west back into the dark, leaving the slowly graying sky behind.

"How did they get here?" Blondie moaned, "Running in the night?"

Luis shook his head, "Too slow. Against the rules, too."

"Well, then, how?" Blondie wondered. "It must have been a drop."

Luis nodded, "True. That is illegal at night also."

"And they beat the shit out of us with clubs. That can't be right."

"Also illegal. Hard to see in the dark, though. Clouds maybe block the old sat eyes. They wait until the ref-drone come, too, before they attacked. What it take, ten minutes?"

"How can they get away with this?"

Luis grimaced, "They have the ball. That is all that matters. We were running away with the race. Maybe the league look the other way to get fans more interest."

Blondie sighed. "So, now what do we do?"

Luis twisted his mouth almost into a snarl, his hands clenched tight.

After a moment staring at nothing, Blondie said, "Maybe we should call in for a drop."

Luis quickly shook his head, "No, no, we cannot. Zelek will be very mad we lost the ball and don't know where the Pig-Dogs run. He will drop us back with the rest of the team to be safe, to start over. We do this, we run out of time. The game is another tie."

What he said was true, Luis knew, that calling in a drop would infuriate Zelek. But, also, he might bench Luis and Blondie and put in their backups. If so, the Rats could not win. Luis would lose his talá.

"How your legs feel?"

Blondie flexed them both. "They're beat up black and blue pretty bad." Seeing Luis's expression, he went on, "I can still run."

"Okay. We go now after them hard. We catch them, take the ball, and run back."

"You're kidding," Blondie said, startled by Luis's intensity. "How're we gonna do that? We don't have any shoes."

"We make shoes for you from our scrum caps, shirts, shorts. I can run barefoot."

"But we'll never catch them," Blondie said, "They're way out front even now."

"No matter. We must try."

"That's good, but how do we find them?"

Luis rubbed his jaw. "There are only so many places they can go before dark."

Blondie murmured, "Places we've already passed." He paused, then looked at Luis. "Daday's lazy. He's always ready to break early to eat and sleep, especially when he thinks he's ahead."

Luis looked skeptical. "You sure?"

"Absolutely! I swear, every guy on the team calls him out for dogging it. He just laughs them off. Nobody does anything, they all think he's kind of a psycho."

"Okay." Luis thought out loud, "We run hard now, slow down near dark, move in quiet."

"Okay, when we find them, how are we going to get the ball back?"

Luis replied, "They surprise us. We surprise them."

"With what? Daday's big and crazy and Abrebe's mean as a snake."

"This time we have the clubs."

Blondie tightened his face into a wince. "With just clubs, I don't like our chances."

"So, what do we do?" Luis asked almost petulantly.

Blondie shrugged. They lapsed into silence for a moment, Luis becoming more agitated as time went by. Then, Blondie lifted his head.

"Just before we pulled up to camp last night, I saw a sign on the ramp for Mall Boulevard heading up to the crossover. There must be some old stores around here, not too far away. They're probably wrecked or cleaned out by floaters, but maybe we could check them out, see if there's anything there we can use. You know, a little more clout than a tree branch."

Luis said nothing.

"Look," Blondie said, "it's a long shot. But how far out do you think Daday and his partner will go? You have an idea, right?"

"If Daday runs slow for half a day, they get out fifteen, maybe twenty klicks."

"So, we could catch up to them in two, maybe three hours easy. That's plenty of time for us to hunt around a while, see what we can find. We'll have to be careful, especially now. Lots of floaters out there, probably."

"They always watch the strips," Luis said.

"Okay," said Blondie, stretching out the word. "And," he said, "we can't let the ref-drones or spy sats spot us. If they see us way off the strip, they might eject us out altogether."

Luis said, "Probably not. They like action for their viewers, so maybe they will forgive us. But they will give more drops to the Pig-Dogs. If one of them is a squad drop, we lose for sure. Better to leave everything here."

"Yeah," Blondie said, "run buck naked in Buckhorn at daybreak."

Luis said, "It still cloudy. We might be okay."

"At least without our unis on the drones might think we're floaters

199

ourselves," Blondie said, now shorn of his shirt and shorts. "This should help us out, though," he said, holding up his laser lighter."

"How do you still have that?" Luis asked. "The Pig-Dogs took everything."

"They missed it. When we bed down, I always take it out of my go-pouch to keep it next to me at night. It'll help us poke around any old ruins we might find."

Luis grunted. "Better hope drones don't pick it up."

"Like you said, it's still cloudy."

Luis didn't respond. Instead, he said, "You shit yet?"

Blondie blinked. "Not yet. My body's holding on to all the fuel it can get."

"Try to squeeze some out to leave for DNA scopes, throw them off."

"I'll see what I can do," said Blondie wryly. "You do your part, too."

They set out up the ramp to the overpass, Blondie leading the way. He opened his eyes as wide as he could in the dim light, trying to save his bare feet from stepping on pebbles and pieces of aggregate peppering the crumbling road. When they returned to the strip, it would be much better even in shoes just made out of scrum caps. With this in mind, Blondie winced along silently. Luis followed him stone-faced, showing no signs of pain from his hardened feet.

At the top of the overpass, they headed south on a two-lane road. After a few minutes, they spotted a dilapidated building on a degraded macadam plot north of the road. A giant sign stretched above the ruined structure, its faded letters reading Sunshine Diner, and smaller ones below adding Breakfast All Day.

"I wish," Blondie said.

They padded on in the growing light, passing several other collapsed buildings until they came to a wide blacktop expanse. In the middle stood a half dozen or more interconnected buildings winding around in a U shape.

"This must be the mall. And look over there," Blondie said, pointing at a building centered opposite the U. Luis turned his head

200

and saw a two-story building, Murray's Field and Stream.

"That's it," said Blondie.

Luis nodded, and they quickly trotted over to the old store. The front doors hung wide apart, metal rectangles around large, open spaces where glass had been smashed out long ago. Luis tip-toed inside, moving to his left silently to stand still while his eyes adjusted to the dark. Blondie slipped in next to him.

"Think we can chance the lighter?" he whispered.

Luis held up his hand, then moved forward turning his head back and forth until he found a round piece of metal he could use as a club. He nodded, and Blondie flicked on the laser lighter. He picked up a piece of a broken two-by-four and used the laser to light one end. Once the flame blossomed, he handed the makeshift torch to Luis. Luis held it straight-armed out in front to survey the store, Blondie doing the same with the lighter.

The second floor had fallen in to form a towering pile of debris in the middle. They could see the edge of a broad stairway peeking out from the pile bottom. Other than that, they found nothing else.

"Picked clean," said Blondie. He glanced at Luis, "Let's go to the big ones across the ways."

The other side of the large, macadam lot fronted the inner curve of the U-shaped structure stretching around to its opposite leg of connected stores. Lowes Home Improvement stood at the far eastern end with Marshalls next to it in the complex center. On its right stretched a vast, dominating edifice topped by a huge sign, Walmart Supercenter, directly across from Murray's.

"There's our best chance," said Blondie pointing at the Walmart.

Luis dipped his head in agreement, and they loped across the buckled blacktop to the giant warehouse. The front doors were gone, leaving a wide-open hallway in the middle of the building. By this time, the sun had risen enough to cast the mall in enough light to allow them to peer inside for a considerable distance. Nothing moved.

Blondie relit Luis's torch and one of his own, a broken table leg. They stepped quickly through the hallway, separating from each other as they cast their eyes around opposite sides.

201

Unlike Murray's, the Walmart still housed a good number of items strewn across the floor. Luis looked closer at one pile, prodding it with the end of his makeshift club.

"This stuff is rotten," he said, "full of old rat shit."

"Check these out," Blondie replied. Luis turned to him and saw a pair of pink, high-heeled pumps in his hand. "Perfect for us," Blondie said. "We can cover some serious klicks in these. Great style, too."

Luis laughed. "Not much here."

They heard something move. Both crouched low and peered into the darkness deeper inside the store. Luis put his finger to his lips, dropped his firebrand on the floor, and quietly darted down the long hall. Angling from one side to the other, he reached the rear doorway, also wide open. His eyes had adjusted well enough for him to see as he scouted the floor. Finally, he pivoted to hurry back. On the way, he saw a light to his left illuminating a sign hanging from the ceiling, Workman Tools.

Luis clutched his metal club tightly in both hands and crept closer to the light. Blondie stood at a counter, moving his torch around. Luis huffed a sigh and stepped over. "What're you doing, man? I almost hit you. We gotta get out of here."

"Nothing but broken crap," said Blondie, holding a wooden hammer missing its metal head. "Not a knife or screwdriver in sight. Floaters must've cleaned everything out long ago."

"Blondie," Luis said, "don't you wonder how the hammer got broke?"

Blondie stared at the handle and dropped it. "Let's go."

"The back way's closer," said Luis. "Better to get outside quick and go around the building in the light."

They headed down another aisle cluttered with detritus but more direct to the rear exit. Luis led them, feeling his way in and out of the piles. One heap blocked the entire aisle. Rather than go around, Luis gingerly tested it with his foot. Before his weight could shift the mound, he bounced over and turned to wait for Blondie. Blondie straddled the pile causing it to slide away beneath him, splitting his legs wide apart. He fell sideways into a crossing aisle out of sight.

"Blondie!" shouted Luis, "You okay?"

"Yeah, yeah," Blondie muttered. "Just annoyed."

"Well, get up, man, we been here almost an hour, we gotta run."

"Just give me a minute."

Luis listened and watched as his lanky companion straightened his legs. Blondie flexed his head back and forth, then stopped.

"Hey," he said. "Look at this."

Blondie reached under the display counter and pulled out a crooked, black object. He sat up quickly and held it out in the light.

"Jesus Christ, get a load of this, Gobernador!"

He held the black article in front of him for Luis to see. It was a rifle, broken and missing its stock, a scope sticking across and out of its back. Its barrel and trigger seemed to be intact.

"Can you believe this?"

"It's broken," Luis said as Blondie rose to his feet.

"Sure, but maybe we can fix some sort of wood to it so that it can shoot."

"Shoot what?" said Luis.

"Well, maybe there're some bullets around here," Blondie said, his eyes cast down searching the floor around him.

"For what?" Luis said. "We cannot shoot Pig-Dogs. We lose the race and they put us in jail!"

"All right, but we can scare them with it. They beat us up, remember."

Luis rolled his eyes.

"Shit," said Blondie. He held up a long box.

Luis looked at it and read, "Daisy Powerline 880 Air Rifle, Black, with Scope."

"It's a toy," Blondie said, pointing up at a sign suspended over their heads, Toys. "A fucking toy." He dropped it on the floor. "I remember seeing these online at Christmas. My old man loved it, said he'd had one when he was nine. His old man had one when he was a kid, too." He sighed, "Let's get the hell out of here."

Not paying attention, Luis lifted the rifle off the floor. He held it up to his head and squinted. "This scope, it still works." He lowered the rifle, "The glass is not broken. It is not a toy."

Blondie stared at Luis, his mouth open. He reached to take the rifle from Luis and peered through the scope. "This is a thermal vision scope, solar powered." He lowered the Daisy and locked eyes with Luis. "For hunting at night, "he said, "even on a toy gun."

Luis said, "Bring it. It might help us to find Daday and Abrebe if we catch up with them."

"You mean when we catch up with them."

They ran west back over the ground they'd worked so hard to cover through the bludgeoning rain. Though still overcast, the clouds this time did not open up. Blondie wore crude covers made from their shirts, scrum caps, and Luis's shorts bound over his feet. Running on the grassy strip in Luis's footsteps, he managed to avoid cuts and abrasions. But the ties around the improvised trainers kept coming loose, slowing them down while he stopped to yank them tight.

Running only in his sitagola, Luis kept a steady pace ahead of Blondie, hiding from him the growing pain in his knees. He knew he could push through this day, though he worried about the toll it might take on him in those to come. His feet hurt some without the sandals, but not enough to slow him down. Retracing their path, they still managed to move more quickly than yesterday by avoiding the obstacles and dead ends that added time during their first run.

In midafternoon, Luis took note of two traffic lanes gradually beginning to slope up. He slowed down and said, "We must be close."

Blondie stutter stepped to a stop. They stood before a half-cloverleaf circling north below the interstate lanes. "The crossing over Continental Boulevard" Luis murmured.

"You think they're here?" asked Blondie.

"Beneath the overpass. We slip up on top, see if we can spot them."

"What if we don't find them?" Blondie said, his voice brittle.

Luis lifted his shoulders and let them drop. "Then, we keep running. Check Klondike Road, Narehood, Creek Road, any road passing under I-80 all the way back to the West Susquehanna. If we
204

don't find them by then, we call in a drop."

Blondie looked skeptical.

"But we will find them. Believe me."

They scurried up to the overpass above Continental Road and scrutinized the area around them with the Daisy rifle scope. By then, the clouds had disappeared, and though the air still carried a chill, they were bathed in sunshine. But the Pig-Dog runners were nowhere in sight, so they ran on.

"You know the spy sats will see us running off the strip on top of the overpasses."

"Can't be helped," replied Luis, "we need the ball."

An hour past noon, they spotted them, resting in the shade of the bridge over Klondike Road. Luis slipped down the grassy slope and silently slid close to them while Blondie watched overhead. Daday and Abrebe slept opposite each other, snoring almost in counterpoint.

Luis saw the ball tucked under Daday's head as a pillow. Between the sleeping men, he took note of the stolen ration packets. He craned his head up at Blondie peering down from the overpass and dipped his head.

"All right, assholes get your asses up!" Luis shouted.

Daday snapped up sitting, Abrebe close behind. The big redhead stared at Luis completely startled until he noticed that the small Wharf Rat runner stood before him empty-handed.

"Why you little brown shit, you have the balls to wake me up? What the fuck you gonna do now?"

Also surprised, Abrebe relaxed, his smile almost a sneer.

"I'm not going to do anything," Luis said, "he is." He jerked his head up in the direction of Blondie training the rifle down on them.

Daday and Abrebe both seemed to pale. Frowning, Daday said, "Where the fuck did you get that?"

"An old armed-forces reserve not too far from here. Lucky, no?"

"You can't use that, they'll throw you out of the league for good, lock you up."

Luis grimaced, "You beat us with clubs, no problem. Anyway, we need the ball. Strip and lie down on your bellies, face in the dirt."

Looking furious, Daday pulled his shirt, shorts, and shoes off. He slowly lowered himself face down in the browning grass. Abrebe followed suit and Luis went to work. He quickly tied the men's arms and feet together with their shirts and shorts. Then, he grabbed the ball and ration packets and put them aside. He looked inside of a shoe from each of them, then called up to Blondie. "Size ten, right?"

"Right."

"These are ten and a half. Abrebe's are eights. You can stuff socks in the big ones."

"Can you wear Abrebe's?"

"No need," Luis said, "my feet are good. Let's go."

Blondie dropped the toy rifle on the roadway and smashed the scope with a piece of concrete. Then, he dashed down from the overpass to meet Luis in stride back toward the east. Back at the spot where they had stashed their uniforms and go-pouches, they put them on and ran hard for another four hours, all the way to Mifflinville and the crossing at the Susquehanna, the Great Island River itself. They collapsed beneath an overpass, fully spent. But they had hold of the ball again, just an easy two days from the finish line.

IV.

The runners woke up the next morning still feeling worn out from the previous day's ordeal. Luis suffered from his old injuries, unwelcome visitors that never disappeared for good. His feet stung and throbbed from a half-dozen pin pricks, punctures, and contusions picked up while treading on sticks and stones again and again. Worse, his knees ached continuously, a given that he expected toward the end of any race. At this point, however, he knew that he still had a lot of running to do.

The drone had dropped off their ration packets, which they tore into like famished floaters. They especially savored the energy drinks, feeling every gulp coursing through their entire bodies. Afterwards, they sat again beneath the massive concrete stanchions, sated and not ready to run.

206

"You know, Blondie," Luis said, "If we win, this is my last race."

Blondie looked startled. "You can't be serious. Look at how good we've done together, despite everything that's gone on. We're a hell of a team, why quit now? We could win a ton of races for a good, long time."

"Maybe so," Luis said, "but I don't think I can run like this much anymore. I don't think I want to."

"Aw, Luis, don't say that," Blondie said plaintively. "What am I going to do without you, Gobernador Brownie?" He hesitated. "I'll miss you, Luis."

Surprised, Luis said, "Don't worry, Blondie, you will do great things by yourself. You are a true runner; you will win a lot!"

Blondie smiled wryly. He played with a stick, rolling one end around in a patch of dirt. Gazing at the ground, he said, "So, what're you gonna do? Keep house with your gorgeous trophy wife?"

Luis ignored the slight. "Maybe. Marie is a good person." He shrugged, "She always complain about my rough feet in bed." Blondie laughed. "So, I don't know," Luis trailed off. "I don't know what I will do when I don't run anymore."

Blondie turned his head, smiling again, sadly this time. "Tough to quit, isn't it?"

Luis dropped his head slightly.

Starting to rise, Blondie said, "Well, you still got plenty left for a couple of days anyway."

They walked out from beneath the concrete arch into a brilliantly sunshiny day. Heading toward the bridgehead across the Susquehanna, they pulled up short. In front of them, they saw a grouping of portable palisades separated by the strip. One flew the red and gray colors of the Wharf Rats, the other the purple and chartreuse of the Pig-Dogs. The full teams for both clubs had been dropped just in front of the west end of the bridge crossing over the river. Players jogged and stretched outside of their camps, readying themselves for a full scrimmage.

"Jesus Christ!" Blondie uttered, "Squad drops by both teams. I've never ever seen that."

A figure loped from the Rats practice over in their direction. As he closed in, they could see his long, lean limbs, lightly bronzed skin, and sandy hair bouncing back, framing him like Achilles on the beach.

Just as he reached them, JonBalliet said, "Good to see you fellows in one piece."

"Good to see you, Jon," said Luis. "What's up?"

The tall backer shook each of their hands as he spoke. "Ref-drones assessed both teams for major infractions, the Pig-Dogs for beating the shit out of you, and us when you left the strip and threw down on them to get the ball."

Blondie swallowed and said nervously, "Nothing about the gun?"

JonBalliet shook his head, "Nothing. Maybe because it was a toy. We saw it all on VR. Everything."

Blondie looked guilty, but Luis said, "We had to do it. The Dogs gave us no choice."

"I can see that," JonBalliet said, "but Daday and Abrebe are over the top nuts about it, especially you guys still being in the race after pulling a gun on them."

"A toy," said Blondie, "a Daisy 880. We can't help they fell for it."

JonBalliet shook his head, "But, now they're out for blood. All of them."

A disquieting stillness descended on the three men.

"Where's Jezek," Luis asked.

"They broke his leg," JonBalliet replied. "That's why I'm here. Compound fracture. It wasn't an accident. We'll do the same if we get the chance."

Luis stood silent for a few minutes, mulling over what JonBalliet had said. At length, he asked, "So, when do we start? What's the first play?"

The team grouped around JonBalliet watched closely as he wielded a stylus above a white board. "Lightfoot, you're point. Luis, you're number one, Blondie, number two. Split runners behind.

"First play, we'll power sweep hard left. Second, hard right. Then, we'll set as though we're running right again, Luis, behind Lightfoot. Blondie, you'll slot at the right end and go in motion to the left. Wait

208

until Blondie's near me, Lightfoot, before calling for the ball. As soon as it's snapped, Lightfoot leads the run left with the front liners sliding left. Luis, you jab step left, then go right to the end. I'll pull right, Lightfoot hands me the ball, and I run for the end, Luis on my flank."

He looked up at Luis, "As soon as I turn up field, I lob the ball to you, Luis." He turned to Blondie, "By this time, you loop around and crack back on the nearest chaser to Luis. God willing, Luis will break away across the bridge. Questions?"

Luis said, "Blondie's a fast sprinter. Why not toss him the ball?"

JonBalliet nodded, "He's faster than you, Luis. If you try to crack back on a chaser, I'm not sure you'd recover fast enough to catch up with Blondie. We need both of you out front together to deal with the other chaser."

Luis dropped his head, embarrassed. He clenched his jaw tight, determined to outpace them all, Blondie included.

The ref-drone signaled, and the Wharf Rats crashed into the left side of the Pig-Dogs. Luis hit a backer causing them both to collapse together on the field.

"You're dog shit now, Wharf Mice!" shouted Daday. "We gotcha good, you ain't goin' anywhere."

Luis glanced at him before heading back to the huddle. Daday smiled wickedly, drawing his thumb across his throat.

A chill shot up and down Luis's spine. He stood close to Blondie and said, "Daday wants blood." Blondie turned his head to stare at Luis, who rasped, "You need to be careful, don't get near them; run like the wind!"

Lightfoot broke the huddle and the team lined up. He called for the ball and darted left, slipping it to JonBalliet bursting right at full speed. Luis forgot the jab step and followed him to the end. JonBalliet whipped around the edge, flipping the ball perfectly as he slammed into two Pig-Dog backers trailing the play. Luis plucked the ball out of the air at full speed and raced toward the bridge, catching a glimpse of Blondie hitting Abrebe in the back of his head with an elbow. Abrebe went down, and Blondie caught up with Luis. The two runners reached the bridge together and dashed across it as fast as they could.

They kept up a furious pace, hoping to make it all the way to the spider web of lanes that joined I-80 with I-380. The wide split between the east and west lanes of 80 and north and south 380 created a large delta full of places to hide from chasers closing in on them.

"We've covered maybe 10K from the bridge past Mifflinville," huffed Blondie, "leaving us 60 more to get to the 380 triangle. I don't think we can do it. We're up from six minutes per K to nine." He glanced at Luis, "We might get there, but we'd be toast trying to finish the next day even if the finish is just 47K away."

Luis barely heard him, his knees ached so much. His feet hurt, too, but he paid them no attention. His real concern rose with the dull pain he felt growing in his groin.

"What do you suggest?" he asked Blondie.

Blondie replied, "I have no idea."

Luis thought back, then said, "There is a cloverleaf at Rt. 93, but only 25 klicks from here. Too easy for their chasers to drop ahead. Plenty of places to hole up in the spaghetti cluster at 80 crossing over 81, maybe 41 klicks. The Lehigh River, 56 klicks. Sixty klicks to the PA Turnpike. Those are the majors. A lot a little ones along the way, too."

"Man," said Blondie, his breath labored, "you got some kind of prodigious memory."

"I been down this road many times."

They pulled up at Honeyhole Road, just past the I-81 intersection, betting that the Dogs chasers would spend time looking for them amid the mass of over and underpasses connecting I-80 to I-81. Honeyhole Road ran next to the Nespopeck Creek coursing perpendicularly beneath the two I-80 lanes. Once a heavily forested part of the old state park, only a few spindly trees dotted the landscape now. Luis and Blondie staggered down the slope and plopped themselves under the curve of the bridge above.

Luis rubbed his throbbing knees and feet, his left leg in tight to ease the pulling tension within his groin.

"Only 45 klicks," moaned Blondie, "but I just couldn't 've gone another step."

Luis snapped his eyes up at Blondie rubbing his feet, suspecting that the lean runner spoke to make his little brown teammate feel better.

"Anyway, here comes the drone," Blondie went on, peering up at the reddening sky. "We can stock up on our carbs, get ready for the long one tomorrow."

Luis wondered if he could make a long run.

In the early morning, they stuffed themselves with as much protein and carbs as they could and drank plenty of high-test power drinks. Afterwards, they relieved themselves against the bridge abutment, hiked up their ration packets and go-pouches, and waded across the Nescopeck. Blondie held the ball high over his head.

Luis found the cold water soothing. Maybe he would be ready, he thought. They clambered out on the western bank and lumbered up the slope. When they reached the top where the strip paralleled the two lanes, Blondie turned and looked back.

"Shit," he said, "There they are."

Luis whipped his head around to see Daday and Abrebe just a soccer pitch length away.

"Let's go!" he shouted, and they took off at a sprint into the orange glow of the rising sun.

Despite their fatigue, Luis and Blondie still outpaced the chasers, the Pig-Dogs players clearly chosen for their quickness and strength rather than speed. Soon, they were out of view of the Wharf Rat runners. But the ball-runners were slowing down, too.

Luis labored to keep up with Blondie, who obviously lagged to stay with his teammate. This was no good, thought Luis. If they continued to give ground, they would be caught, and these Dogs would show no mercy. At the very least they would turn the ball over, and he would see his talá disappear like smoke. That could not happen.

When they'd been out for an hour and a half, Luis stopped near a small stream, the Oley Creek. He barked to Blondie still running ahead.

"Blondie. Blondie!"

Blondie turned his head around and came to a stop.

"Listen to me, Blondie," Luis yelled. "This is not working. I am holding you back. They will catch us and we will lose."

"No," said Blondie, "at our slowest we can still outpace them."

Luis shook his head, "I must stop sometime soon. You must keep running. There is time for you to win. I can trail them off."

Blondie gritted his teeth, "No way, Luis, never. If they catch you without the ball, they'll hurt you, bad!"

"I don't care. This is my last match anyway. I rather win, then I can laugh in their faces." He suddenly stopped and pointed to Blondie, "Keep the ball in your hood. I'll fill mine with my uni, my go-pouch, other things to make a bulge they can see. Maybe lead them away. You run fast to the 380 triangle and hide." He hesitated. "Find a nice, tall tree with a good fork. Climb it so they cannot see you if they show up. When you can, run and win."

Blondie smiled slightly. Luis pushed his go-pouch into his hood. He took off his shorts hood and stuffed them as well to fill out the bag. "There. That look more like a ball."

Blondie laughed and clapped Luis on his shoulder. "Back to the loincloth, huh?"

"Sitagola."

"Right." Blondie searched around the area and looked back to the west. He turned to Luis and said, "Well, okay, Gobernador. See you at the finish line."

Luis nodded, and Blondie took off. Luis watched as the tall, pale runner hit a stride well past what they had been marking before. He sighed, turned, and waited for the Pig-Dogs.

Daday and Abrebe didn't show up for an hour. Luis appreciated the rest, drinking and eating in a methodical way while waiting. As soon as they appeared on the horizon, Luis showed himself. When he saw them both speeding up, he turned and ran hard the other way. He followed the Oley Creek to an old pond bed and skirted its edge toward the north. He glimpsed the two chasers on the curve, a good half-kilometer behind. They had slowed, too, Luis recognized. If he continued at his current pace, ten minutes per klick, he could keep them at the same distance until nightfall. If his knees and groin held out. Dióse Damano, Diose Damiyé, he mouthed silently, let it be.

Five hours later, Luis knew that his pace had fallen off badly,

212

maybe fifteen minutes per klick now. When he looked back, he saw that Daday and Abrebe had made up some ground. But their rate had dropped, too. He looked at the overhead sun. An hour away from setting, he estimated. They would push soon to catch him if they could. They might even call for a quick drop in front to try cornering him. If so, he'd go to his escape plan; run off of the strip. Blondie should be so far ahead by this time that losing another klick or two for an out-of-bounds penalty wouldn't matter. Luis hoped so, anyway.

He had covered about 30 kilometers, making the most out of cloverleafs before and after the bridge over the Lehigh at White Haven. The chasers had to search each clover pretty carefully to make sure their prey wasn't hiding out. Luis made it all the way across the I-476 Northeast Extension and over the Tunkhannock Creek to the Blakeslee cloverleaf. He'd managed to keep the chasers after him all that time, but his body screamed pain. He needed to hide out for the night.

The intricate spaces around the Blakeslee clover beckoned to him, but he knew that Daday and Abrebe would catch up before the last light faded. In any case, there were few places to hide in the burnt grass areas, bare from vast forest fires years ago. He needed to push himself just a little bit farther. But, where?

Luis racked his brain until he remembered that an old natural bog reserve lay two kilometers down the road, off south of I-80. Most likely the swamp had dried up, but enough water might still be left to grow some green outside of the median. He would be committing a major race violation, but at this point he had to take the chance. Even so, he thought, he could strip down and hide his gear in the dark, maybe divert the spy sats and drones. If the Pig-Dog chasers found his ration pack and uni, so what? They'd still be way behind Blondie.

The plan provided Luis with renewed energy. He almost sprinted the last two kilometers to the spot on the median adjacent to the bog. Sure enough, tall trees covered the strip and other brush grew plentiful in the surrounding area.

Luis took off his hoodt, slung it over one shoulder and scaled a tall maple. Ten meters up, he tucked it into the crotch of a large limb and

213

the trunk, then slid down. A meter away, he stuck a stick behind another tree trunk to mark the place. He turned and ran south, bending a branch here and there to mark his trail. In no time, he crossed over the I-80 east lane out of bounds into high brush to search for a good place to bed down. He settled in to deep sleep, hoping that he wouldn't be awakened too soon by floaters.

Next morning, he stretched luxuriously. Nothing had disturbed him during night. Even the temperature had remained tolerable despite the changing season. Easy to stay warmer in some places these days, he thought. He picked himself up, urinated, and headed back to the interstate, keeping a lookout for Daday and Abrebe.

He slipped back over the eastbound lane onto the median and quickly scrambled down to a tree trunk, his eyes darting everywhere. Nothing. He carefully retraced his route from last night and easily found his way to the maples where he'd hidden his gear. When he found the stick and peered around the tree next to the one he had climbed, he froze stock still.

On the ground beneath the tree lay his shirt, ripped apart to reveal what remained of his ration packet and go-pouch strewn around it. Somehow, the Pig-Dog chasers had found the tree and his gear before he could retrieve it. How? Among all these trees, how could they find anything so fast? Unless they knew beforehand. Luis shook his head, it didn't matter. They discovered that he didn't have the ball and they'd taken off after Blondie immediately. Now, he had to chase them down and pass them to warn Blondie.

Luis put on his torn shirt and readied himself to run when the morning drone flittered down between the tall trees, a ration packet suspended between its wheels. He couldn't believe it. Quickly, he grabbed the packet, tore it open and began to consume the protein bars, washing each bite down with the power drink. After a few minutes, he filled his H^2O reservoir and stuffed the leftovers into his shirt hood. He started to rise when a flash of silver caught his eye in the ration packet debris. He stooped down and pulled out a safety-wrapped item. He opened it delicately and saw several pharma capsules in a row.

214

Luis lifted his head. The medi-trackers had taken note of his pain and sent drugs for his knees and groin. He jammed them into his mouth and swallowed them down with the dregs of the drink. He set out then, knowing that in a short amount of time he would feel no pain.

He ran as fast as he could, building to a six-minute clip per kilometer as the painkillers took hold. The I-380 triangle lay just 17 klicks down the strip. He could reach it in an hour and a half, maybe sooner. Unless he ran right up Daday and Abrebe's butts. Then what? He shook his head, no matter. He'd figure something out when he caught them. But first he had to catch them.

The flat terrain helped. Once a northern resort full of trees, lakes, and ponds, the entire area was desolate now, except for the fastidiously maintained median. After a few days running without sandals, his feet had toughened enough so that he hardly felt the grassy ground. Even the occasional pebble didn't set him back. At this point, his only worry was worry.

After an hour, he arrived at the span where I-80 gradually separated, the west-bound lane curving north, the east veering south in a gradual descent down the Poconos. On the way, he saw no sign of the Pig-Dog chasers. He couldn't be sure if he had passed them somewhere among the foliage growing lushly within the various segments of the strip. If they took the west leg of the interstate, he easily could have missed them altogether. Or, they still could be ahead.

The sun floated just above the tree line an hour past dawn. Luis slowed down, padding carefully toward the rendezvous spot that he and Blondie had chosen. He worked his way through a thick stand of silver maples to the edge of a meadow. A formation of huge rocks jutted up in the center of the grassy field. Luis glance around, then scurried silently to the rock pile. He came to an abrupt stop, crouching below the rocks. He heard sounds ahead, voices, and a cry of pain.

Luis pulled himself up and carefully looked through the V separating the tops of two stones. Not too far distant, five men stood around a copse of elms. Familiar looking, they wore stained white t-shirts, dark khaki trousers and thick tool belts with rip saws dangling at their waists. Their orange hardhats with black letters identified them, Tree Experts. Two held high their long poles, snapping their scissoring clips again and again in the branches above. Each clip elicited a horrible, terrifying scream of pain from a squirming form hidden amid the leaves above.

The foreman craned his neck gazing up, twisting his mustache with his finger and thumb, resting his other hand on his hip. He called out to his men in Spanish, "Don't just keep pulling and letting go. Clip hard, hang on, and yank him down."

The men tried to follow the foreman's orders, causing more agonizing shrieks from above. Luis felt sick hearing them, dreading what they meant.

"Go for the arms, the legs."

At last, they latched on and jerked their poles down, tumbling Blondie out of the tree headfirst into the ground. His ration packet trailed after him to rest next to his silent, still form. The foreman gestured with his head at the other two men, who ran to Blondie, open clasp knives in their hands. Luis turned away and dropped down below the outcrop.

He heard fragments of conversation among the tree experts, muffled by the rocks. The foreman yelled for them to search around. Luis listened and quickly dashed low to the ground scurrying back to the maples. A dozen meters in, he climbed one, as high as he could go.

Three of the tree experts entered the stand, searching around the trunks. Luis clung to a limb, petrified that they would look up. But, they didn't. They left the woods and rejoined the others.

Luis stayed high in the maple for hours, afraid to climb down. He struggled with his thirst and hunger, his fatigue, his need to go to Blondie, and his overwhelming terror. Finally, he lowered himself carefully to the ground. Painstakingly, he dodged his way to the rock formation. Seeing no one around the trees ahead, he girded himself and slunk over.

He found the ration packet torn apart and bloody, with more blood on the ground where Blondie had laid. But he was gone. The tree experts had taken him with them.

Luis sighed deeply, aching. He turned and saw Blondie's go-pouch and many of his belongings strewn about. His murderers had rifled through everything thoroughly. Luis crouched on his haunches and pawed at the go-pouch, almost whimpering. He picked up the solar laser lighter as he stared at the rations and power drinks thrown aside. They had come to kill Blondie, not steal from him.

Except for the ball. The game ball was missing. The tree men killed Blondie to keep him from winning, perhaps, but also to get the game ball. Luis stood up. But, did they find it? Maybe not, he thought. While searching below him in the maples, they sounded as though they'd been stymied. If they hadn't found it, where was it? Blondie could have hidden it anywhere.

Luis rubbed his chin, then looked up. He scaled the tree in no time, soon finding the fork where Blondie had tied in to sleep. Luis gazed around, up and down, and back up again. A large limb curved out of the tree trunk, about as high up as Blondie could have reached. Luis grasped the limb and pulled himself up and saw it, the game ball wedged in a crotch. A tree and a good fork, Luis recalled sadly. What did I do to you, Blondie, he thought mournfully.

Back on the ground, he gathered up what he could use from Blondie's go-pouch and H^2O reservoir. Luis stuffed the ball into his shirt and started to run.

The Delaware Water Gap Bridge stood just 33 klicks away, less than a four-hour run if he maintained a ten kph pace. He wasn't sure he could do it. Even if he could, he'd be spent for the sprint across the three-quarter kilometer span. The medians across both bridges consisted of half-meter high, 40-centimeter wide concrete safety walls, impossible to run on. The eastbound bridge, however, featured a four-meter wide pedestrian walkway connecting the old Appalachian Trail between Pennsylvania and New Jersey. To get over the bridge without being hit with a major penalty, runners had to speed across an adjacent trail walkway before their opponents could block them.

The trouble, however, Luis realized, was that the Pig-Dogs somehow seemed to know when and where to intercept the Wharf-Rats runners at all junctures. Without any doubt, he expected to find

217

all of the Pig-Dogs squad-dropped and waiting for him right in front of the eastbound span. If he tried to dodge them by speeding over the westbound bridge, he would be called for another major infraction. This would give the Dogs the use of one more squad drop to place them on the other side right in front of the finish line.

He brooded as he ran, roiled by images of Blondies' brutal butchering. He also felt dread mounting over other questions. Why did the tree experts do it? What larger betrayal was at work?

He pounded along, unable to manage his rate of speed. He wanted to run away as fast as he could. If he did that, though, the Pig-Dogs would catch him. They had found Blondie and him at every point along the way. Now that he was alone, Luis knew that they would run him down, too, no matter what. He needed to change direction, he needed a new plan. After covering another five klicks, he decided what he would do. He started to slow down.

After crossing Rimrock Drive in Bartonsville three hours later Luis pulled up, 17 klicks from the Delaware Bridge. He settled down beneath the curve of the I-80 overpass above Pocono Creek. After a few minutes, a ref-drone arrived with his evening rations. Luis ate and drank, swallowed his meds, and stretched out to sleep.

When night fell, he quickly stripped off his uni and piled it next to him. Still lying on the ground, he emptied his shirt of everything except for the ball and Blondie's laser lighter. Using the laser, he cut a hand-size slit in the ball. As it deflated, he thrust his hand inside until he found what he was searching for, the small league tracking sensor. Luis laid the tiny mechanism on the pile formed by his clothes. He stood up, the flattened white ball gripped in one hand and Blondie's laser lighter in the other. Wearing only his sitagola, he struck out east toward the Delaware Water Gap guided by only a few faint stars above.

Luis stood under desiccated trees on the other side of the old toll plaza just past Oak Street. He had walked and jogged from Bartonsville throughout the night, crossing creeks and streams by walking on the interstate itself. Another talá, he thought, betting that by stripping down he had eluded any detection by the spy sats. As old as they were, they weren't all that effective at night. He felt exhausted now, but he dismissed it. Even if he had bedded down for the night, he never would have slept. Blondie crowded his mind, and thoughts of Margara, and Marie, too, though not as much. Eighteen years since he'd seen Margara. How much had she changed?

He stared down the highway at the lanes closing together in the distance. Just two klicks away, the Appalachian Trail joined with the walk across the Delaware Gap Bridge. He would start moving slowly as the sun appeared ahead of him. By the time half of it topped the horizon, he would be at the bridge entrance with enough light to take off.

The long walk in the black night had cost him. Unseen pebbles and sharp rocks had bruised and cut his feet. His knees ached and his groin throbbed. At least the ankle had held up, he thought, for now. No matter. For just over a kilometer he would tear across the bridge to the finish. He would run like the wind.

He moved stealthily forward, eyes darting side to side, front and back. When he came upon a collapsed building that afforded him some cover, he halted to compose himself, then dashed to another hiding place. Finally, he stood just a hundred meters from the bridge walkway.

He crouched close by the broken concrete, ready to go when he heard the heavy drumming behind him. He stood halfway up as the drumming became the whining turbines of a hover craft, their deep-throated din telling him it was big. A drop, a full squad drop.

Luis straightened up and whipped around. Héna díse damano, let it be the Wharf Rats, he prayed. The dull, gray machine alighted, its oversize cargo door dropping from the rear as a ramp. The Pig-Dogs spilled out at full speed, racing directly toward him. Luis turned and darted to the pedestrian walkway. As he reached it, he heard another set of thunderous turbines behind him. The Wharf Rats drop, too late to block his hunters.

He ran onto the narrow causeway as fast as he could, glancing back once to see Daday and Abrebe out front, breathing heavily, tongues lolling like mad dogs. He faced front, pumping his legs furiously. He came to the first span over the river, a short hundred-meter stretch. It curved a bit, allowing him to check on the chasers. Daday and Abrebe were no longer in sight. Instead, the Pig-Dogs' new young runners galloped behind him, steadily closing the gap.

Luis tried to accelerate, but his legs wouldn't respond. He gritted his teeth and kept on running, hoping the youngsters would wear themselves out.

He cleared the first water crossing, which brought him to a 60-meter segment over the tip of an island. He raced low to the pavement, trying to avoid the limbs and browning leaves of the trees growing over the edge of the bridge wall. Maybe the young runners trailing him would hit one of the branches, knocking them both off their stride. He hoped so, but he dared not look back for fear of losing speed.

Passing the island tip, he reached the final half-kilometer of the bridge, 200 meters of it in the center suspended over the last of the river. If he could keep his pace, he would be at the finish line in a minute and a half. He could see the far edge of the bridge in the distance, seeming to draw closer. He would finish, he realized, they would never catch him now. He would be the Gobernador one last time.

As he approached the end of the section over the river, a dart flashed past his head. He dropped to the concrete and watched a flight of other darts and arrows fly above him coming from the other end of the bridge. Héna díse íyerugame, he cried out silently. He rolled over on his side to glance behind him. Joined by Daday and Abrebe, the young Pig-Dog runners had dropped to the deck. They stared at him fiercely, waiting.

Luis turned back to the front to see a few more projectiles wing above, clattering on the pavement at his rear. He dropped his eyes to see a mass of men rushing toward him from the finish line. Lean, bearded men running fiercely, shreds of clothing covering their bony bodies. Some of them wore wildly colored, beaded headdresses, others old straw farmer fedoras and a few brimmed caps.

Floaters, he realized, more in one place than he'd ever seen before. He oddly took note that they ran barefooted like himself. He knew then that he was finished. He could run no more. The race now pitted

220

the Pig-Dogs against the floaters with himself the prize in the middle. Sure enough, a peek behind him showed the Dogs on their feet stalking toward him and the floaters. A glance up front revealed the floaters also moving methodically in his direction. Both groups had slowed their pace, clogged by their numbers on the narrow trail and the sight of approaching hostiles on the other side.

"A la mierda," Luis spat. He pulled himself to his feet and yawed his way to the outside wall. Glancing over the side, he saw the water 92 meters below. He whipped the ball, now a flattened, white leather disk, over the edge and watched it fall, slowly wafting in wide arcs, finally touching down on the river to be quickly carried away.

Luis turned around and rested his elbows on the bridge wall. Both bands of men pushed toward him, three abreast, and Luis readied himself to leap.

Another hovercraft suddenly swept down over the eastbound lane spraying wide, rapid volleys of taser bolts, scattering the men on both sides back away from Luis. A side door on the hovercraft opened and an arm waved furiously at Luis beckoning to him. Luis took a single step to clear the inner wall of the walkway and climbed into the flier.

Crew members wrapped him in an alpaca robe as the hovercraft lifted off. Luis collapsed on one of the faux leather seats, and two medics kneeled to gently place his cut and battered feet into soothing booties. Another gave him a blast of anodynes.

Luis closed his eyes just for a second.

He opened them to see Harry sitting across from him.

"Quite a show, yes?" Harry said.

"Where did all those floaters come from?"

Harry made a face. "God knows. Never saw so many before, never like that in one place. Acting up like that in a league match?"

"Why did they do that?"

Harry lifted his hands, "They're wild. Making some kind of point or something? I don't know. They had no chance."

Luis frowned, lips pressed together.

"No matter. You don't look the worse for wear," said Harry, handing a maté to Luis.

Luis stirred the herbs around with the silver straw. He had learned to enjoy maté after living in Rio for so long. So long ago.

"I feel the worse," he said. He stared at his agent, middle-aged and fat, red-faced with thinning red hair, an hombre blanco for sure. One of the world's richest men. But he liked Luis, enough to keep an eye out for him, protect his interests despite the runner's impulsive nature.

"Well," said Harry, "we'll get you back up to snuff. You'll feel like your old self again in no time." He laughed, "Especially when the good doctor's palliative kicks in."

"It already has."

"Wonderful! Soon, you'll be ensconced in your apartment in Rio, planning your next conquest."

"You know I am finished running, yes?" Luis asked him, almost out of curiosity.

Harry dropped his head, "That's certainly your decision to make. Either way, you are a successful man, a winner indeed."

Luis frowned, "I lost the race. I broke all the rules. The league could ban me for life for trashing the ball, throwing it away."

Harry grimaced, "These things are negotiable."

"I lost the talá, Harry," Luis said. "I didn't win the race. I lose everything, except maybe a little bit, league consolation pay."

Harry swung his head down in a long curve. "That isn't exactly correct," he said. He lifted his eyes to Luis, smiling broadly, yet still a bit fearful. "You didn't lose the talá," he said, "because it was never placed."

Luis's eyebrows pulled together. "Never placed? I place it with Pascal."

Harry lifted his hands to Luis, then pulled them back and folded them between his knees.

"I talked to Pascal. I convinced him it was a bad idea. He agreed. I asked him to rescind the bet, return the money. He did. He's something of an honorable man, Pascal is. He likes you, you know?"

Wonderment swirled in Luis's head. He felt furious and relieved, treated like a child, cared for like a friend. Mierda. He peered up at Harry. "Pascal likes Marie."

222

Harry averted his eyes. "Sure he does, but he likes you, too."

Luis closed his mouth in a sneer. "So I am back at the beginning."

Harry grinned. "No, you're not. You are, in fact, in better shape than before, much better. You understand?"

Luis sighed impatiently, waving one hand at Harry, "What are you talking about? Come on, spit it out."

"Well," said Harry, "After receiving Pascal's voucher, you had a lot of capital sitting around, liquid capital. In fact, it was fortunate, the timing was right. So, I invested it for you." He smiled again broadly, as though already being congratulated for his fine work.

Luis shook his head ruefully. "Tell me what you did, Harry, por favor."

Harry took a breath and said hurriedly, "I couldn't get your approval on this, you were already out on the strip. So, I had to act with your best interests at heart, and I did. As a matter of fact, I did indeed." He breathed again, "I invested the bulk of your capital into," he paused for effect, "into VirtuReel Ltd."

Again, Luis's brow scrunched up. "VirtuReel? What for? Why VirtuReel?"

Harry swallowed to get ready to explain. "VirtuReel is overwhelmingly the largest virtual reality holocaster in the entire world. They not only own all rights to every median strip football game, which is plenty in itself." He paused again, "The stroke of luck here is that VirtuReel has acquired the entire MSF League, including holoreality rights to each and every player!"

"That's in my contract?" Luis said, looking puzzled.

"It's in every player's contract," Harry replied, "every employee's, in fact. VirtuReel can do anything they want with any player's image, game performance, and VR cast, anything with any player's likeness, period!"

"Okay. That's good," said Luis.

"It's not just good, Luis, it is great!" He sat back in his seat and held his hands up to continue. "VirtuReel intends to revolutionize the game. How? By replacing live action games with virtually real CGI players on fabricated strips."

223

"What are you talking about? That won't work, you can't replace the players, they're the best in the world!"

"Very true, no question. But," Harry said, "they get hurt. They get old. They demand more money. Sometimes they underperform. There are ties, unexpected losses, little in the way of innovation. With CGI players and fields, things can be fine-tuned. Oh, I don't mean controlled, I mean eliminating the little glitches that annoy viewers. Through targeted use of quantum computers VirtuReel has developed very sophisticated megalgorithms that ensures random outcomes for all VR matches. No one knows what will happen until it happens."

Luis shook his head, "This will never work. People will know."

Harry said, "Not so. The field testing has been done, real games versus VR games. VirtuReel technicians have advanced augmented imaging to such an incredibly high level that viewers simply cannot tell the difference. Test after test group hasn't known what they were watching. It's indisputable. Virtually real median strip football is the future, only the future has arrived now! And you're in the thick of it."

Luis felt bewildered. How could all this be happening; how could everything change all at once?

"What about the players? What happens to them?"

Harry's expression suddenly grew solemn. "They all will receive severance packages that set them up for life. VirtuReel is both grateful to them and accordingly generous, believe me."

Luis grasped his head between both hands, "Then, why all these games, why keep doing it this way if you can make it all up to look so real?"

Harry blinked. "Why, to build databases. We need the data to further refine the VR casts."

Luis stared at Harry. "Why all the ties?"

Harry sat back. "A cost-saving measure pushed by some major shareholders. It really wasn't necessary, but those guys grew up poor, I guess. The severance packages will compensate for the ties, though, I assure you."

Anguish filled Luis's eyes. "What about Blondie? That was a cost-saving measure? I caused him to die, Harry. I almost died, too. How much did this tie save? One retirement payoff instead of dos? How does VR explain that?"

Harry swallowed, his face ashen. "It was a tragic mistake. Signals horrifying mixed. Those responsible have been apprehended. The authorities are investigating the perpetrators. Absolutely."

Luis shook his head, "It was a horror, Harry. Make for a good VR story, no?"

Harry didn't reply.

"Viewers will want to play too, right Harry? VirtuReel will make them star runners?"

"Uh, not just yet," Harry said, "they need to sort out the liability issues first."

"Too bad. A lot of money there. But, no problem, they can still make the talás. They don't know what happens until it happens, right Harry?"

Luis spent the rest of the flight gazing out at the clouds, pink blossoms in the sky. Harry had told him that Pascal and Marie intended to meet them at the port when they landed. But Luis decided otherwise.

"You can't be serious, Luis," Harry said. "I know you've been through a terrible experience and you need to heal. I think the best way is to go home to familiar surroundings, to Marie and your friends."

"I am going home," Luis said. "Back to my ranchería. I might even run the delaphípu again. I might find Margara."

Harry sat back. "You think she'll still be there? Alone, waiting for you?"

Luis shrugged. "Probably not. But I want to see. Maybe she has a familia, I would like to see that. And, my other people, too. I want to go back to my home."

Saddened, Harry reached over and grasped Luis by a knee. "The way the world is now, Luis, there may be nothing there anymore."

Luis nodded his head sorrowfully. "True. But I want to go and see."

Harry lowered his chin slightly. He raised it and said, "What about

Marie, Luis?"

"She'll be happier with Pascal. She always was happier with him."

"That could be," Harry said, "but she loves you, Luis. She'll love you forever."

Luis smiled sadly, "I want her to be happy now, Harry."

Harry slumped a bit.

"You, too, Harry."

Harry lifted his head, "And, you, Luis?"

Luis shrugged. "I want to. Maybe be just more happy."

Acknowledgments

Short stories set high bars for writers in that they require the same care as novels in developing characters, dilemmas, and conclusions, but in a very confined space. Speculative stories, especially science fiction, compound the challenge by adding the need to create plausibility. A tall order indeed, and the only way writers can hope to approach these standards depends upon the help of a rich and varied supporting cast of editors and readers. Since I'm very far from the exception in these needs, I'm happy to list those who have helped me achieve any success in these stories. I thank them all with my deepest gratitude and love.

Pat Wallace, my brother, also my roommate when we were little, read everything I sent him with great gusto while also giving me the straight skinny on myriad ways to improve. A master storyteller and matchless musician himself, it is my pleasure to dedicate this volume to him in humble appreciation of his spectacular, speculative mind.

My beloved wife Ivey proved again her gift as a consummate editor of content by helping me clarify ideas to benefit all readers.

If I have read a thousand science fiction stories, my brother George has read tens of thousands. He aided me in developing my tales from beginning to end, providing research, feedback, and genuine criticism of my efforts. My sister Lucie not only encouraged me at every turn, she took on always with great cheer the heavy slogging of copyediting and proofreading.

Jim O'Donnell read everything, offering the perspective of a literary scholar who knows how to improve a story regardless of genre.

Also, of course, my sisters Anne and Ellen weigh in as well. Their enjoyment of the stories accompanied by bits of welcome criticism make my day every day. And lastly, I thank my son Conor and daughter Molly, rising stars who light my skies.

About the Author

Dan Wallace worked in book publishing for 37 years, most of them at Gallaudet University Press. In 2014, he turned to writing full time. He has written five novels that include *Tribune of the People: A Novel of Ancient Rome* and *Run West: A Novel of the Civil War.* He has completed two other short story collections and also writes poetry and essays that can be read online at his writing exchange *In the Wallace Manner* (inthewallacemanner.com). He lives with his wife Ivey in the Washington, DC, area.

Mainstream Stories
by Dan Wallace

A young West Virginia girl trained as a boxer by her father strikes up a troubling, long-distance friendship. Hoping to live the dream, a master plumber crosses the ocean to compete for a fantastic prize. In a small city museum, an ambitious curator crosses paths with two aspiring artists at an avant-garde exhibit. Humiliated after dropping a fly ball, a disillusioned boy's love of the game hinges on the actions of an old major leaguer. A young woman considering her tenth school reunion reminisces to decide.

These stories comprise an array that mine the country's cultural history during the past half century. Each offers vivid characterizations of common people and places as pieces in the puzzle of an ever-changing world. Insights abound in this wide-ranging collection well worth reading through and through.

Blossom Gold and other stories
By Dan Wallace
ISBN 978-1-7335725-6-9 trade paperback
ISBN 978-1-7335725-7-6 Kindle E-book
Wylisc Press, Silver Spring, MD
Available at Amazon.com

City Stories
by Dan Wallace

Summoned to jury duty, a divorced carpenter finds himself neck-deep in a Philly mob case. In the high-stakes urban real estate trade, a young agent makes his move to join the heavy hitters. A housecleaner seeks a unique form of justice for her upscale clients only to run into unlikely speed bumps. Tired of his mundane work buying microchips, a computer tech road warrior stops in Las Vegas for twenty-four memorable hours.

These stories and their companions cast stark light on various characters striving to succeed in circumstances singular to life in urban settings. Far removed from the natural world, people are the game and currency is the currency. For many of those shaped by society's strictures, survival defines success. This collection reveals in striking fashion the means an assortment of individuals use to work out their own formulas for success in the city.

Jury of Peers
City Stories
By Dan Wallace
ISBN 978-1-7335725-0-3 trade paperback
ISBN 978-1-7335725-1-0 Kindle E-book
Wylisc Press, Silver Spring, MD

Novels by Dan Wallace

In the winter of 1861, East Tennessee mountain boy Billy McKinney finds himself marching with the Rebels to engage the Yankees at the Cumberland Gap. He never wanted to fight for the South because his preacher taught him that slavery was wrong. Mostly, though, Billy fears getting killed. In his first battle, he charges through a storm of gunfire and cannon shot amid a driving, icy rain. All around him his friends fall, their mouths bubbling bloody webs of agony. Terrified, Billy decides to run. In his mad dash, he meets up with four runaway slaves led by Bev Bowman. They take him along on their flight, though as prisoner or partner remains to be seen.

Run West is a compelling story of survival in a time of anguish and conflict that no one could escape.

Run West: A Novel of the Civil War
By Dan Wallace
ISBN 978-1-7335725-2-1 trade paperback
ISBN 978-1-7335725-3-8 Kindle E-book
Wylisc Press, Silver Spring, MD
Available at Amazon.com

Publishers Weekly—Wallace's epic novel triumphs with a vivid historical account of ambitious elite Roman politicians and generals.

Library Journal— This thoroughly researched novel is as dramatic and gory as any swords-and-sandals epic and demonstrates how educational historical fiction can be. A wide cast of characters including soldiers, senators, slaves, mothers, and wives expand the reader's understanding of life in this time.

Midwest Book Review—A deftly constructed, exceptionally well written, and consistently compelling read from beginning to end, "Tribune of the People" is a truly impressive novel of the old Roman Empire by Dan Wallace. This is the stuff from which block-buster movies are made!

The US Review of Books: Professional Book Reviews for the People— Wallace's epic tale vividly depicts the opulence and grandeur of the ruling classes while simultaneously detailing the sights, sounds, smells, and squalor of those not born to wealth or position. His battle scenes pulse with excitement as he couples the weapons, tactics, and strategies of war with the carnage they wreak. No less compellingly does he describe the deceit and scheming in the porticos of power as well as the intrigue and hidden agendas in intricate familial relationships. RECOMMENDED.

The Historical Novel Society—A most timely novel; the characters are engaging and well-formed and the story well told. The novel gives you a feel for ancient Rome in the last years of the Republic.

Tribune of the People: A Novel of Ancient Rome
By Dan Wallace
ISBN 97917335725-0-7 trade paperback
ISBN 97817335725-1-4 Kindle E-Book
Wylisc Press, Silver Spring, MD
Available at Amazon.com